Daughter of Venice

* * *

Other books by Donna Jo Napoli

Three Days

Changing Tunes

The Bravest Thing

Jimmy, the Pickpocket of the Palace

The Prince of the Pond:
Otherwise Known as De Fawg Pin

Shelley Shock

Shark Shock

Soccer Shock

On Guard

When the Water Closes Over My Head

The Magic Circle

Zel

Song of the Magdalene

Trouble on the Tracks

For the Love of Venice

Stones in Water

Sirena

Crazy Jack

(with Richard Tchen) Spinners

Beast

Albert

(with Richard Tchen) How Hungry Are You?

The Hero of Barletta

The Angelwings *series*

DAUGHTER OF VENICE

Donna Jo Napoli

WENDY LAMB BOOKS

Published by
Wendy Lamb Books
an imprint of
Random House Children's Books
a division of Random House, Inc.
1540 Broadway
New York, New York 10036

Visit us on the Web! www.randomhouse.com/kids
Educators and librarians, for a variety of teaching tools, visit us at
www.randomhouse.com/teachers

Library of Congress Cataloging-in-Publication Data
Napoli, Donna Jo.
Daughter of Venice / Donna Jo Napoli.
p. cm.
Summary: Frustrated with the restrictions her gender imposes on her life, fourteen-year-old Donata, disguised as a boy, sneaks out of her noble family's house to roam the streets of late sixteenth-century Venice and then must confront the repercussions of her actions.
ISBN 0-385-90036-8 (lib. bdg.) — ISBN 0-385-32780-3
[1. Sex role—Fiction. 2. Venice (Italy)—History—16th century—Fiction. 3. Italy—History—16th century—Fiction. 4. Family life—Italy—Venice—Fiction. 5. Jews—Italy—Venice—History—16th century—Fiction.] I. Title.
PZ7.N15 Dau 2002
[Fic]—dc21
2001032426

The text of this book is set in 13-point Adobe Jensen.
Book design by Trish Parcell
Manufactured in the United States of America
March 2002
10 9 8 7 6 5 4 3 2 1
BVG

To the spirit of Elena Lucrezia Cornaro Piscopia—

scholar, musician, artist

* * *

ACKNOWLEDGMENTS

Thanks go to my family, particularly Barry, Eva, Robert, and Noëlle. I also thank Piero Brunello, Luisa Corbetta, Silvia Gasparini (legal historian extraordinaire), Giulio Lepschy, Susan Proctor, Diana Wright, Alvise Zorzi, Rosella Mamoli Zorzi, the librarians at the Biblioteca Nazionale Marciana, the archivists at the Palazzo Ducale and at the Archivio di Stato, and my editorial team—Mara Bergman, Kate Harris, Jodi Kreitzman, Alison Root, Jamie Weiss, Jennifer Wingertzahn, and Jane Winterbotham. Finally, I am so grateful to Wendy Lamb, my editor.

* * *

Venezia

1592

Ghetto

CANNAREGIO

Rio Terrà di Maddalena

Chiesa di San Marcuola

Palazzo Mocenigo

Canal Grande

DORSODURO

Canale della Giudecca

Isola di Giudecca

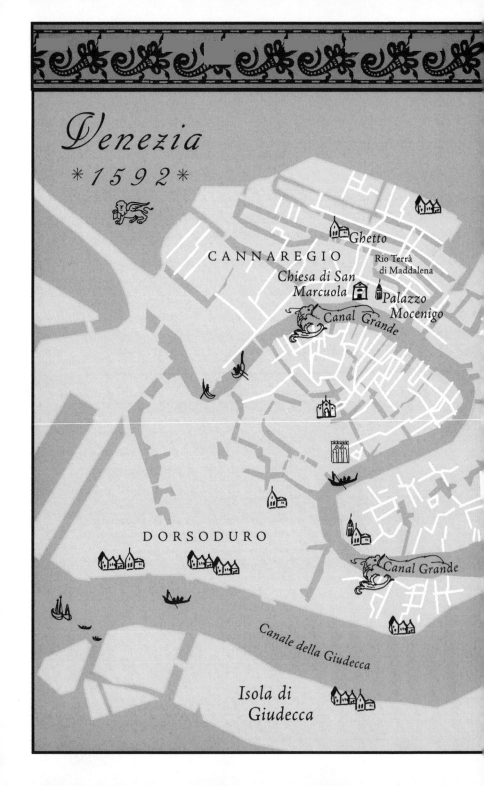

Torcello
Burano
Laguna Veneta
Murano
San Michele
Venezia
Giudecca
San Giorgio Maggiore
Isola di San Michele
Fondamente Nuove
Canale della Navi
Arsenale
Merceria
Piazza San Marco
Bacino di San Marco
Isola di San Giorgio Maggiore

CHAPTER ONE

MORNING LIGHT

A big fruit boat passes, rocking our gondola hard. Paolina tumbles against me with a laugh. I put my arm around her waist and hug her.

Paolina squirms free. "It's too hot, Donata." She pulls on one of my ringlets and laughs again.

Yes, it's hot, but it's a wonderful morning. The Canal Grande is busy. That's nothing new to us. From our bedchamber balcony my sisters and I watch the daily activity. Our *palazzo* stands on the Canal Grande and our rooms are three flights up, so we have a perfect view. But down here in the gondola, with the noise from the boats, and the smell of the sea, and the glare of the sun on the water, not even the thin gauze of my veil can mute the bold lines of this delightful chaos.

Our Venice, called *La Serenissima,* "The Most Serene," is frenzied today.

My feet start to tap in excitement, but, of course, they can't, because of my shoes. Whenever I go on an outing, I wear these shoes. They have wooden bottoms thicker than the width of my palm; I have to practice before venturing out, or I'll fall. And even then, I go at Uncle Umberto's pace—a blind man's pace. I look in envy at Paolina's *zoccoli,* her sandals with thin wooden bottoms. Paolina is only nine and she hasn't been subjected to high shoes and tight corsets yet.

"Can I take my shoes off, Mother? Just for the boat ride, I mean."

"Of course not, Donata."

"But I hate these shoes. They keep me from doing what I want."

"That's exactly why you should wear them." Mother reaches across Paolina's lap and gives a little yank to my wide skirt so that it lies flat over my lap. "High shoes make sure young ladies behave properly."

"Because we're afraid of falling? But you always say proper behavior comes from proper thoughts."

"Keep your shoes on, Donata. And don't make remarks like that when we arrive." Mother sits tall herself. "We're almost there now. Be perfect ladies, all of you."

Laura, my twin, sits facing me, with our big sister Andriana beside her. Laura stretches out her right foot so that her shoe tip clunks against mine. She's grinning under the white veil that hides her face, I'm sure of that. The very idea of my being a perfect lady is absurd. I grin back, though, of course, Laura cannot see my face, either.

Andriana's hands are in her lap, the fingers of one squeezed in the other so hard that her knuckles stand out like white beads. Mother's words make her throw her shoulders back and stretch her neck long. Underneath Andriana's veil, she is far from laughter; I bet her lips are pressed together hard.

Mother grew up the daughter of a wealthy artisan—a citizen, not a noble. There are three kinds of Venetians: plain people, who cannot vote; citizens, who vote but cannot hold office; and nobles. Mother was lucky to marry into Father's noble family. We all know that, but Andriana is the one who worries about it. She worries that our questionable breeding casts doubt on her worthiness as a bride. But she needn't. Andriana is sixteen, two years older than Laura and I. She's ready for a husband. And she'll get one easily. The oldest daughter in any noble family marries, even if she's ugly. And Andriana, with her wide-set, hazel eyes and delicate, pointed chin, is stunning. The mothers at the garden party today will all want her as a daughter-in-law.

If Andriana is lucky, she'll marry someone young and handsome. How I wish that for her. There are too many old widowers around looking for brides. The breath of decrepit Messer Corner, his exaggerated limp, the gray hair from his ears pollute my thoughts. That can't happen to Andriana. Father would never choose poorly for her, no matter how rich a suitor was. Andriana will marry someone vigorous, most certainly. She will have children.

Children. The youngest in our family is Giovanni—already three years old. There are twelve of us: Francesco, who is twenty-two; Piero, twenty; Antonio, seventeen; Andriana, sixteen; Vincenzo, fifteen; Laura and I, fourteen; Paolina, nine; Bortolo, six; Nicola, five; Maria, four; and Giovanni, three.

Giovanni is Mother's last child. That's what Mother says, at least. Father likes to say, "Things happen," and he winks. But I'm old enough to understand that Mother is probably right about this. Giovanni is our only brother who still sleeps on the same floor of the house as the girls, and I adore him. We all do. He'll probably move down to the small boys' floor soon. I miss having a baby in the house.

My heart squeezes. I want to take Laura's hand, but she's sitting too far from me. Laura and I have to be careful today—as careful as we can. The perfect ladies Mother wants us to be. For we, too, hope to marry someday. Both of us.

We've never voiced that hope to anyone else—it's a whisper between us in the dark. We know very well that if we hadn't been born twins, one of us would be the third sister and unmarriageable, for a nobleman is lucky to marry off one daughter and blessed to marry off two—he cannot hope to marry off more than two. But twins should be a special case—it's impossible to think of one of us marrying but not the other.

I place my feet primly together and sit up tall like Mother and Andriana.

The gondola veers into a side canal and the water is instantly calm and quiet. And smelly. This small canal is shallower than most, so the filth people throw into it can stink for days before it's finally washed out to the open waters of the lagoon. Hot weather brings the most foul odors.

The *gondoliere* in the front leaps onto the step and offers his hand to us, while the *gondoliere* in the back steadies the boat against the docking pole. I stand and hold on to one of the supports of the tent we've been riding under in the center of the gondola. Sweat rolls down my thigh. It's hot for late spring. I'd like to lift my skirts high and let a breeze tickle my bottom. But that's exactly the sort of behavior I must avoid today. I raise my skirts only high enough to allow me to step out of the boat.

We open our parasols immediately, for the sun must not darken our skins. Girls with alabaster complexions are more highly prized. Mother nods at us in approval, and leads us through the gate into the walled garden.

We're among the last to arrive, naturally. It is fitting that others await us. We are not only a noble family, but one of the wealthiest in all Venice. Only 105 families declare their fortunes to be greater than ours. And, while Father is but an ordinary member of the Senate, his brothers hold some of the most prestigious government offices. Everyone respects the Mocenigo family.

We take off our veils ceremoniously. Some girls and women hardly ever wear veils, except in church. We wear them wherever we go because Father insists. But even Father allows us to go without them in the company of women. And the men servants here don't matter.

Signora Brandolini, the hostess, rushes up to greet Mother, then kisses each of us girls. With a scoop of her arm, she sweeps Mother and Andriana away. In an instant, they are surrounded by the women who matter—the mothers of eligible sons.

We are left to our own devices, Laura and Paolina and I.

Laura takes my hand. "Let's see who's here."

I reach for Paolina with my other hand. "Come on."

Paolina backs away. "The Brandolini family's magnolias are in full blossom," she says. "They came all the way from the New World. I have to touch them." And she's gone.

My eyes follow her.

"People first," says Laura in my ear. "Magnolias later."

Laura's right. What a funny little sister we have, who prefers plants to humans. But, then, that's why Mother allowed her to come along today, even though she's too young—the Brandolini family has one of the most wonderful gardens in Venice and Paolina begged so sincerely. Mother has a soft spot for gardens herself. She grew up on the island of Murano and I heard her speak once of her childhood garden.

Laura leads me by the hand around the groups of women to the girls our age, clustered by the food table. The smell of sardines under vinegar prickles my nose. Onions and olives and pine nuts fill the bowls. Thin strands of dried horsemeat swirl to a peak on a platter. Roasted blackbirds from Perugia and cold strips of spiced tripe from Treviso and stuffed peacocks from Lombardia, and oh! Beyond all the meats a gigantic bowl surrounded by cut flowers brims over with early strawberries, the tiny kind that grow on the island of Torcello.

A pang of longing for our summer home makes me blink. In late June we'll go to the Colli Euganei, on the mainland. Paolina and I will climb the hills and gather blueberries and raspberries. Paolina has made that her special job and, of course, I help; I'd never give up the chance to climb those hills.

Uncle Umberto accompanies us everywhere in the country. He says it's only right; he says that even in the countryside a girl's reputation needs to be guarded. But I know it's because he loves the freedom that the countryside offers his blindness—the freedom of walking without fear of falling into canals—just as I love the freedom of walking outside without my awful high shoes. Sometimes the two of us run hand in hand for the pure joy of it.

If the weather is good, Paolina and I take along our younger brothers Bortolo and Nicola. This year we can take baby Giovanni as well, for he's become a little wild man and he'll need to run free. And, most fun of all, we often take our cousins: Elena and Eva and Michele and Nicola and Roberto. All five of them are the children of Father's sister Aunt Rosella. They're younger than us because Aunt Rosella is much younger than Father. She had two older sisters—but they died in infancy. Aunt Rosella married into a family in Padua and we don't get to see her most of the year—so we spend almost every summer day with her and her children.

I stop dreaming and look back to the bowl of small berries. Are they as good as our hill berries? I go around the table and stuff a handful of them into my mouth.

"Glutton." Cristina Brandolini is beside me, her hands on her hips. Teresa Lando leans out from behind her, looking equally scornful. "If all the girls did that," says Cristina, "the women wouldn't get any at all."

I swallow and flush with embarrassment. "I couldn't help myself. I'm sorry."

Cristina bursts into a grin. "The kitchen is full of them."

Teresa laughs.

I should have known. Cristina loves to tease.

Cristina's braided hair is pinned up in a cone shape, like that of the older girls. She wears a tiara with a red stone at the center. The bodice of Teresa's dress is cut so low, her breasts are half-exposed. I brush my own ringlets over my shoulder and smile, but I feel suddenly childish beside these girls, though we've played together for years.

Cristina hooks her arm in mine and whispers, "There's cream, too. Mother decided not to put it out because of the heat. Teresa and I are off to plunder the kitchen. Want to come?"

Ah, this is the Cristina I know, after all. I search the groups for Laura. She's surrounded by friends, busy and happy. She won't mind if I'm gone.

The three of us walk swiftly with our eyes down. When we enter the shade of the ground floor of the *palazzo*, we close our parasols and lean them by the doorway. I follow Cristina and Teresa up the stairs to the first-floor hall that runs the full length of the home, with windows that open to the canal on one end and windows that open to the alley on the other. The hall has doors on each side. I can guess what lies behind them—a library, a map room, an uncle or two's bedchamber, a music room—much the same as in our own *palazzo*.

The girls go straight to the kitchen, where the door is open. But there's another open door along the way.

I peek in. It's a map room. In the center of the floor, beside the mosaic with the Brandolini family crest, rests an enormous globe on a wooden stand. Piero, my second oldest brother, has spoken of the two globes in the Palazzo Ducale—the Doge's Palace. Piero is a true scholar; he races off to see whatever new inventions come to town. But our family doesn't have a globe. And I've never seen one before. In fact, I've only looked at maps in passing; a map room is man's territory, and ours is often used for tutorials, so I can't sneak in.

I take a silent step into the empty room. The globe is covered with the constellations—a celestial globe. Winged horses and tiny cupids and mythical creatures float through the clouds. I circle it, enchanted.

And now I see the morning light shines bright on the wall beside the door; it shines on a very different sort of map. A map cluttered with homes and canals and bridges. I rush to it. In the bottom corner is the signature of the mapmaker—but I can't read, so I cannot learn his name. Still, I know this mapmaker is a master, for he has painted Venice, my dear Venice, as seen from above, through the eye of an angel.

My own eyes travel the Canal Grande. I've been along much of it in our gondola, going to parties. And once Laura and I got to go to a festival in the great Piazza San Marco. Father is stricter than most of my friends' fathers, many of whom take their daughters to all sorts of celebrations—but at least he allowed that. Mother dressed us like princesses to show us off to the world.

Still, the gondola took us from our home doorstep to the *piazza,* with no stops along the way. That's how it always is: we girls go from doorstep to doorstep. I've never walked on the paths between the canals, except to follow the little one out our back door, down the alley and across one bridge, to the church of San Marcuola.

There are so many alleys on this map. Why, there must be hundreds. And what Francesco, our oldest brother, has told us girls is true: the alleys don't go in one direction for very long. They cut across each other all helter-skelter, and some end abruptly in canals. I can see why the boys talk about getting lost in Venice. I imagine it.

It dawns on me that I don't recognize a single alley or street on this map. I can't even be sure which *palazzo* is ours, which church is San Marcuola. It's almost as though I'm a stranger in my own city.

I go cold with the odd sensation of being lost and alone. I know hundreds of facts about Venice. Thousands, probably.

But I know them from memorizing what others say. I know almost nothing from my own experience. I've seen almost nothing with my own eyes. I hug myself and rock from side to side.

"There you are." Cristina stands in the doorway. "What are you doing in this stuffy room? Is something wrong?"

I shake my head.

"Then come along, goose. You're missing the fun." She holds out a strawberry covered with cream.

CHAPTER TWO

WORK

"So?" says Laura, giggling in anticipation. "Did anything momentous happen at yesterday's garden party?"

We older girls are sitting in a circle on the floor of the workroom, just the three of us. This is my favorite kind of talk—when no parent and no little one is near—and we can speak freely.

Andriana shakes her head and tries to look nonchalant. "No one's description of her son overwhelms me with passion yet."

I pinch her arm teasingly. "Or maybe everyone's does?"

Andriana blushes. "Anyway, Mother warns me I mustn't get carried away by what the women say. I am allowed to make suggestions—but in the end, Father will choose wisely for me. Being picky is a mistake."

"*Maritar o monacar,*" whispers Laura—marry or enter a convent—an old Venetian motto. "Tiziana Erizzo was picky."

Tiziana is a few years older than Andriana. She refused the man her father chose, so her younger sister, who was about to enter a convent, married him instead, and it was Tiziana who got whisked off to the convent. The last time we saw her, when she was visiting her family for a party, she told Andriana she's better off in a convent than in a miserable marriage, like her good friend Anna. It is rumored that Anna's husband brutalizes her. Still, Tiziana admits she hates it in the convent. The company of pious women stifles her.

Unless I marry, a convent lies ahead for me, too. As it is, probably my dear Paolina will be pressed to enter a convent within the next two years. And little Maria, who is only four, will do the same when she comes of age. Thus far Laura and I have escaped such a fate merely because of the accident of our birth order—because a second daughter just might, with luck, get a marriage offer.

I fold my arms across my chest and shudder. "I'd die in a convent."

"Don't be so dramatic, Donata. If that's where we end up, we'll make the best of it." Laura turns her head away and plays with the end of a yarn strand from the giant spool in the center of the room. Her face is hidden from us, but she can't hide the tremble in her voice. "Neither of us will die."

"Maybe both of you will marry," Andriana says brightly.

Laura quickly looks at Andriana, then at me. I share her shock at hearing our secret hope spoken so baldly.

When we don't answer, Andriana takes each of us by the hand. "I shouldn't have said that. I didn't mean to make light of what I know lies too heavy on you. I'm sorry." She squeezes our hands. "Maybe you can both be like Aunt Angela, and live here to take care of Francesco's children when he marries. We can go to him together, the three of us, and ask him."

Aunt Angela is Father's youngest sister, and, though I love her, I can't help pitying her. I pull my hand back. "Laura can do that, if she wants. She loves anybody's children. But I couldn't bear a life like Aunt Angela's. Always trying not to be a burden. Tiptoeing around the house and never speaking my mind. It would drive me crazy."

"You couldn't keep from speaking your mind anyway," says Laura flatly. "Francesco's wife, whoever she turns out to be, would strangle you within a year of her first baby's birth."

It's so true that I laugh in spite of myself.

Laura purses her lips. Then she laughs, too.

"Not a convent, and not a life like Aunt Angela's," says Andriana slowly. "What other choice are you thinking of, Donata?" She leans toward me. "Nothing else is mentionable."

She's talking about becoming a courtesan. The houses of prostitution are filled with the daughters of failing merchants and poor men. No noble daughter would choose that wretched trade.

I stand up and pace.

Paolina comes in, breathless. "I'm sorry I'm late. I had to dress Maria because Aunt Angela isn't feeling well." She stops and blinks. "You haven't even started the work yet? What's the matter?"

Andriana gets to her feet. "All this yarn." She runs her hand along the giant spool. "We're supposed to get all of this onto the bobbins in a single morning?"

"We've done a full spool in a morning before," Laura says, ever the obedient one. She's standing now, too, with the end of a yarn strand still in one hand. "The weavers depend on us."

I look toward the window, where the noises from the busy

canal outside come spilling in. I'd rather sit on our upstairs balcony and watch the world. "The weavers can wait. Who wears wool in this weather anyway?"

"Are you complaining, Donata?" Mother walks in. "Summer is Venice's best trading time. I'm surprised you don't know that. Your sisters obviously do." This is my typical luck: Mother didn't hear Andriana complaining, only me.

"Other girls from noble families don't have to do guild work," I mutter.

"You'd be surprised the work that goes on behind doors." Mother picks up a bobbin. "Yesterday morning spoiled you. We can't go to parties every day. The storerooms still hold ten giant spools from the early spring wool, and all of them have to be transferred to bobbins for the looms before we leave for the hills in two months." Mother loosens a strand at the top of the giant spool and walks around it slowly, winding the yarn onto the bobbin with just the right tightness to keep it free of snags, yet just the right looseness not to strain it. I imagine her at my age doing the same. And at ten and eight and maybe even six. Mother's been an expert at this probably as long as she can remember.

Laura picks up a bobbin and works from the center of the giant spool. Paolina and I follow. We aren't as expert as Mother, but we're good at it.

The business of producing woolen goods is not ours, naturally. Nobles are not even allowed to be members of guilds. Nobles run the government—that's their duty. Most of my friends consider crafts beneath their dignity. They'd never guess that a noble, and a girl at that, had passed so many mornings doing this sort of work. Just yesterday, upon taking my hand, Teresa exclaimed at how soft it was. People say that to Andriana and Laura and Paolina, too, even to Mother. The lanolin in the wool nurtures our skin.

Uncle Alvise, Mother's brother, inherited his wool business from Mother's father, who died before I was born, like all my grandparents. Uncle Alvise is the chief officer of the huge wool-weavers' guild—1,541 members. The only guild with more members is that of the boatmen—1,741 members.

I know these wonderful numbers because I am a master eavesdropper. I eavesdrop when Father gathers my older brothers to discuss business. And I eavesdrop outside the library when my brothers are having their afternoon tutorials—if I'm lucky enough to slip out of my music lessons, that is.

Father talks a lot about the wool industry, because woolen cloth is what our family sells. That, and pepper. While nobles cannot make goods, they can trade them. That's how Father met Mother; she was the daughter of his major supplier of woolen cloth.

Mother had to do this work when she was a girl, but she doesn't have to anymore. She does it because she wants to stay within the tradition of her childhood family.

I duck past Laura and Mother as I walk around the giant spool. We don't do this work nearly as often as Mother did it when she was a child. Still, we do it too much. "The wool industry is a bore," I say.

"This part of it, perhaps." Mother winds steadily.

"This is the only part of it I know," says Paolina.

"Tell her the details, Mother," I say, "like you told us when we were Paolina's age."

Mother keeps winding, but she looks at me thoughtfully. "There are the beaters and the carders and the combers and the spinners and the weavers. And, finally, the sellers, like your father. It's a wonderful industry. The weaving, especially. Learn to appreciate it, for it's your heritage."

"Have you actually seen weaving?" asks Paolina.

"Of course."

Of course? This is something I haven't heard before. My step quickens. "When?"

"My family's factory is across the Canal Grande, on the waters of the Rio Marin in Santa Croce. Most of the wool industry is there. Because I lived on the island of Murano, I couldn't just walk into the factory anytime I pleased. But now and then I'd beg my father, and he'd take me along."

"Describe it to us," says Paolina.

My head buzzes. Mother's father took her places. And the way she's talking, it sounds as if she had the freedom to walk around Murano. How different must the childhood of a citizen be from that of a noble. I wish Mother would tell us all about her childhood. We've asked many times, but she rarely offers details.

"The apprentices warp the looms. Then they operate the pulley strings that control the heddles that raise or lower the threads of the wool. That's all they do. All day long. My brothers were apprentices when they were young and they'd complain about cramps in their shoulders.

"The journeymen often operate the pulley strings too, because it takes two men—one to each side of the loom. But sometimes the master lets the journeymen actually weave. That's where the skill comes in—the weaver is responsible for gauging the tightness and ensuring the evenness. And that's where the artistry comes in, too. For it's the weaver who chooses the colors and their arrangements. A master weaver sees the fabric that lies dormant in the waiting yarn, so that his cloths please the eye as well as the skin."

We are silent, caught up in Mother's description. I realize I've never before heard Mother say so many words without stopping.

"You know so much," says Laura finally. "I don't even recognize some of the words you said."

Mother gives a laugh. "Nothing's difficult about it. Nothing's mysterious."

"Everything's mysterious if you haven't seen it," I say.

Mother walks just ahead of me. Now she glances over her shoulder. "When you're a woman, if you like maybe I can get your uncle Tomà to take you to a factory someday."

"Me too," says Paolina.

When I'm a woman. Maybe. Does that mean when my reputation no longer matters? When I've entered a convent and am beyond scrutiny?

"Talk about the colors," says Laura.

"What?"

"You said the artistry of weaving is in choosing the colors. Tell us about that," says Laura.

"Actually, I was talking more about my own little ideas than about what happens."

"What do you mean?" asks Laura.

"The colors of the wools are muted. I always thought that if I were a boy, I'd break tradition and tell the dyers to make the wools as vivid as silk threads or blown glass."

Venice's silk is famous for its colors, especially scarlets and crimsons. So is the blown glass. We have blown glass chandeliers in splendid colors.

"Have you seen glass blown, too?" asks Paolina.

Mother nods. "The Gritti family factory is on Murano. Every child in Murano has seen glass blown."

"Even noble daughters?" I ask quickly.

"Some of them, maybe. Not all," says Mother. Her tone is a warning. She's not in the mood to hear me complain about Father's strictness. But I have no intention of complaining now. I don't want to do anything to stop Mother from talking to us like this.

"I know something about the Gritti factory," says Paolina.

"Is that so?" Mother laughs. "Do tell."

"It used to be here in Venice, but they moved it out to Murano because of the danger of fire. Glass factories have hot hot fires, and it's too dangerous to have them near homes. Giulia's mother talked about it once."

"That's true," says Mother. "But it's not the only reason, or even the most important one. They moved the factory because the dyes in the Gritti factory are the best of all the Venetian Empire—it's important to our economy to keep those dyes a secret. It's easier to protect the factory from spies if it's isolated out on Murano."

Spies. Mother makes the business of Venice sound alluring. I want her to talk and talk and talk.

"Mother?"

We all look over at Andriana. She's sitting on a stool by the door. She hasn't been working with us at all. I'm immediately curious. Andriana is not as scrupulously obedient as Laura, that's true, but she's also never been a rebel.

Mother stops circling the spool, so we all do. "What is it, Andriana?"

"Yesterday, at the party, Signora Lando remarked on how dark my hair is." Andriana curls a lock of her hair around one finger. "I was wondering if I should bleach it this morning. What do you think, Mother?"

Signora Lando is Teresa's mother. And Teresa's oldest brother is several years older than she is. He must be thinking of marriage by now.

Mother's face is quiet, but I can guess she's made the same calculation I have, for she puts down her bobbin. "I'll go ask Cook to gather the herbs. You find the widest-brimmed hat in the house."

Andriana stands with a smile. "Thank you, Mother. And ask Cook for lemons, no? I've heard lemons make the herbs work better."

"Get to work, you three," Mother says distractedly to the rest of us.

The world of Mother's childhood has been swept away. But that's all right, because I'd like to know about the present, too. Some of my friends bleach their hair, it's true, but I've never been there when anyone did it. "Can't we see first?" I ask. "We could help Andriana find the right hat, at least."

"All right. Go help your sister." Mother rushes to the kitchen.

We girls race upstairs to the *piano nobile*—the noble floor—where our parents' bedchamber and all the girls' bedchambers are. It turns out that Andriana secretly chose the hat last night. And she already cut a hole in the top of it with a knife she snatched from the kitchen after dinner. Everything about the way she acts now is strange—sure and independent. The authority in her voice excites me as she explains what we each have to do.

Andriana dips her hair into the large bowl of fresh bathwater sitting on the floor in her room. Paolina holds the hat upside down, at the ready. Now Andriana stands and bends over the hat, letting her hair fall loose in front of her. Laura and I tuck and carefully pull Andriana's hair through the hole in the hat.

"It's all in," I say.

"Stand back." Andriana straightens up, flinging her hair, so that it flops over the edges of the hat. She goes to the balcony and sits with her back to the sun, her face and neck shaded by that wide brim.

Paolina spreads Andriana's hair evenly in every direction.

Mother comes out holding a bowl of fragrant herb paste. She has on a wide-brimmed hat herself. "Don't stand in the sun without a parasol," she says to no one in particular.

We get our parasols and run back to the balcony.

Mother smears the herb paste along the locks of Andriana's hair, moving from the scalp to the tips. It glistens green and bright yellow. I sniff several times. Ginger, I think. And juniper? Perhaps that brassy yellow is Spanish saffron. Translucent blobs of lemon pulp cling to Andriana's hair here and there like tiny baubles.

The assurance in Mother's actions surprises me, just like Andriana's assurance in having the hat ready. No one has ever bleached their hair in this house, so far as I know. Yet Mother clearly has experience in this task. Did she and her sisters do this when they were girls?

Mother had only two sisters, and both of them died in the

smallpox outbreak that left Uncle Umberto blind. It happened at their summer home in Treviso. Mother and her other brothers were lucky enough not to have joined the others at Treviso yet. I watch Mother now for signs of sad memories. But her face shows nothing but concentration on the job.

Andriana's hair isn't really dark. It's light brown. Nowhere near as dark as Laura's and mine. Paolina's hair is even darker—the color of summer nights. This paste would never work on any of us, I bet.

"You've seen all there is to see." Mother gestures toward the inside of the room. "Go on back to work. The three of you can do at least half the spool."

We go back to the workroom slowly. Even Laura takes her time. We pick up the bobbins and walk round and round the giant spool.

"Francesco? Is that you?" calls Paolina. She was the one to call out, but we all heard the footsteps.

Francesco comes into the room. "Working, my lovelies?" He smiles. "Where's your big sister?"

"Getting herself beautiful," says Paolina.

"Is the Lando son looking for a wife?" asks Laura.

Francesco shrugs. "I don't know." He turns to leave.

"Tell us a story before you go." I drop my bobbin. It rolls across the room, undoing almost all my winding. But I don't care. Francesco's stories are how my sisters and I learn about the Venice we never see—the Venice my brothers are part of. I rush to block his way. "You were out late last night, weren't you?"

"I'm always out late." Francesco grins. "That's the fun of

being young and male." Francesco is twenty-two years old, old enough to take a wife. But so far he's shown no interest in settling down. Instead, he enjoys the company of many women. And sometimes, though I'm not supposed to know this, he sneaks a woman into his room.

My cheeks heat up at Francesco's words, but I'm so hungry for news that I persist, even at the risk that his tale will be bawdy. "So what did you see?"

Laura and Paolina put down their bobbins and come over to us now. "Tell us," says Paolina.

"What is this? First Bortolo, now you girls. Does everyone need amusement today?"

"What do you mean, 'first Bortolo'?" asks Paolina in a loud whisper. Her eyes brighten. "Did you hold his arms while he stood on the balcony railing again?"

"I'd never tell." Francesco raises his eyebrows and smiles mysteriously. Standing on the balcony railing is expressly forbidden. And it's something Bortolo loves. Francesco is the only one of us who dares to let Bortolo do it.

"Well, no matter what you did with Bortolo, telling stories to us is not simple amusement. It's edification," I say firmly. "And you hardly ever spend time with us anymore. Please, Francesco."

"I did see something wonderful, and it has a great story behind it." Francesco sits on the floor and we sit before him, like believers before a priest. He looks at each of us slowly, reveling in his power.

I pinch him on the leg. "Speak."

"I saw a painting by Paolo Veronese."

"A painting?" Laura's face falls. "Just a painting?"

"No, not just a painting. A very special painting. It was entitled 'The Last Supper of Christ.' "

I'm puzzled. None of my brothers is particularly pious, least of all Francesco. Nor does Francesco have a strong love of the arts. "What's special about the painting?"

"The apostles use forks to pick their teeth; the soldiers hold mugs of wine; the servants have bloody noses; silly people stand around in the background with parrots on their shoulders." Francesco's hands paint the scene in the air as he talks.

"It sounds raucous," I say.

"That's precisely what the representatives of the Inquisition said."

I draw closer in confusion. The Inquisition is the church tribunal that seeks out and punishes heresy.

"The Convent of Santissimi Giovanni e Paolo commissioned the painting, then the Inquisition denounced Veronese for it." Francesco's voice rises and his words quicken. "They said it was an offense to the eucharist and they demanded that everything that made the painting so vital and exciting be changed."

The painter was denounced—my heart pounds. What terrible punishment did he receive?

Paolina turns to me, her eyes big. "Father doesn't like the Inquisition telling Venice what to do. He's said that before, many times."

But Francesco laughs. "No one really tells Venice what to do. Or, rather, Venice never listens."

"So the Senate found a way around the denunciation?" I ask, incredulous.

"A most elegant, and, thus, Venetian way." Francesco's eyes

shine. "The Committee on Heresy simply changed the name of the painting to '*Il Convito in Casa di Levi*'—the banquet at Levi's house."

Elegant indeed. The lucky painter. I'm laughing.

"Who was Levi?" asks Paolina.

"A man in the holy testament who offered a banquet for Jesus," says Laura. "You know that story, Paolina."

"So Veronese is a free man and Venice got our wonderful painting as is." Francesco stands and wags a finger at us. "Remember that, my lovelies. To be Venetian is to be practical." He leaves.

I wonder where he's going. It could be anywhere. Anywhere at all. That's his right.

We are silent.

Finally, Laura picks up her bobbin. "Shall we be practical, my Venetian sisters?"

Chapter Three

THE XILOGRAFIA

It's late afternoon and I've finished my lessons—dance and music. Laura remains in the conservatory, practicing violin. She's good at it. I, on the other hand, have a stone ear; I'll never make anything but screeches with my violin, no matter how many years I practice. So I'm standing in the bedchamber I share with Laura, picking up the bronze statues of animals that Uncle Leonardo has given us. Every time he returns from his travels, he brings us another. The boar with the real bone tusks is my favorite. But the bumpy toad and the wide, scuttling crab are almost as precious.

The canals of Venice teem with crabs. Small boys crab all the time. I know that because of my brothers.

And I have a secret. Once, when I was Maria's age, I overheard my older brothers as they went down the stairs, talking about which baits they'd use to lure the crabs and who would get to swoop down with the net at the just the right moment. I snuck into their bedchambers and searched through their clothes until I found the shirt I wanted. I was such a little fool,

I picked one that had long sleeves with red lace at the cuffs and collar. I even put on a red cummerbund with lace, too. Somehow my four-year-old brain thought the boys would take me in as another brother if I wore boys' clothes—and I chose the clothes I loved the best.

I raced down the stairs and found the boys on our *fondamenta*—our bank on the canal—squatting in a huddle. They laughed when I came up decked out in party clothes. All but Antonio. He handed me a string and told me to try crabbing. And he called me "little brother." I actually believed he thought I was a boy. And, to everyone's amazement, within minutes a monster-sized crab tugged on my string. But then Cook came outside and shooed me back upstairs with the threat of telling Mother if I ever tried that again.

What fun it was. What fun, just to go crabbing.

I glance out over the balcony at the canal below. A small boat, a *sandalo,* carries four young men, standing tall. It turns onto a side canal.

I don't know the name of that canal. I've never been down it. And there it is, opening to my eyes, then disappearing behind the buildings.

Everything disappears behind buildings, around bends. Everything teases.

I think of the map in Cristina Brandolini's home, the one that shows every alley and canal of my dear Venice.

And now I'm rushing down a flight of stairs to our map room. I pass the library, where the door is ajar, and I can hear Messer Zonico, the boys' tutor, talking with Father. So the lessons must be over—the boys are gone, and Father is there. It's odd that Father's home this early.

I step closer and listen.

"Piero, at twenty years old," says Messer Zonico, "is the most persistent at his afternoon studies, though Vincenzo is the most brilliant."

He doesn't mention Francesco. That's not surprising. Francesco recently refused to study anymore with this tutor. He's too busy having fun.

But Messer Zonico doesn't mention Antonio, either. Antonio is seventeen—two years older than Vincenzo. If the tutor is talking about Piero and Vincenzo, he should mention my sweetest brother Antonio, as well.

Messer Zonico bids farewell. He'll come out the door any moment now.

I run to the map room and duck inside. The afternoon light hangs heavy. Maps are mounted on the top half of every wall, reaching practically to the ceiling. I see large land masses with mountain ranges, and lots of seas, and one vast ocean. Where in all this is the Venetian Empire?

My uncles could tell me. They have been almost everywhere.

Our only uncle who stays home with us is Mother's brother Umberto—because he is blind and never travels. I'm glad that he's always around, though of course I wish for his sake that he hadn't gone blind. He's my favorite uncle because he's always been the most patient. And he knows a lot, because, as he likes to say, he was adventurous before he went blind, so he had all sorts of experiences, even though he was but Francesco's age at the time. When I was small and everyone else would get annoyed at my incessant questions, Uncle Umberto would pull me onto his lap and answer question after question, until I was satisfied—at least for the moment.

But I have four other uncles. My father's brothers. When

they are in town, they live in rooms on this floor. They like living close to one another, and they gather often in this map room. The whole world matters to them. That's where they are now, off in that wide world. Uncle Leonardo is on a trade mission to Constantinople, undoubtedly buying barrels and barrels of pepper. Uncle Giacomo is on a peace mission to the Sforza palace in Milan. And, most important, Uncle Girolamo is finally governor of Cyprus, after three separate times of being ambassador, and Uncle Giambattista is ambassador to no less than His Holiness, the Pope.

I can say the place names easily. But I don't know where Cyprus is on these maps. I don't know where Milan is. Or even the Vatican.

One wall has smaller maps. In a sense, they aren't maps at all, but pictures of *campi* with churches. I find Piazza San Marco. It's the only one I recognize. Though I was but a little girl, the facade of that basilica is painted in my memory permanently from my one festival there, as are the bell tower and all the arches—arches and arches and arches.

I remember standing on a long balcony with Andriana and Laura. Mother sat beside us on a stool. And so many other women and girls lined the balcony. Mother was pregnant and not feeling well. Carolina was inside her—Carolina, one of our three sisters who later died.

Father talks about the census figures, how many people live in each area of town, how many babies die, how many women in childbirth die—so I know that our family is far from alone in these sad matters. Indeed, while Mother's and Father's childhood families had more losses than most, the family they have built together has made up for it by being exceptionally lucky. Mother has lost only three babies to illness, and all of them girls.

It was a dreadful time. A lethal fever swept through Venice, bringing the stink of rot, which hung in the air for months. Loud, raspy coughs racked all the girls younger than Laura and I. Mother quickly quarantined them. Iole and Daria, the other set of twins, died, as did the new baby, Carolina. Only Paolina lived through it, though she was pale and skinny. Mother has made up for it by feeding Paolina the fattiest pieces of meat ever since. She's now on the plump side, to be sure. Everyone knows the fattiest meat is the juiciest and the most delicious. But we don't begrudge it to Paolina. She is everyone's darling.

A rush of love for Paolina warms me. I'm so glad she didn't succumb to the fever.

I remember everything about the day of the great festival. Mother felt so poorly, she almost changed her mind at the last minute and didn't let us go. But Andriana cried and swore to hold Laura by one hand and me by the other, so that Mother wouldn't have to do anything at all—just be there. Mother finally relented, though she sat silent the whole time.

The woman to my left explained what was going on to her daughter, and, naturally, I listened closely. She pointed out who was who in the procession in the *piazza* below. She knew which officials wore the gold and white, which wore the crimson. She knew who the standard-bearers were. Her daughters ate candied nuts from a silk purse on a cord around her wrist and laughed at the rising slope on the rear of the Doge's hat. None of us could see the jewels from where we sat, but the woman described them in detail, as though she had actually seen them herself instead of just hearing about them from her husband. And she said, "Peace to you, Mark, my evangelist." She said it three times.

When we got home, I taught that saying to Andriana and Laura. And later we dressed up and played procession in our bedchamber, chanting those words as we marched around the room. I felt important—as though I were a soldier or even a senator, marching for everything good and holy, unflinching no matter what assailed me. Invincible. We played procession often. Then one day Andriana decided she was too old—and that was the end of it. Just like that.

I walk around the map room slowly now, but there's no aerial view of Venice. Nothing I can study to learn about this world I live in.

On the table by the window lies a picture which must be waiting to be mounted. I stand over it. It shows a ducal procession in Piazza San Marco. I smile; it's as though my memory a moment ago has come alive and materialized on the table, just for me. The men in the procession are talking to one another or playing instruments or marching fiercely ahead. One of them looks remarkably like Father, and I am sure now that the artist has tried to make the likeness of members of the Senate, for these men wear red gowns with fur trim. Why, there's Uncle Girolamo. It's uncanny the way the artist has captured his smile.

Along one side of the *piazza* women gaze down at the procession from a long balcony. That must be where we sat years ago. Beneath the balcony are arches. I remember the arches on the Basilica—but I didn't realize there were arches under where I sat, as well. I count them now. One hundred. Precisely one hundred arches. How perfect.

And now I look at the women on the balcony. I go from face to face. I don't recognize anyone, but perhaps these aren't noblewomen. Wait, this woman looks a lot like another one. Yes, it's the same face, the same dress, the same pose. Twins, like Laura and me. But, oh, the woman next to her is like the woman next to her twin. Two sets of twins? It can't be.

I scan the whole balcony. The women are repeated every twelve panels. They were done from a pattern.

But each man in the procession is unique—even though there must be over a hundred of them.

"Donata? Is that you?" Antonio comes in, carrying Nicola on his back.

I step away from the table. "I could be Laura." Of our seven brothers and three sisters, none can tell Laura and me apart. Unless we're undressed, that is; I have a blue-black birthmark on the bottom of my right foot and another on my back.

Antonio lifts his eyebrows in doubt. "If you were, you wouldn't be here."

That's true. But it doesn't matter, because I know Antonio won't get mad at me. He's the one who showed me how to crab, after all. He never gets mad.

Nicola smiles at me. "Antonio is my horse. I'm going to race him in Campo San Polo."

"I've never been to Campo San Polo," I say.

"I'm going," says Nicola.

I bet that's true. I bet little Nicola will go to Campo San Polo and I never will. He'll watch the horse races and I never will. Maybe he'll even ride a horse in a race some day, though Campo San Polo is not in our section of Venice.

Antonio gallops around the table with an exaggeratedly high gait, so that Nicola bumps wildly, letting out shrieks of glee. He halts in front of me and prances in place. "What are you doing in here?"

"Do you know who made this wood engraving?"

"Matteo Pagan. He has a shop on the Merceria."

"The Merceria," I say. It's the biggest commercial street in Venice.

"When Father and Piero and Vincenzo and I go out in the morning, we take the gondola to the point on the Canal Grande near where the old Rialto bridge stood before it burned down. You know that spot, right?"

I nod. Mother comments on the site of the old bridge every time we pass it.

"The Merceria runs from there to the Piazza San Marco. The four of us walk the full length, listening to trade news. Then Father continues on through the *piazza* to his work in the Senate, while we boys wander back slowly." He smiles. "Getting our fill of current events."

"And going into shops is current events?"

"In a way. We have to know what Venice produces, after all. And it's fun." Antonio grins now. "That's a fine *xilografia*, don't you think?"

"The men are real," I say. "The women aren't."

"What do you mean?"

A thickness forms in my throat. I feel unreal myself, like the women in the *xilografia*, as though everything I am, everything I think, is merely an idea, a dream—and a flimsy dream, at that. I know nothing. "Have you ever seen a map of Venice that shows all the *palazzi* and the canals and the alleys—all from above?"

"Jacopo de' Barbari made such a map." Antonio stops prancing. "Why?"

"I wish we had one."

Antonio frowns. "I could get a copy, I'm sure. But what's on your mind, Donata?"

"Venice," I say. "Simply Venice."

"Keep going, horsie!" Nicola shouts. He squeezes Antonio's nose playfully. "Go go go."

They gallop out of the map room.

CHAPTER FOUR

MIDDAY MEAL

Mother's in the kitchen with Cook. So is Aunt Angela. Even Cara, the wet nurse and laundress, is in the kitchen.

Andriana and Laura and Paolina and I have spent the morning playing with the little ones in Laura's and my bedchamber. Or, rather, Paolina and I played with the little ones, while Laura and Andriana worked on the girls' hair. I'm used to putting my hair in braids, naturally, but the bun Andriana has fashioned on me is not a twist of braids over one another. Instead, it's a clever smoothing into a large puffy ball. And it's not in the ordinary place, on top of the head. No, the new style, according to Andriana, who somehow manages to learn these things, has the bun at the back of the head.

Aunt Angela comes into the room. "Don't you look nice. And just in time. Come along, everyone." The boys run past her toward the dining hall. Little Maria takes her hand.

Andriana looks Laura and Paolina and me over with a discerning eye. "Oh, I forgot something. The most important thing. We'll be there in a few moments, Aunt Angela. I promise."

"Hurry. Your father has announcements to make. He won't tolerate delay." Aunt Angela leaves with Maria.

Andriana picks up her hairbrush, and with quick, deft moves, she loosens a few strands of curls on both sides of Laura's face, so they hang down beside her cheeks. "Isn't that perfect?" she says happily.

And it is—the curls are of exactly the same thickness and length. I smile in admiration.

"Now, Laura, you do that to Paolina. I'll do myself and Donata." Andriana goes to the mirror and primps.

I stand beside her feeling foolish. After all, if Laura can arrange Paolina's hair, then I should be able to arrange my own. I reach for a lock of hair at my temple.

"Don't, Donata." Andriana speaks gently. "You heard what Aunt Angela said. Father's got important announcements to make. That's why everyone's cooking so much. It will be like a party. You want to look your best, don't you?"

Andriana's right; I'll look better if she does my hair. It's not that I'm clumsy. It's more that I'm impatient about certain kinds of things—and hair is among them. I hold my hands behind my back to keep them from acting against my better judgment.

Andriana kisses me on the cheek and fixes my hair. I stare at the mirror transfixed. I look just like Laura—perfect.

We hold hands and walk to the eating hall. Giovanni plays on the floor with a carved wooden tiger that Francesco brought him from the Chinese market—Francesco is liberal with gifts; he loves the markets. But everyone else is seated.

Even little Maria. Andriana and Laura and Paolina and I take our seats.

The table is strewn with delicate pea flowers. Our dining table always has flowers, but not in this much profusion unless we have guests. Cook has scattered rose water on the tablecloth. I feel pampered and happy.

Giò Giò, Cook's primary helper, serves. An antipasto of *folpeti consi*—boiled octopus with parsley. Then a first course of rice with snails and raisins. And, finally, lamb, bitter chicory, bread with honey. It is, most definitely, a feast.

The boys talk together. The girls talk together. Mother instructs Nicola and Bortolo on their eating habits, as she does every meal. Maria looks from face to face silently. When she sees me looking at her, she waves. I wave back. Father waves at us both. Maria giggles. The air feels like a festival.

Cook comes in carrying a plate piled high with cookies of every type—*zaeti* and *amareti* and *baicoi* and *busolai*. He puts them in the center of the table, as always. And, as always, I immediately push them directly in front of Uncle Umberto, who loves cookies almost more than the small boys do.

I don't know how I came to earn the privilege to be the one to push the cookies in front of Uncle Umberto. I'm sure that any one of my brothers or sisters would like to do it. But somehow everyone looks to me—and it has been this way as long as I can remember.

"Thank you, Donata." Uncle Umberto's blind fingers lightly tap until they find the biggest *zaeto*, his favorite. The rest of us wait, out of custom, full of happy expectation at the pleasure we know will cross his face as he takes a bite, and I realize that this is the right atmosphere for asking for gifts.

"Father," I say. Everyone hushes. When Father speaks or when Father is addressed, everyone pays attention. "Do you know the mapmaker Jacopo de' Barbari?"

"Indeed I do." Father looks at Mother, then back at me. "Have you met one of his daughters?"

"Of course not," Mother says firmly. "Donata's friends are all noble daughters."

"But I've seen one of his maps, Father. At the Brandolini home. It shows Venice from above, as though the mapmaker were flying. I think we should have a map like that."

Father's mouth curves up at one corner. "You do?" He leans across his plate toward me. "That's quite a suggestion from a daughter."

"I didn't mean it as a suggestion," I say quickly. Please, I'm begging in my head, please don't sweep this away as an impertinence. "It's more a hope," I say aloud. "The map is beautiful. And Venice belongs to all noble families, after all."

"Venice does belong to all noble families. It's a good idea, daughter. We can think about it later." Father looks across the table. "We have other things to talk about now." He clears his throat. "In fact, though, I'm glad our . . ." Father pauses and looks at me.

"Donata." I'm used to supplying my name, just as Laura is.

". . . our Donata has so auspiciously brought up the fact that Venice belongs to us, and, hand in hand, we belong to Venice—facts that carry certain duties. Yes, I'm grateful to Donata, for this is precisely what I want us to focus on today." Father's voice assumes the tone of an announcement. "By the Venetian law of 1242, all sons share equally in the inheritance of their parents. You know this law well," he says.

We nod.

"It's a good law," says Father, "because it ensures a kind of equality among brothers that engenders family loyalty. In some of the other city-states outside Venice, only the oldest son inherits. The rest must prevail on the generosity of the oldest or join the priesthood or set out on their own, which almost certainly dooms them to a life of meager means."

Yes, Venice's way is better, I think. More fair. For the boys, that is. For the boys it is truly a serene republic.

"So, as you well know, the natural result of this law is that only one son can marry," says Father. "This is not law, but, rather, a tradition based on common sense. If every son married and had sons of his own, the family wealth would be squandered away to nothing in the span of a few generations. So only one son marries, and the rest live *in fraterna*—in a state of brotherly companionship—in the ancestral home, with plenty of money all their lives." He looks meaningfully from one to the next of his sons, all the way around the table. "When these brothers die, their wealth passes to their nephews—only one of whom, in due course, will marry and have sons. And so it goes, on and on, conserving the wealth and protecting the family forever."

Nicola grabs something from Bortolo under the table. Bortolo jabs him with an elbow.

"Excuse us, please," says Aunt Angela. She gets up and lifts Nicola into her seat and takes his, placing herself between them.

Bortolo makes a face at Nicola across Aunt Angela.

The little ones are restless—and with reason. Nothing Father has said so far is news.

"Francesco is twenty-two," says Father, "only three years from manhood."

"Three years from when I clothe myself in a black gown," says Francesco. "But I am already a man, Father."

"I stand corrected." Father smiles at Francesco. "In any case, it is time to discuss the future of this family, and, hence, the future of my sons."

"And not just marriage, Father," says Piero. "Our educations must be discussed. My best friend has already been attending university for years, but I'm still working with a private tutor, after thirteen years."

"For good reason," says Father. "By having you boys study at home, I have the chance to talk with your tutor and to watch you. I understand your different strengths. And you have the chance to find your own preferences."

"How can I find a preference when the lessons are so easy?" Vincenzo says. "The tutorials bore me, Father. Completely."

"I agree with Vincenzo," says Francesco. "I learn everything I need to know by walking round the markets, listening to the traders."

"You see?" says Father. "Francesco has just proved my point. He's learned things about himself. Your friends, Piero, may already be at the university, but they are pursuing a course of study chosen for them, not by them. A good life is one of service to the Republic, and, thus, to God. But a happy life is one in which that service brings personal satisfaction as well. Your grandfather was wise enough to teach me this."

"And your father is wise enough to teach you, in turn," says Mother.

"Francesco," says Father, "your words reveal what I myself

concluded. Your strengths lie in the love of the hustle and bustle of the marketplace."

Francesco's eyes shine and he smiles close-lipped, with appropriate dignity. Father is saying what we all know is true.

"I see a future for you in exports, wheeling and dealing."

Francesco nods, his smile wider now.

"You can have this *balestreria*—a position on a merchant ship. The government will endow part and I can pay the rest. This will give you a chance to learn the arts of Mediterranean trading."

"I've always wanted to travel," says Francesco.

"I thought so. I've seen you enthralled, listening to Uncle Leonardo's stories whenever he comes home." Father's eyes grow very serious. "And I can see more in your future. Eventually, I see a place in the Senate committee that regulates foreign trade."

Francesco's immediate surprise turns slowly to glowing pleasure. With his willful ways, not a one of us imagined him rising higher than a minor magistrate.

"We need contentious souls to hold our strength abroad," says Father, "and I know no soul more contentious than yours, Francesco." He laughs.

The sense of celebration in the air makes us all laugh, even little Giovanni, playing on the floor again, who cannot possibly have any idea of what this conversation is about.

"To do this well, an education is needed. If you're willing, my son, you'll study law at the University of Padua beginning at the start of the next term. A year will suffice."

Francesco gets up and comes to Father's side. He kneels and kisses Father on each cheek. "I'm more than willing,

Father. I see a purpose to my studies now. I will add to our family fortunes, you'll see. I won't disappoint you."

"You never disappoint me, Francesco."

Francesco goes back to his seat.

"Piero," says Father.

Piero leans forward. His cheeks filled with color when Father spoke of the University of Padua. Though university study is not that common even among nobles, Piero has been wanting that openly for so long. Father has already committed himself to paying for Francesco's *balestreria* plus a year of university. But he has to be willing to pay for Piero's education, too. He simply has to be, or Piero couldn't stand the disappointment.

"You're a thoughtful scholar, though you're but twenty."

I watch Piero's Adam's apple go up and down as he swallows his anxiety.

"And you excel at teaching your younger brothers. They respect you."

Piero lifts his chin, accepting the well-deserved praise. For it's true: When Piero plays with the little ones, the game usually transforms itself into a lesson of sorts. Father has observed carefully, to notice this in him.

"But a year at the university wouldn't serve you well."

Piero's face goes slack, as does mine. I don't want him sad.

"You have a developed sense of both precision and justice. The combination makes you suitable to govern men, my son. You will practice your legal skills in the *Saviato agli Ordini*, then move on to the Senate, without a doubt. So, with your assent, I've arranged for you, as well, to start studies at the University of Padua. But your education, unlike Francesco's, will take several years. You must be able to converse well with the heads of states in perfect Latin and Greek. You must know jurisprudence to the last detail. You must represent your family, your country, and God in the best way you know how."

Piero sits a moment, clearly stunned. His future rolls out before us. Several ambassadorships, then a governorship. He'll be like Uncle Girolamo. Or maybe even like Uncle Giambattista, who talks with the Pope himself. My skin prickles into gooseflesh.

Francesco laughs. "It's perfect, Piero. I'll rake in the ducats, and you'll spend them."

Oh, I hadn't even thought of the money. Most ambassadorships are unpaid posts. So it will cost our family a lot.

Piero grins. "But my prestige, dear Francesco, will allow you to get that eventual post on the foreign trade committee." He lingers teasingly over the word "eventual."

"I take it the plan is acceptable to you," says Father.

Piero gets to his feet so fast that his chair falls backward. We all laugh. He rushes to Father, kneels, and kisses Father's cheeks. "I will do everything in my power to be worthy of your trust."

"And expense," calls out Francesco. But it's a good-natured jest.

"And expense," says Piero, with a smile.

"You are already worthy of both," says Father.

Piero returns to his seat.

We all look to Father. Could there possibly be more announcements?

He smiles at us, obviously enjoying the way his proposals have been received thus far. "Antonio," he says. "It's your turn."

Antonio's chest rises and falls visibly, he breathes so hard. "I love Venice, Father," he says quickly, before Father can continue. "But I have no inclination for trade or travel—unlike Francesco—nor am I clever at studies—unlike Piero. I hold dear the values of the Venetian Empire, and of the city of Venice, and of our own cherished family. I will always toil faithfully. I want to stay here, in this city, a member of the Senate, eventually, if I am fortunate enough to be elected. That is the life I want, serving however I can."

I hardly breathe. Antonio is my most placid brother. I've never heard him take control like this. And with Father, of all people.

But Father shows no surprise; he doesn't hesitate. "Precisely my assessment, Antonio. The family will thrive in your hands someday."

Antonio blinks. He's confused, as we all are. All of us but Mother.

Mother reaches across the table and puts her hand on Antonio's. "You're the one to marry."

"Me?" Antonio looks from Mother to Francesco. "But what about Francesco?"

Exactly my question. Father was the oldest of the brothers in his generation, and he was the one to marry. And his father was the oldest of the brothers of his generation. The custom in our family is clear.

Francesco lifts both hands, palms facing Antonio. "In my opinion, there are too many lovely gardens in Venice to enjoy only one."

Paolina perks up. "The *palazzo* of the Nani family is said to have the most wonderful garden in Venice."

We laugh, Paolina joining, though our silly little sister doesn't know the joke's on her.

"I'll keep that in mind," says Francesco.

"And you, Piero," says Antonio. "What about you?"

"I've never hoped to marry," says Piero. "I took it for granted that Francesco would be the head of the family." He speaks slowly, as though working his way through his thoughts. "With all my serious studies ahead, and then the hardships and dangers of life abroad, a wife would have no place in my future. And, Antonio, the very fact that your first reaction is to check the response of your older brothers is proof that you value the peace of the family above all else. Father and Mother have not erred."

Antonio smiles. "I would enjoy a family, it's true. My own children." His eyes are warm with joy. "My own children to climb all over me."

"Just as you've let your younger siblings do." Father smiles. "An education serves a father, as it does a senator," he says. "The more you've studied, the better decisions you make."

Antonio nods. "I see that, Father. I see that in you."

"So, then, it's settled. You will join your older brothers in Padua next term. They will commence the study of law at the university of jurists. You will commence the study of philosophy at the university of the liberal arts. For how long is up to you."

Antonio gets up and walks to Father's side. He kneels and kisses Father's cheeks. "Thank you, Father. You will be my model."

"Not in physique, I hope." Father puts his hand on his large belly and laughs.

Antonio goes back to his seat.

Father picks up his napkin and wipes his mouth, a gesture of finality.

"But what about me?" asks Vincenzo.

"You're the quick one," says Father. "No one doubts that. But you still have much to learn about yourself. It's not time yet to discuss your future. The next order of business is the family's marriages. Antonio's and Andriana's. Andriana's first, since Antonio's must wait until he finishes his education."

Andriana jerks to attention.

"But not this moment. I have several matters to deal with now. These are enough decisions for one day." Father gets up and leaves.

Once he's out of the room, Vincenzo scowls. "All the good choices are taken." He counts off on his fingers. "Francesco will make the money, Piero will spend it, Antonio will make laws and babies. What will I do?"

But everyone is getting up and going about their business.

Everyone but Laura and me. We look at each other in perfect understanding. Father has said the next order of business is the family's marriages. Antonio's and Andriana's.

He said nothing about Laura and me.

CHAPTER FIVE

LOVE

"You look so glum." Paolina squeezes my hand. "Come with me. Please. Giulia's mother is going to a garden party at the Fiorazzo family's *palazzo* in San Trovaso. She's taking Giulia. And she invited me. I know she'll let you come, too."

San Trovaso is in the neighborhood called Dorsoduro. They'll go in Giulia's family's gondola, directly to the steps of the *palazzo;* they won't travel any intriguing alleys.

Still, there are many things you can see from a gondola, even through a veil.

And the Fiorazzo garden might be marvelous.

But when Paolina gets home, she will describe every wide leaf of fig, all the white bells of japonica, the scent of laurel. I will shut my eyes and feel I'm walking through grass, and think I breathe the wisteria. I don't need to actually be in the garden myself.

Besides, if I went, I would watch the mothers' faces as they beamed on their marriage-bound daughters, the way they'd insist the girls stay in shade to keep their skin perfect, the way they'd hover.

"You'd get to miss violin lesson," says Paolina, coaxingly. "I know you hate it."

Not even her slyness can bring a smile to my lips. "You go and enjoy yourself, Paolina." I look over at Laura, who stands by our bedchamber balcony, just inside so that no one can see her from the outside. Her back is to us, and the curve of her shoulders carries the sadness I feel. "I need to talk with Laura, anyway."

"Both of you should come with me," says Paolina.

"We don't love gardens the way you do," says Laura softly, without turning.

"You need to learn to love something," says Paolina. "Something besides men."

Laura and I both look at our little sister.

Paolina stands solemn-eyed. "A garden is a like a whole group of children. Very quiet children—but very beautiful children, too. If you take care of plants, they grow and bloom. And sometimes they grow in ways you don't want them to; they can be naughty."

My silly little sister isn't silly at all. I cup Paolina's round face in my hands and press my cheek to her forehead.

"How long have you known?" asks Laura.

"Giulia's mother told me two years ago. She explained why she allowed me to dig in the sun with her gardener when she wouldn't allow Giulia."

"I'm sorry, Paolina," says Laura. Tears roll down her cheeks. "I'm sorry for all three of us. And for Maria, too."

"Don't be sorry for me." Paolina goes to the door. "I'm going to spend my life in wonderful gardens—maybe even here in our *palazzo*. I could make the most fragrant garden ever if Father would let me." She stops, her hand on the doorknob. "Do you want to come?"

"Not today," I say.

Paolina leaves.

I put my arm around Laura's waist and she folds herself against me in sobs. Beyond her shoulder, I see the traffic on the Canal Grande. The nobles and citizens are like a sea of black gowns and *barete*, dotted here and there with the crimson of a senator. I watch the standing men sway with each movement of the gondola oar. From this angle, I don't see a single woman in the boats. "In a few years our brothers will join the men in those boats." I work to keep bitterness from my voice. "And they'll get a wonderful education. All those years at the university. We should be glad for them, at least." I swallow. "And especially glad for Antonio."

"Don't be brave, Donata. I can't bear it. It's terrible enough that little Paolina has to be so stoic." Laura rolls her forehead hard against my collarbone.

I put my hand on her neck. "You're right." I pull the pins out of Laura's bun and smooth her locks free down her back.

And now a brush is passing through Laura's hair. Mother has come in silently. She moves the brush rhythmically. How much did she hear?

I step back, but Laura remains curved toward me, her torso forming a bereft hollow for her tears.

I take the pins out of my own hair and shake it free. Mother is still brushing Laura's hair. Laura is still crying. She cries double, for both of us.

"Can't we both stay here to care for Antonio's children someday? Please, Mother," says Laura.

"Rooms will be needed for Antonio's family to grow. No one can know ahead of time how many rooms. And it is custom to have only one maiden aunt at home. If two are kept, then they'll argue." Mother's words lack emotion. They come in regular beats, like the movement of the brush.

I don't even want to take care of Antonio's children—but I want even less to go to a convent. "The boys all get to live here forever if they want—and they take up rooms, too."

"Men can vote. It's important that the family voters stay close and all vote the same way." Mother shrugs. "Women can't vote. It isn't practical to keep daughters at home."

Practical. I remember Francesco saying that to be Venetian is to be practical. I want to scream. "Is it practical to lock girls away in convents?"

"I don't know any girls who were locked away, Donata, and neither do you." Mother reaches with the brush for my hair.

I step away and shake my hair as though it's a mane.

Mother goes back to brushing Laura's hair. "Girls go into the convents voluntarily, for the good of the family."

"Voluntarily?" I stare. "Who would volunteer for such a life?"

"The convent has its advantages."

"What advantages?" I demand.

"Women are protected there."

"Protected? Mother, they're trapped. They have no freedom."

"That's not true, Donata. They can continue their music studies. They can have parties with lovely foods and any guests they like. And those who are so inclined can talk to diplomats and influence the direction of government."

The last thing I want to do is continue my music lessons. And what's the point of parties, if all I wear is long, black, shapeless gowns?

No one speaks.

"If I hadn't married," says Mother, at last, "I'd have entered a convent happily."

"So you could influence the direction of government?" asks Laura.

Mother laughs. "A girl of my background couldn't do that. But nuns can work. Many of them weave. That's what I would have chosen."

I know it's true the moment she says it. Just yesterday morning her voice filled with joy when she talked of weaving. "That's why you don't feel sorry for us now. But look at us, Mother. We're not lucky like you were. We have no trade to pursue. We've never had a chance to know a trade. Noble girls have no chances."

Mother's eyes cloud with pain and for an instant I'm sure she does understand, after all. But she blinks, and her eyes change again. "This from the one who always laments when asked to work? My dear Donata, you can't have it both ways. Lucky, indeed. Your childhood has been full of pleasures. Your adulthood will be, as well, if you allow it."

How does she do this? How does she manage to make me feel ungrateful whenever I complain? I want to argue more.

But Laura steps forward, cutting me off purposely, I know. "How often can nuns visit home?" Her very question smacks of resignation. I want to shake her.

"Suora Luciana came home for every important family event."

Suora Luciana was another of Father's sisters. She drowned in a boating accident when I was small. I don't remember her. "That's not enough," I say. "This is our home. Not some dreadful convent."

"There's nothing dreadful about them. Oh, my daughters, the families of Venice recognize the sacrifice, and they are tolerant of behavior in the convents. They shut one eye."

"As well they should, Mother." My voice is firm, but already the practical side of me, the Venetian in my veins, wonders exactly what behavior is tolerated. I cannot ask, though. I will do nothing to suggest the convent is an option to consider.

"Don't play the rebel now, Donata. It will serve you well to accept your future. What can you do about it anyway? This is the way things are."

Laura sniffles. "Girls in convents do not fall in love."

"Many girls outside of convents don't fall in love, my daughter."

I think of the whispers about unhappy marriages. Maybe by the time women are Mother's age, they accept the idea of loveless marriages. But how can anyone accept that idea at the start of a marriage? "Andriana wants love," I say. "I know she does. When the girls our age talk at parties, we talk about love—that's what we talk about—and about the boys we've seen at Mass on Sundays and about who might like our brothers. Andriana wants love, Mother."

"We will do our best to find Andriana the proper husband, but she will have to do her best to be happy with him, whoever he is. Old or young. Ugly or handsome."

A proper husband. Mother always talks about proper this and proper that. She's always trying to prove to everyone that she's proper—that she's worthy of Father. I'm so sick of being part of her proof. "What makes someone the proper husband, Mother, if not love?"

"Don't talk nonsense, Donata. You know very well that a noble girl needs a husband who can offer her the kind of life she's accustomed to. Falling in love has little to do with a good marriage."

"Father fell in love with you," says Laura. "He married you out of love."

"And he paid for it roundly." Mother puts the brush down and turns Laura to her. "Your father has the makings of a governor. There is no one smarter or more diligent than he. But when he chose a wife outside the nobility, he cut himself off from that kind of success."

"I didn't know that," I say, instantly going limp inside. Father has always seemed content in his world. He talks of his brothers' achievements without rancor—he boasts of them, even.

"That's why he's been so careful with you children." Mother talks softly now. "The boys have been educated at home longer than most—so that Father could keep an eye on them. You girls have been more sheltered than most—so that no one can question your virtue and noble character."

"Father got love, but we never will," whispers Laura.

"There are all kinds of love." Mother goes to the large canopied bed that Laura and I share. She sits and rests her hands in her lap. "Convents are bursting with the love called charity."

"But they're not bursting with children," Laura says. "I want children, Mother."

"Oh, my daughters, what you don't know." Mother motions us to her. Laura sits on the floor and puts her head on Mother's lap. I remain standing, but close enough that my skirt presses against Mother's. "The courtesans of Venice run a high risk," says Mother, in a grave voice. "Many of them have children they neither want nor can care for. Venice has so many illegitimate children, her orphanages overflow. Besides that, many mothers die in childbirth, and their infants often go straight to the orphanages."

I tremble slightly. When Mother gave birth to Giovanni, she was sick for months afterward. So sick that we had to get the wet nurse, Cara. When Mother first said Giovanni was her last child, I was grateful. I'd forgotten how grateful until just now.

"Clergy help in the education of these children," Mother says. "Nuns teach the girls to sing and play instruments. They teach the boys the virtues of discipline and hard work. You can be like mothers to tens of children. You can do so much good with your lives."

I don't want to teach music. I don't want to be surrounded by tens of children and pious women. I don't know what I do want anymore, but it's not that, it's nothing like that.

Mother pats Laura's cheek with one hand and takes my hand with her other. Her clasp is tight. I cling to it.

CHAPTER SIX

CLOTHES

I'm wrapping the white cloth around my chest. It's soft, filmy silk, the finest Venice makes, which means the finest in the world.

Mother would blink at such a claim. Her cheeks would go ruddy and the corners of her mouth would pucker just a little and she'd wait for me to continue—for me to say, "That notwithstanding, the quality of this silk is clearly second to that of Venice's wool." Then she'd smile hugely and continue her rushing about.

My hands tremble a little as I tuck the end of the swath in place. It's been three days since Father's announcement of the family marriages, but it feels like forever. Everything has changed. I stand in profile and examine my changed self in the mirror.

"Flat as a man," says Paolina with a giggle. She slinks up behind me and gives me a conspiratorial grin in the mirror.

I twirl around and kiss the tip of her nose.

Laura makes a tsking noise and plucks at the silk swath that binds my breasts flat. "Someone's going to guess. Someone outside."

"No one outside will guess," says Andriana. "Neither of you will ever have enough bosom to arouse suspicion."

"That's the truth." I laugh teasingly. "I saw you sitting in profile at the balcony windows yesterday. No one in Venice is ignorant of your ample charms. I bet half the bachelors in the city long for you."

But Laura's chewing on her bottom lip. She doesn't give even the smallest smile. "Do you have to bind yourself so tightly, though, Donata? That can't be good for your growth. Think of Chinese women's feet, after all."

Francesco has told us stories he's heard about Chinese women's feet, contorted so unnaturally from binding that the women cannot walk. They have to be carried around. And stories about their nails, grown so long that the women cannot use their hands. They have to be fed and washed. A spasm of distaste jerks me tall. I don't want to be a man. I simply want the privileges of a man. Or at least this one privilege: free passage. And I must seize this privilege now, before it's too late. But I wouldn't give up my womanhood for it.

I loosen the silk swath and breathe deeply.

Laura's face softens in relief.

"Laura's right," says Andriana. "You're going to get caught. Not by strangers. By Mother. Then we'll all get in trouble. And if that happens, I'll say I told you not to do it. I mean that, Donata. I won't get in trouble over this—not now—not when Father and Mother are looking for a husband for me."

"That's all right. I wouldn't ask you to take any blame on my behalf. Besides, there won't be any blame to take. And think of it, sisters. Francesco has been practically ignoring us lately—he almost never tells us stories anymore. But today I'll go out and have adventures myself, and I'll bring home wonderful stories for all of you, and no one will be the wiser."

"We don't need wonderful stories, Donata." Andriana presses one hand against the spot between her eyebrows. I know she's trying to keep her brow from furrowing—she does that to prevent those ugly lines that worriers get. "Don't do it. You will get caught."

"How?" My hand goes to my mouth and I look at Laura. "Oh no, you're not going out yourself today, are you? You're not visiting a friend?"

"No no," says Laura. "But you will get caught."

"Not if you pretend you're me when Mother comes asking, as you promised." I catch her right hand in both of mine. "You will be true to me, won't you?"

"Of course. I'll curtsy for you and hurry to whatever task Mother sets. I'll be the most obedient and sweetest self anyone could want. All in your name, I swear."

"So that will work," I say. "Mother is so busy these days, carting Andriana around to the dressmaker's and all those . . ." I stop myself. I was about to call the things Mother and Andriana do foolish. Jealousy can make me unkind. That's truly foolish. Besides, I am happy for Andriana. I must remember that. "Mother's never in the workroom. She hardly notices I am here now. She won't notice when I'm not here."

"She'll notice," says Andriana. "How could she not, if Laura is as obedient as she promises to be?"

I look at her quickly. Then Paolina laughs, and we're all laughing.

I pull on the black hose and slip into the blousy, thin shirt common to noble boys in summertime, and, finally, the light sleeveless jacket. I stole these clothes two days ago from a pile of my brothers' castoffs that Cara had gathered for the poor bin at the church of San Marcuola. It was actually that pile of clothes that started everything. It sat there, like an opportunity.

I snatched this outfit before my head could even think what I would do with it.

But, really, the thought was always there. After all, it was wearing boys' clothing that gave me my one chance to go crabbing years ago.

If my adventure is successful, if I am not caught, life will be very good. At least until Father dispatches us to the futures he chooses for us. I am going out into the world today. Me, Donata. Out into the world, on foot.

"Your patch is less than artful," says Laura. She's plucking at me again, nervously trying to arrange my sleeve so the patch doesn't show so much.

I put the patch on last night, working under the oil lamp late into the dark. What a pity that the one shirt I grabbed from the charity pile had a rip in the sleeve. But by the time I had the chance to spread the outfit out in my room and examine it, it was too late to pick another shirt; Uncle Umberto had already bagged up the rest of the pile and lugged it off over the one little bridge to San Marcuola yesterday, before Sunday Mass. When I asked him what had happened to the pile, he didn't even question why I should want an old shirt. He just offered me one of his own. I didn't take it—Uncle Umberto is three times my size—but I kissed him and thanked the Lord for the ripped shirt I already had.

"Who cares?" I say now, though I am promising myself silently that I will be extra careful not to get new rips in this outfit. It must last me, if I am to go on lots of adventures. "The boys who walk the streets don't all look refined, you know."

Laura's eyes grow large. She didn't know that, really. None of us know it with our own eyes. All of us understand that anything I say at this point comes indirectly via a brother, probably Francesco. Yet the very fact that I am about to go out in my disguise has somehow already lent me an air of authority. I warm to my subject. "Most of the boys outside aren't at all like our brothers. They aren't the sons of nobles, but of citizens. And not always well-to-do citizens. They're rough characters."

Andriana presses both hands to her brow now. "You need to look like one of the refined boys, Donata. Absolutely respectable. You don't want someone picking a fight with you."

"Or worse," says Laura.

"What's worse?" I ask.

"I don't know," Laura whispers. "I don't want to know."

Paolina claps her hands suddenly. "Ha!" she says, and climbs onto our high bed. She carefully spreads her skirt out around her in a circle. "You don't have to worry about that patched shirt. I've taken care of it."

"What?"

Paolina's fat little cheeks almost burst with pride. "A boy is coming here. A guild member."

Andriana steps close to the bed. "What do you mean?"

Paolina clasps her hands together and bounces on her bottom in glee. "I arranged a trade. Donata will give him her clothes—her boy clothes—and he'll give her his."

"My clothes are patched and worn threadbare. Did you tell him that?"

"Yes."

"If he's willing to take them, then, his must be just as bad," I say.

"Not at all," Paolina says. "His are good. I made sure of that."

"Why on earth would he trade good clothes for bad?" Laura asks.

"Because . . ." Paolina sits up tall. "I also promised one of my outgrown dresses for his little sister."

"But what about your own little sister?" Andriana's voice is a scold.

"Maria won't fit into it for years. And by that time, Mother won't remember it. Besides, I wore it gardening at Giulia's home. It's so stained, Maria would be glad to avoid ever wearing it." Paolina beams. "See? I thought of everything."

I know the dress Paolina means. Last fall she wore it almost every day. Cara had to practically wrestle it away from her to wash now and then, muttering little angry words in her native Friulano dialect. Paolina has so many funny ways.

But stains or no stains, the boy is getting the better end of this bargain, I bet. He is assuredly less well-off than we are. So Paolina's outgrown dress, despite the stains, will be far finer than this boy's sister's other clothes.

I take off the hose and sit on the floor cross-legged so I can rub at the birthmark on the bottom of my right foot. This is how I wish for luck. "Where is this boy?" I ask.

"He's supposed to deliver fish within the hour."

"A fisherman?" Laura's voice rises in a squeal. "You talked with a fisherman?"

"A fisherboy. He's nice," says Paolina.

"A fisherboy," says Andriana in a murmur. "I've never even been allowed to talk to the spinners when they take away the bobbins of yarn, but here you talked to a mere fisherboy. His father probably isn't even a citizen. Did anyone see you with him?"

"Cook, of course. I went down to the ground floor with Cook and helped him select the eels yesterday," Paolina says. "And when he was out of earshot, shouting orders to Giò Giò about where to lug away a barrel, I asked the fisherboy. And he said yes. Just like that."

"Aren't you something," Andriana is saying slowly. "You may have as much mischief in you as Donata does." She looks slantwise at me.

I stare at Paolina. A fisherboy? I'll be wearing fisherboy's clothes.

"Fishers wear terrible clothes," says Laura. "Trousers and big, loose shirts. Donata would never want such clothes."

"Yes, I do," I say, suddenly realizing the possibilities. Fishermen don't live in our section of town, in Cannaregio. The fishing industry is in Dorsoduro, the only section of Venice that is larger than Cannaregio—much larger. If I'm going to blend in wearing those clothes, if I'm going to be an anonymous fisherboy wandering the alleys, I'll have to go to Dorsoduro. Alley after alley, all the way to Dorsoduro. "The fisherboy's clothes will be perfect."

"You can't be serious," says Andriana. "Fishers aren't refined.

You can't go out dressed as a fisher. Someone awful could come up to you. Don't do this, Donata. Forget the whole thing."

"I'm going out," I say. "No matter what." Out.

My heart flutters, then slowly begins to pound, louder and louder. I feel like I'm passing through the giant, thick doors of a cathedral.

Chapter Seven

THE EXCHANGE

"There he is." Paolina points.

The other three of us press together on the balcony and look out on the Canal Grande. There's much to see in both directions. Too much. "How can you pick his boat out from the others?" I ask, counting three fishing boats in the direction Paolina points.

"I can't, really." Paolina takes the brown paper parcel that holds her old dress and runs to the door. "I have faith. Come on, Donata. We have to get down there."

I snatch my satchel, which holds the boy shoes, the clothes for exchange, plus the *bareta* that Vincenzo used to wear over his messy hair. I stuff it under my nightdress, which I put back on after Paolina's announcement about this fisherboy. The hidden satchel sticks out fat in front. My eyes meet Paolina's and we've got the same thought. She puts her parcel under her skirt, too. We smile and parade our fake pregnant bellies for a moment.

Paolina peeks out into the long corridor. "All clear."

Cara passes by just at that moment, with a bucket and a scrub brush. She doesn't count. None of the servants count.

At least not so far as Laura and Paolina and I are concerned. We girls are old enough to go about our day within the *palazzo* without interference from them.

So the only ones who might question what Paolina and I are doing are family members. Father is undoubtedly working already; he leaves at dawn and doesn't return till the midday meal.

That means Mother is the one we need to avoid on this floor. But I cannot hear the shrill voices of Maria and Giovanni, so Mother may well be off somewhere with them—probably in the kitchen. At yesterday's evening meal Maria blurted out that she missed Mother, she missed making treats with her in the kitchen. Mother said that was silly; she was right there. But her face showed that she knew she's been too scarce lately. She's allowed the whole marriage business to consume her. She must be in the kitchen with Maria and Giovanni now—I'll bet on it.

Paolina and I walk to the stairs, our hands clasped in front under the secrets of our fat bellies. We could run, we're both so excited. But that might arouse Cara's suspicions.

The next two floors down present the greatest dangers: our other six brothers.

Cristina Brandolini once said she envied me for having such a large family. I was happy when she said it; I love all of us. But this morning I wouldn't mind if I had fewer brothers to sneak past.

Piero and Antonio and Vincenzo are hardly a threat, of course, because they're probably already strolling the Merceria, on their way back from walking Father to the Senate. But Francesco could easily be home still, especially if he spent his night frisking around with courtesans. If he caught us on the stairs in our nightdresses, he'd demand to know what we were doing. When we didn't answer, he'd shoo us back to our floor and start who knows what kind of teasing tonight at the evening meal. And teasing like that could lead to a family inquisition.

Paolina takes the parcel out from under her skirt and puts it under her arm so that both her hands can hold the stair railing. Solemn, she walks on tiptoe.

I kiss her cheek and toss my own satchel over one shoulder. Then I take Paolina's parcel from under her arm, so that she can hold the railing more firmly. We hardly breathe as we pass the entranceway to the rooms on the next level down.

And now there's only one floor to go before the ground floor. This is where Bortolo and Nicola sleep, with Aunt Angela to watch over them. This floor is also where the kitchen is, though Cook and Giò Giò sleep on the fourth and fifth floors above the ground floor, with the rest of the servants. And this floor is where Uncle Umberto sleeps. But if he hears us, all we have to do is run. He's slow in his blindness, and so long as we don't say a word, he'll never know who passed on the stairs.

That's everyone. For now, at least.

We're halfway down the stairs when laughter rings out—unmistakably Nicola's. Aunt Angela's lament predictably follows. Nicola has played some naughty trick on her again.

No sound of Bortolo. Oh, no. Sure enough, there he is, lying on the floor in the middle of the doorway, watching us come down the stairs. His big head rests on the back of his folded arms. His eyes shine like one of Venice's zillions of cats. He lifts his brows without saying a word.

I nod, equally silent.

We've just agreed with our faces alone that I will bribe him, as I have many times before. For, although this is my first time going out on my own, I've had other secrets of various types and Bortolo has developed a special knack for discovering them. I'll have to bring him a treat from outside.

Now he points at Paolina, ready to extort from her as well.

She shakes her head.

Bortolo gets to a sitting position and opens his mouth, but I rush to him and clap my hand over it.

"Please, Bortolo. It's only me who has a secret," I hiss. "I'm the only one who owes you. Paolina is going right back upstairs."

His eyes bore into me over the top of my hand. He doesn't look convinced.

"I'll show you," whispers Paolina, squatting beside him. "I'll come by on my way back up. I'll even take you up with me, to play."

Bortolo peels my hand away from his mouth. "None of you other girls are fun. The only one who plays good is Donata. She's almost as good as Antonio."

I warm with pleasure. Antonio has always been the most fun to play with. It's an honor to be compared to him.

Paolina takes a deep breath. "I'll get Andriana to hold you steady as you stand on our balcony railing."

"Andriana won't agree," Bortolo whispers. "Only Francesco dares do that." That child is no fool.

"Yes she will," says Paolina.

"Bortolo!" calls Aunt Angela, from down the corridor. "Where are you?"

"Nowhere," calls back Bortolo. He shakes his head at Paolina and leans toward her. "And what if Andriana doesn't agree?"

"I'll bring you a plant from Giulia's garden," says Paolina. "A flowering plant."

Bortolo wrinkles his nose. "Who cares about plants?"

Paolina takes a loud breath and I know she's preparing to argue.

"I'll bring you an extra-special treat," I say quickly.

"A treasure," insists Bortolo.

"Yes, a treasure."

Bortolo gets up and runs down the corridor. "I'm coming. I'm coming to get you, Nicola, and turn you into a big fat goose with my big fat goose magic and eat you. Yum," he screams.

Nicola shrieks in fear that is only half a game.

I stifle a laugh, and Paolina and I run the rest of the way down the stairs.

The ground floor is full of the noise of outside, for the big gates that open onto the Canal Grande have been pulled back completely and all Venice pours in with the unfettered stream of sunlight. The fishing boat already bobs in the water channel that cuts into the central foyer of the ground floor. Cook haggles with the fish vendor, who barks orders at a boy. The boy jumps here and there about the boat, finding exactly the fish the vendor wants to show Cook.

Paolina and I hunch in the cool, damp shadows and work our way along the wall until we can duck into the first storeroom.

"Give me those," Paolina says. "And stay here."

I'm not used to taking orders from Paolina. But this is her plan—so I hand her my satchel and her parcel and move a little farther into the storeroom. The strong odor of clean wool thread, the odor I'm familiar with from so many mornings of preparing bobbins for the looms, is at odds with the strangeness of the situation. I slowly wind a strand around my arm from wrist to shoulder. When I can't stand the suspense any longer, I peek into the foyer.

Paolina sits on the stone floor behind Cook, perched on the satchel, which lies on top of the brown paper parcel. In that position, she seems tiny and much younger. Not even Father could be upset that she's not wearing a veil in front of these fishers. Every now and then she says something to Cook. No one suspects her. She could get away with murder, that's what Mother says. I bet when she finally enters a convent, the nuns will find her so unruly, they'll try to marry her off even if it means putting up a dowry for her themselves.

At last Cook leads the fisherman up the stairs and Paolina tosses the parcel and satchel onto the boat. She stands now, with her hands on both hips, imperiously.

I watch for the boy to hand Paolina a satchel in return. But he opens the one she gave him, says a few words, then strips off his shirt. Right there in front of my sister. We've seen shirtless boys and men from our window on occasion, but never up close like this. Except for our brothers, and they don't count. Though Paolina will never marry and, thus, her reputation doesn't really matter, she shouldn't be subjected to this sort of thing. I come out of the storeroom, despite the fact that all I have on is my nightdress. "What do you think you're doing?"

The boy throws the shirt on the stone floor and turns his

back as he pulls off his trousers. I go hot with embarrassment, but, even more, I'm amazed at the muscles of his back and bottom and thighs. And astonished that he is as brown under his clothes as on his neck and feet. Why, he must fish naked. The image of the lagoon littered with rocking fishing boats full of naked fisherboys leaves me speechless.

He has already donned the old black hose from my brothers, which look ridiculous, actually, and he's pulling on the shirt, when we hear the fisherman as he descends.

I race back to my storeroom and peek out.

Paolina picks up the boy's old shirt and trousers.

"What's this?" asks the fisherman.

"A trade," says the boy.

The fisherman looks from the boy to Paolina and back to the boy. The brown paper parcel is nowhere in sight. He turns up his hands. "Why?"

"For fun," says Paolina. She gives her most charming smile and the fisherman finally laughs with confusion. In a flash I see her as the Mother Superior to her flock of nuns. No one could fail to take her word for anything.

The fisherman gets in the boat and they push off and paddle those long oars, almost as long as the oar of a gondola.

It's only when Paolina thrusts the boy's fish-stinky clothes into my face with a triumphant laugh that I put my hands into my long hair and gasp in realization. "A *bareta!* He didn't give me his *bareta*. Or shoes, either."

"Wear the old ones you stole from the charity pile," says Paolina.

"They're in the satchel."

But the fishing boat is gone.

CHAPTER EIGHT

BAREFOOT

Paolina helps me braid my hair tight at the back. We work silently. There's no one to hear us, even if we did talk; Giò Giò already came down and closed and secured the great gates to the Canal Grande. But somehow the dim light of this storeroom calls for quiet. The only sun is the thin strands that sneak in through the bars over the small, high window.

Paolina tucks my braid inside the fisherboy's shirt, which is so long on me, it comes down to midthigh. "Watch where you step," she says, her voice strangely nasal because she's holding her nose against the stink of these clothes. She smiles and leaves.

I wish the fisherboy's shirt gathered tight at the throat like my brothers' shirts. Then at least I could be sure my hair wouldn't work its way out as I walk along. But I'll just have to hold my neck stiff.

I climb over giant spools of wool thread and hide my nightdress in a corner. Then I go to the tall doors that open onto the alley side of our *palazzo,* turn the key in the hole, and slip out. There's no way I can lock these doors from the outside, so I simply close them firmly.

The stone under my feet is cool because this alley is in continual shade, with a *palazzo* on each side, both facing onto the Canal Grande. Only people coming to one or the other *palazzo* pass here. Luckily, the alley is empty. It's so quiet, I can hear the hens cluck in the neighboring courtyard.

I walk to the end of the alley and turn. If I were going to Mass, I'd continue on, and over the small bridge ahead. But now I go only halfway down this alley, and, with my heart pounding in my ears, I turn down a side alley I have never ever walked before. I go to the end of it, and stop. The way I'm panting, you'd think I'd been running. I feel almost dizzy.

The wide street in front of me is raucous. I recognize it from the talk at our dining table: This is the Rio Terrà di Maddalena. It was a canal until a few years ago. Now it is among the most traveled passageways of Venice. It's also one of the filthiest, for although the sweepers clean every night, merchants have been passing here since dawn. I gulp.

We go barefoot indoors all the time. But I've never before been outside in bare feet. When I go to church or to a friend's home, I wear my fancy shoes—the ones I hate. But at least those high soles keep me safe from the mucky street.

Nothing protects my feet now.

I remember the fisherboy's brown feet. Why, he doesn't even have shoes. Of course not. It's so obvious, I almost laugh at what a fool I was. And he probably doesn't have a *bareta*, either. If he fishes with no clothes on, he certainly wouldn't put a hat on his head. I was an idiot to put mine in the satchel. He's probably sold them both by now.

Well, if he can walk back and forth from his boat to his home every single day with no shoes, then I can certainly go out just this one day with no shoes.

"Move, boy." A water-carrier pushes me aside with a rough swipe of the arm. The two deep buckets swing heavily from the beam balanced across his shoulders.

I shrink back from the touch of his large hand. We have a courtyard with our own cistern. But many homes get their water from the public cisterns in the *campi*. The job of carrying water takes enormous strength, because it's unending. This man will trudge all day long from that cistern to every home in our parish that doesn't have a private cistern.

I walk in the direction that would be to the right as we look out our balcony window onto the Canal Grande. That's the general direction of Dorsoduro, where the fishermen live. I stay close to the walls, trying to ignore the bits of rubble that tickle my arches and stick between my toes. Every man I pass seems larger than normal, more powerful. I know this is just because the water-carrier gave me a scare. I know I can manage this adventure. There's nothing really dangerous about it. Just bare feet, that's all.

A boy my size but a couple of years younger walks toward me. He's barefoot and in trousers, too, though he has a *bareta* on. I press against the wall to allow him passage. But he catches my eye, and his own glints. He also hugs the wall closer. I swerve out to go around him, but he quickly swerves himself and our shoulders bash hard.

"What you think you're doing here?" His face is mean. Three rings of dirt circle the creases of his neck. His breath smells of rancid figs. It warms my cheeks.

Warms my cheeks! No veil. I'm outside without a veil. That's what it means to be a boy—but, oh, it makes me feel as if I were naked. I fight the urge to cover my face with my hands.

"This spot's mine."

His language is crude and hard to follow. I have to get away from his nastiness fast. I lower my head and try again to pass.

He grabs me by the hair at the nape of my neck. "What's this? What you doing with hair like this?"

I twist away, but he pins me to the wall.

"Whatever gimmick you've got, boy, go use it someplace else." His face is so close to mine, I fear his lips will brush my cheek. "Don't ever let me see you begging around here again."

So that's it. "I'm not begging," I say reasonably. "I'm a fisher-boy."

"With this white skin?" He pinches my cheek. "If you beg as bad as you lie, you'll not last long in this world. Take your fake fancy talk and go die someplace else." He spits in my face and walks on.

I'm breathing heavily as I wipe the boy's saliva from my nose and brow. I want to go straight home. Now, this very instant. Straight into the arms of my clean, cooing sisters. But the beggar boy went in the direction of home. Oh, I spy him now, leaning against the wall by the opening of the alley that leads back to my *palazzo*. I have no choice; I hurry in the other direction, shaking with disgust.

I don't want to go to Dorsoduro now. The beggar boy was right—I'd stand out, with my fishbelly pale skin against all the deep tans of the fisherboys. People would look, and then someone would notice my hair tucked into the back of my shirt and who knows what would happen then. I wouldn't even be able to talk my way out of trouble; they'd all accuse me of acting fancy.

If only I could find a way to circle back through the alleys and home again. But I remember the confusing maze of alleys on the map in Cristina Brandolini's home. I remember how Francesco laughs when he talks about all the times he's gotten lost. I must stay on this street—I must walk in a straight line, so I don't get lost. As soon as I'm sure the beggar boy is gone, I'll go home.

What am I thinking? Here it is, my first venture into the world I've wanted so much to explore, and I'm about to run back home. What a fool. There is so much around me—so many marvels. I can't let one vile boy ruin it all.

I must find strength. Strength and pride. The kind I had when I used to play procession with Laura and Andriana. I remember the words of the woman on the balcony beside me as we looked down on the Piazza San Marco that one wonderful day. "Peace to you, Mark, my evangelist," I say inside my head. And I'm marching, marching.

Ahiii! I lift my right foot. A large splinter of wood has embedded itself in my sole, smack in the center of my birthmark. I lean against the wall for balance and try to pull it out. The end that protruded breaks off. Now the only way to get it out is to dig at it with a needle. And, Blessed Mary forgive me, but it burns like the fires of eternal damnation.

I want to cry. Who'd think that a thing so insignificant as shoes could ruin an adventure? For want of shoes, I've been labeled a beggar and banished from the alley that leads to my home. For want of shoes, I'm now a cripple.

I hobble along the street, my bottom lip trembling with self-pity. My path winds carefully around stray objects that might cause further injury to these poor feet of mine. Every step hurts.

The bell of San Marcuola rings loudly. The church is off to the left somewhere beyond the next bridge. It couldn't be that hard to find.

The clothes for the poor mount high in a bin just inside the doors of the parish rectory. I could go to the rectory and ask for a pair of shoes. They're sure to have wooden-bottomed *zoccoli,* at the very least. And I could beg a *bareta,* too.

But I would recognize the priests. They're always slavish around Father and Mother, and they mumble pious words to us girls as we leave the Mass. So there's a chance, no matter how small, that they'd recognize me, even though they've only seen my face when they've lifted the veil to offer the Communion wafer and wine.

And maybe there are other beggar boys watching me, too, not just that one boy. Maybe asking for shoes would count as begging to them.

I can't go to the rectory.

My foot hurts worse with each step.

I come to the bridge. A group of boys swim naked in the canal. I blushed at the sight of the naked fisherboy this morning—but now all I feel is envy. A fine reprieve on a hot day. I'd smile if my foot didn't hurt so much. I look back toward the alley I think of as mine. So many people clutter the street that it takes several minutes before there's enough of a clearing for me to see—alas, the beggar boy stands beside the opening of the alley talking to a man.

I fight back tears and look ahead. On the other side of the bridge the pathway opens to the right into a wide street. I can see the opening to the first alley off of that. No one comes out of it. No one goes in. I'd be safe there, at least for a little while.

A cart loaded with summer melons from somewhere far south of Venice rolls past noisily. The vendor and his two helpers bump it up the steps of the bridge, roll it across the center, then bump it down the steps on the other side. The bridge is narrower than the passage, so walkers cluster impatiently behind the cart as it crosses the bridge, then quickly fan out and pass around it on the far side. I wait. When the hubbub quiets down, I limp over the bridge. I stay right behind the melon cart as it turns into the next wide street. Then I turn again, into the quiet alley.

I lean against a wall. It seems my whole body throbs now with the pain of the splinter.

A man comes out of a house and walks past me without a glance. But I cannot take my eyes off him. He's a Jew. I know from the little cap on his head. Mother explained about those caps once when we passed a boat full of Jews. She said all Jewish boys and men wear them.

This must be the path to the Jewish Ghetto. I've heard Francesco talk about it. The newest synagogue of Venice stands in the Ghetto Nuovo—the New Ghetto. Why, I can go there and ask for shoes. Jews are famous for their charity. That beggar boy won't care if I seek help in the Ghetto. He's not a Jew, for he wasn't wearing a little Jewish cap. And, yes, I can ask at the synagogue for one of those caps, too. Then no one will question me about my hair.

I move along the shadowed alley as fast as I can manage. The smaller alleys to the side are dark and cool and soothing, like the little alley beside our own *palazzo*. I realize that's because the buildings here are extra tall, some of them taller even than the biggest *palazzi* of Venice. And the alleys here are hardly dirty at all. I don't have to keep scanning the ground for sharp objects.

There's light ahead—light and music. Children sing in another language. Not Venetian, and not the Latin I hear every Sunday at Mass. This must be the ancient language Hebrew. I get to the end of the alley and stop just within it, having a clear view of the *campo*. Small boys, ranging from perhaps six or seven to ten or eleven, stand shoulder to shoulder in rows before a tall, heavyset man of perhaps twenty years old—maybe twenty-five at the most. The high, sweet voices rise into the late-morning sunlight like doves.

When the boys finish singing, they drink from a basin of water and disperse. The choir master, or whatever he's called, sends greetings to their families in a strong voice and in clear Venetian.

I wait for him to disappear down an alley, then I manage

my way painfully to the basin and dip my sore foot in the water. It's surprisingly cold. The shock almost numbs me, like the Chinese balm that Mother administers to our cuts.

A dark boy, much darker than the fisherboy, walks up to me and stands with a bucket, waiting, his eyes black stones in clear white. He stares at my foot.

I realize with a gasp that I have dirtied the water he's come to fetch for drinking. I turn aside quickly, ashamed. "I beg of you," I say softly, beckoning him to take the water. "Surely you can still use it for cooking."

The boy doesn't answer. He doesn't wear the Jewish cap. He must be a slave.

Father keeps no slaves. He believes it is unjust for one human being to own another, since all human beings have souls. He's right, as always. But some noble families disagree, and even ordinary citizens own slaves if they can afford them. This boy is probably Turkish. In our recent war with Turkey many slaves were taken.

The slave fills the bucket and drags it by the rope handle, walking backward. His eyes flicker from the vacillating surface of the water in the bucket to me. The water and me—we both worry him. Maybe he'll get a beating if he spills too much water. But why would I make him worry?

I wait till he's gone. Then I dip my hands in the water and let it trickle over my sore foot.

"Do you have a disease?"

I practically jump at the voice. "No, gentle sir." The man has a small start of a beard. He looks around Antonio's age—seventeen. Or perhaps eighteen.

"Your foot is turning black."

"What? No it's not." I look down at my feet, which seem obscenely white against the gray stone.

"Hasan told me."

The boy. I wonder if he told that I had my whole foot in their drinking water. "Your slave boy was mistaken, as you can see." I offer a small smile.

"Hasan is no slave. We don't keep slaves here." Scorn sharpens the man's voice.

"My father doesn't keep slaves, either," I say quickly.

The man's eyes narrow. Then he laughs. "Your father, who cannot even keep his son in shoes, does not keep slaves. What a surprise."

He's laughing at me, as though I'm a fool. I go hot.

He stops laughing and squats, so that his head is now at my waist level.

The unexpectedness of his action makes me fall back a step onto my right foot, my injured foot. I wince from the pain.

"Let me see," he says kindly. "Hasan said the blackness is on the underside."

Ah, now I understand. "It's a birthmark," I say, twisting my foot upward. "But I got a splinter in the center of it." The splinter forms a ridge under the skin. It's long. The sight of it makes it hurt more.

The man takes my foot in his hands. I pull back instinctively, but he holds firm. His hands feel around the edges of my foot. He looks up at me with questioning eyes.

"If you have a needle, I can work it out," I say at last. "Please, sir."

"Why did you come here?"

"I saw the basin," I say. "I came to wash my injury."

"Tell the truth."

"As the Virgin Mother is my witness, this is the truth."

The corners of the man's mouth twitch. I'm almost sure he's holding back a smile. "The Virgin Mother, indeed," he says. "But why here, in the Ghetto?"

I try to free my foot, but he's got a strong grasp. "I was going to visit your synagogue and beg for shoes and one of your caps."

"A yarmulke? What does a Catholic boy want with a yarmulke?"

There's nothing to respond to that.

"All right, boy, we're used to people seeking refuge. We turn no one away. But if you're spying, that's another story."

"I'm not a spy." The idea is absurd. "Who would I spy on? And why?"

The man turns his back, still in a squat, still holding me by the foot. "Climb on my back and we'll take care of that splinter."

I've both gotten rides and given rides before. But only with my family members. The young man waits, tensed in his squat. The very position makes his shirt press against his flesh, revealing the outline of muscle. What if he senses my femininity? Or, worse, feels the evidence against his back? But what else can I do? Barely breathing, I climb onto his back and curl my hands around his shoulders lightly, holding my torso stiff and as far from his spine as I can.

He carries me across the *campo*, up an alley, to a doorway. He kisses the fingers of his right hand and touches a metal marker on the doorway. Then we pass through the dark storage area of the ground floor, and up the stairs. He opens the door of that first floor above the ground floor and walks inside, me still on his back.

I am in the home of a Jew.

CHAPTER NINE

QUESTIONS

An older woman, with a basket over her arm, is clearly on her way out. She gives me a glance, hears about my splinter from the man, and leaves, without a word.

The man deposits me on a bench at a kitchen table. "One minute." He goes into another room.

I'm alone with a strange man in a strange house. The thought makes me shake. Mother would be appalled. So would my sisters. And I can't begin to describe the way Father and my brothers would react. I should go down the stairs and out as fast as I can.

But I don't want to limp home, a failure. Laura and Andriana would argue that this is proof that I shouldn't go out in disguise ever again. Only Paolina would take my side, and she hardly counts. If this were my only reason, I'd have no choice but to go immediately.

But there is another reason: simple curiosity. The very reason why I've come on this adventure. I never even hoped to find myself in someone else's home, much less that of a Jew, much less alone in his kitchen so that I can freely look among his things. And it isn't dangerous to be here, because the man doesn't know I'm a girl.

The ceiling is low. The wood of the furniture and counters and door and floor is as dark as Paolina's hair. I run my hand along the table. The surface is worn smooth; it feels almost soft. I stand and hop on my left foot as quietly as I can, over to the counter. The wood dips in one spot, forming a shallow indentation. This must be where they grind nuts, or maybe pound meats. Our counters at home have similar dips, but the counters are marble, so the dips are but slight.

The smell of onions permeates the air, but I don't see any bins of them. And there's another smell, a sour smell I don't recognize. And the odor of sweet wine.

Plates, bowls, cutlery are stacked neatly on the sideboards in a funny arrangement. Some of the bowls are on one board, and others are on the other board. The same number of bowls, in fact: eight. And exactly half the plates are on each board. I count the spoons.

"Hello." A girl comes into the room from the stairway. Though she's small, her face shows she's at least Bortolo's age—six.

"Good day."

She wrinkles her nose and I remember the reek of fish in my clothes—I've become used to it. "What happened to your yarmulke?"

What a funny first question. She doesn't even ask who I am. But at least she didn't say something rude about my smell. I smile at her and quickly put down the spoon I'm holding. It clacks against the others.

"No!" The girl rushes to the sideboard. "Now look what you've done."

"What?" I clutch my hands together in front of my chest. "What did I do?"

"Sara? Is that you?" The man comes into the kitchen. "Can you find me a needle?"

"This boy mixed the spoons." Sara picks up the spoon I was holding.

The man takes it from her. His other hand goes to his head in dismay, and he knocks his yarmulke off center.

I look again at the sets of spoons on each shelf. They are identical. I merely set the spoon on the wrong shelf in my haste.

Sara spreads out the spoons on both shelves and counts. "See, Noè?"

"Did you move anything else?" the man called Noè asks me. His voice holds a frightening fierceness.

I press my clutched hands to the underside of my chin and shake my head.

"Tell the truth," Noè says. "This is important. We separate our eating utensils by what they are used for. We cannot mix them."

Sara gasps. "Doesn't he know how to keep a Kosher home?" She looks at me with awe. "So that's why you don't have a yarmulke. Are you a Lutheran, then?"

"A Lutheran? Of course not." My eyes burn. I know in a moment I'll cry. "The spoon is the only thing on those shelves that I touched." I turn my head away and blink fast. "I'm sorry," I mutter. "I didn't know. I'm sorry."

Sara comes around in front of me. "Don't cry. Sometimes

babies make the same mistake. The rabbi can fix it." She lifts her chin coaxingly. "We'll use forks in the meantime." Her tone is that of a mother.

I smile in spite of myself.

Noè puts the offending spoon in his pocket. "What are you doing home at this hour, Sara?"

"I came to fetch a cushion for Mother's back."

"Then fetch it and be gone."

To my surprise, Sara runs off obediently, all her spark suddenly subdued.

"Sit back on the bench," Noè says. He picks up a wine jug and a knife.

"You're not using that knife on me." I sit on the bench and tuck my right foot under my bottom.

"I won't cut. You'll see." Noè puts out his hand for my foot.

I don't move.

Noè laughs. "I won't cut. I promise."

Grudgingly I extend my foot.

Noè pours wine over it. It stings. Then he uses the point of the knife to nudge the splinter toward the hole where it entered.

I suck in with a hiss.

"This might take some time." Noè's voice is casual. "So. What are you doing in the Ghetto?"

"Exploring."

He uses his thumbs now to squeeze toward the splinter. It hurts a lot. "Exploring what?"

"I already answered one question. It's your turn," I say, more boldly than I feel.

"All right. Ask."

"Did I make a terrible problem with the spoons?"

Noè smiles. "It can be fixed. So what are you exploring?"

"Everything," I say. "Why are the buildings here so tall if the ceilings are so low?"

"Don't you know about the decree back in 1516? All the Jews of Venice were ordered to move to the Ghetto. So the buildings have to be built tall enough, with enough floors, to hold us all."

"How sad that they had to leave their ancestral homes."

"But they didn't."

I cock my head in confusion. "What?"

Noè jabs the point of the knife a little too deep.

"Ahiii!" I yelp.

"Sorry. This splinter is stubborn."

A bubble of blood forms on my sole. I look away. "What do you mean, they didn't leave their ancestral homes?"

"Some of them had their ancestral homes here. Jews have lived in the Ghetto for the past five centuries. But others have lived on the island of Giudecca even longer, so they stayed there. And there are plenty on Murano."

"They didn't obey?" I ask in alarm. State punishments can be severe. "So what happened to them?"

"Nothing."

I can't believe that.

Noè squeezes from the sides of my foot again. "Ah, at last."

I look down. An end of the splinter sticks out.

Noè puts his head to my foot and, with his teeth, he pulls the splinter out. "Ta-da!"

I'm still amazed at the fact that this man's mouth was just on my foot. But the relief of having the splinter out surpasses the amazement. "Thank you. It's maddening that something so small could cause so much pain."

"You owe me," Noè says, pouring wine over my foot and finally letting go.

Now the wine stings worse than before. I cradle my foot in both hands and blow on it. When the sting stops, my foot feels much better. I look up at Noè. "I owe you for more than just this. I owe you for the water in the basin. I dirtied it with my foot. It was thoughtless. I'm sorry."

Noè smiles. "Hasan told me."

"I'll pay for it. I have no money on me. But I can bring some back."

"I bet you can." Noè puts the wine jug away. "But that's not what I meant. You asked several questions in a row. So you owe me several answers in a row. Where do you live?"

"Do you promise not to tell anyone?"

"No."

"Then I won't answer."

Noè folds his arms across his chest. "You said you wanted shoes. We have *zoccoli* that will fit you, but we can't afford to simply give them away."

"Sell them to me then," I say eagerly. "I'll bring you back the money."

Noè makes a small whistle. "Now, why is it that you'd rather buy *zoccoli* than simply borrow them? I know you've got shoes at home. Your feet are too soft and tender to travel the streets barefoot. I bet today is the first time you've gone outside barefoot."

"You're the one with the mind of a spy," I say.

Noè laughs. "Answer that one question and I'll sell you a pair of *zoccoli*. Why buy rather than borrow?"

"I want to own them so that I can use them over and over."

"Why don't you use your own shoes?" Noè says.

"I already answered your one question."

Noè grins. "All right. I'll get the *zoccoli*."

"And a cap, too," I say. "A yarmulke."

CHAPTER TEN

TOLERANCE

I run home, despite the small ache that remains in my foot, holding the yarmulke in place with one hand. Noè gave me one that fit just right. But when I went into the alley and twisted my hair up inside it, it no longer fit. Instead, it balances loosely on the coiled braid. These *zoccoli,* likewise, flop a little, and since they are open-toed, I cannot simply stuff a little ball of wool yarn inside each sandal. But I'll find a way to tighten the leather straps. I'll make them fit perfectly. The yarmulke may be a lost cause, but the *zoccoli* are not. And that's all right, anyway, because I'd rather have a *bareta,* which wouldn't mark me as a Jew. I have to figure out a way to get one.

I duck in and out of the crowd on the Rio Terrà di Maddalena, keeping an eye out for the beggar boy. Everyone's going home to eat. I spent more time in the Ghetto than I realized. Please, please, dearest Lord, don't let me be late. And, oh, if I am late, my brothers will have come in already and surely locked the door behind them. I run now.

I go in the side door of our *palazzo,* which is, mercifully, still unlocked, straight to the storeroom where I left my nightdress. Within seconds, I've changed.

The sounds of my four older brothers are loud outside the storeroom door. They've just come home, only steps behind me, and they're joking about something. A woman, I think. A woman from the Castello area of Venice. Perhaps it is not only Francesco who wastes his time with prostitutes, for Castello has so many of them. All of us girls know that.

They pass by the storeroom door, which I realize with a skip of my heart is slightly ajar. One of them closes it. Oh, thank you, Lord. I bet that was Piero. He cannot abide disorder.

And I cannot believe my good luck to have arrived without their seeing me and then to have them be so involved in conversation that they didn't even investigate an open storeroom door. This is a very good day, despite how it started.

I hide my *zoccoli* and the yarmulke in a corner. Then I roll my trousers and shirt tight and hold them under my nightdress, as I held the satchel when Paolina and I played pregnant this morning. When my brothers' voices fade to nothing, I peek out.

The side door opens again.

I duck back into the storeroom, my heart thumping. I cannot risk the noise of pulling the door shut all the way.

Footsteps fall heavy. It must be Father. And he's tired—he passes slowly.

I run to the foot of the stairs. Father clomps upward. His footfalls echo up and down the empty stairwell. I walk as softly as I can, staying a floor behind him. He enters the *piano nobile.* I creep up the remaining flight and peek into the corridor.

Laura sees me; she's been waiting for me. She gives me a quick glance, then she rushes down the corridor after Father. "Papá," she calls, "Papá, tell me about your morning and I'll tell you about mine." She chatters as she pulls him into the dining hall.

I slip across the corridor into Laura's and my bedchamber. I hide the fisherboy clothes in the bottom of the closet and dress as fast as I can.

Andriana comes in. "You're late. But you're lucky; it seems everyone is late."

"Help me," I say, unbraiding my hair.

Andriana sniffs at my hair. Then she takes a jar of rose water and sprinkles it lightly. "Be gone, fishy smell," she says in a mock-religious tone.

I laugh, but I'm grateful to have been saved from difficult questions at the meal. Tonight I will rinse my disguise thoroughly.

Andriana picks up the brush now and works her wonders. "Was it wonderful?"

"I think so."

"What does that mean?"

"Things happened. I'll tell you everything tonight."

We walk down the corridor toward the dining hall. I stop in the hall by the glowing portrait of Father's grandfather. An artist called Bellini painted it. Great-grandfather is in a crimson robe on a black background. Beside it is a portrait of Father's father by a different Bellini. He's in a black robe on a gold background. The colors are alive.

Both Bellini artists were masters whose colors Venice's nobles said could never be equaled. But Venetian painters since then have excelled with colors over and over again. Father just had the famous Tiziano make a portrait of Mother. Her eyes actually glisten in it, and her lips are rosy and seem to tremble. And recently Father's been talking about an artist called Tintoretto, who uses colors so marvelously, he's been appointed to paint ceilings in the Palazzo Ducale itself, in rooms used by the Senate and the Collegium. Father intends to have his own portrait done by this Tintoretto.

What Mother said was true: Venetian colors and dyes are the envy of the world. Venice has to protect them.

That's what Mother said. She talked of secrets and spies.

My eyes burn. I feel as though I will burst into tears. Everything I've looked at since that morning with Mother has conspired to make her words—words that I was so eager to hear more of—gain in meaning and hurt horribly. The mysteries of Venice are like a rainbow—and I am soon to be shut away from them. It's as though my future has lost its color.

"Come." Paolina is beside me. She stands on tiptoe and kisses my cheek. "There's sausage from Modena. You like it. Come."

"Please, Paolina." I clasp her hand desperately. "The next time I go out, if I'm not back before the boys, I'll need you to unlock the side door for me. Promise you'll do that."

"Will you really go out again?"

I nod.

"I promise."

We're the last to take our places, but no one cares. This is an ordinary meal, no announcements today. People talk and laugh. Nicola knocks over Aunt Angela's wine glass. The sweet smell of Malvasia tinges everything. This is wine Uncle

Girolamo brought back from Cyprus last time he was home. As Giò Giò rushes to help clean it up, Aunt Angela kisses Nicola on the cheek and fusses happily, for overturned wine brings good fortune. Bortolo stabs Nicola with a carrot that is so soft from boiling, it smushes on his sleeve.

"Don't do that, Bortolo." I point a finger at him. "Poor Cara will have a terrible time trying to get that stain out of your shirt."

"Since when do you worry about Cara's work?" asks Francesco.

And it's true. I never do. None of us do. The worry over my disguise has made me consider things I never thought about before. I flush and look quickly at Mother. But she's talking with Father; neither of them heard me. Perhaps no one but Francesco and Bortolo heard me, and maybe Uncle Umberto—for his head is turned toward me now and there's a quizzical expression on his face. The rest of them are all busy cleaning up the spilled wine or eating. This is a lucky lucky day.

Bortolo throws a carrot at me. It lands on the edge of my plate. I go to scold him, but he's looking at me hard. Oh no, I forgot my promise to bring him home a treat. And he already rejected the remaining baubles in my jewelry box the last time I had to bribe him. Maybe Andriana will let me give him something of hers. I smile at him reassuringly.

The rest of the meal passes without event, but when Father puts his hands on the table to push himself up to a stand—the signal we recognize as the end of the meal—I blurt out, "Father, where do the Jews live?"

The table goes silent. My brothers and sisters look at me as though I've suddenly gone daft.

"In the Ghetto," says Father.

"All of them?"

"No. Some live on Giudecca and some live here and there around Venice."

"But aren't they supposed to live in the Ghetto, all of them? Wasn't there a decree passed years ago?"

"Yes, there was a decree." Father looks to the boys, as though asking who has told me about this decree.

But I press on: "Why aren't they punished?"

Father's mouth curves up at one corner. "Is my daughter taking an interest in Venice's government?" He leans across his plate toward me. "Don't be hostile to the Jews, my little daughter. They are important to the well-being of our Republic."

"I'm not hostile," I say quickly. "I just want to understand."

"Then your brothers will explain to you later." Father looks across the table. "Francesco and Piero know about these things." He stands and leaves.

Laura and I go back to our bedchamber for our usual rest before the afternoon music lessons. As soon as we shut the door behind us, Laura takes my hand. "Tell me about it."

I shake my head. "I'll tell everyone tonight, when we all gather after dinner."

Laura squeezes my hand. "Then just tell me this: Did it make you happy?"

Her question takes me by surprise. But it is, after all, the heart of the matter. What else could merit the risk of my parents' wrath? "Yes. Bad things happened. But good things, too. I'm happy I went out."

"Then I'm happy for you." Her voice catches.

"You don't seem happy. Did something happen?"

Laura shakes her head. And now she's crying.

I pull her to me and cradle her head in my hands.

"Where's my treat?" Bortolo yanks on my skirt.

"I told you to knock first," I say crossly. I give him a small pinch.

Bortolo goes to the door and knocks. "Where's my treat? And why's Laura crying?"

"Don't talk about me as though I'm an idiot who can't answer for herself." Laura stamps her foot. "Besides, how did you know it was me crying and not Donata?"

"You have different faces."

This is true. But no one else has ever noticed the small differences. Or no one has let us know if they have.

"Why are you crying?"

"I have a toothache," lies Laura.

Bortolo looks at her with respect. Toothaches are common at our age, but he's too young to have ever had one. "Too bad," he says in his most grown-up voice. He kisses Laura on the back of her hand tenderly. But a second later he turns to me with his usual eager face. "Where's my treat, Donata?"

I put my hand on his head heavily and am about to explain that I forgot, when I realize that his head is about the same size as Laura's. So it must be about the same size as my own. "I have a treat for you, Bortolo. But it's special. And, in a way, it's dangerous."

"Dangerous?" Bortolo's eyes narrow. "I have a knife. Francesco won it gambling and gave it to me. The blade is sharp, but I've never cut myself."

"Does Mother know?"

"No. And don't tell her."

"I won't," I say. "But this treat for you also has to be kept a secret. And not just from Mother. From everyone."

Bortolo licks his lips. "I understand."

"But, as I said, this is very special. You don't get it for free."

Bortolo frowns. "I get it because I'm not telling on you for going down the stairs this morning in your nightdress."

"That's not a big enough secret for such a special treat," I say.

"What else do you want?"

"Your *bareta*."

Laura looks at me quickly.

Bortolo sticks out his bottom lip.

"Not your velvet one," I say. "Your plain cotton one. For when you play in the *campi*."

Bortolo shrugs. "All right. If it's a really good treat, you can have my old *bareta*. I'll tell Mother I need another."

"But you mustn't tell her you gave it to me," I say.

"I'm not stupid, Donata."

I smile. "Stay here with Laura while I fetch it."

"I'll go get my *bareta*."

"No!" I don't want him in the stairwell, where he'll see me running past him. I don't want him to know I have business on the ground floor. "Stay here and wait. Promise?"

"Yes."

I go out, shutting the door behind me, and cross to the stairwell quickly. I race to the bottom and into the storeroom. The shoes and cap are exactly where I left them. I take the yarmulke and fold it small enough to fit in my fist. Then I race back up the stairs.

I go into Laura's and my bedchamber.

"There you are," says Piero. "We've been waiting." Francesco sits on our bed.

Laura looks at me and her shoulders lift the smallest

amount, enough to let me know she was helpless to stop them coming in.

"I'm going downstairs." Bortolo runs and stands directly in front of me. "Aunt Angela's looking for me," he says more loudly than normal. His eyes search mine.

I put my hands behind my back. "See you later, Bortolo."

He smiles. As he goes past me, he takes the yarmulke from my hand and slips out the door.

"What are you doing here?" I ask, trying to keep the anxiety out of my voice.

"We came to talk about the Jews," says Piero.

I wring my hands behind my back. What could they know of my morning? Who saw anything? I stare at them.

"Father wants you to understand. He says you're the daughter with a head on her shoulders." Piero looks at Laura with a teasing grin. "No offense, Laura."

My knees go weak with relief. They're here merely to finish the conversation I started at the midday meal.

Laura smiles and I know she's feeling the same relief. "How can I take offense from someone incapable of accurately representing Father's ideas, my poor half-wit brother?" she quips back.

Piero laughs.

"Jews are bankers, little sister," says Francesco. "And they're bankers who take chances. They lend money to the poor. If they didn't, there would be even more poor in Venice than there presently are. And we already have way too many beggars. So it's in Venice's best interests to let the Jews do what they want, including live where they want."

"And it's not right to force people to live in a given place," says Piero. "If we want a serene republic, we cannot behave like brutes."

"But if that's the case," I say, "why was the law passed in the first place?"

"To appease the Vatican." Francesco slaps his hands on his knees to accent his words. "We pass a law, the Inquisition is satisfied. Whether we enforce it or not is no one's business but ours." He looks at me thoughtfully. "The Holy Office of the Roman Inquisition has an agenda against Protestantism as well. Do you want to know about the Lutherans, too?"

Lutherans? That's what the little girl Sara accused me of being. "What have the Lutherans to do with the Jews?"

"Because of the Pope's grumblings, the Lutherans haven't been welcomed into most Venetian neighborhoods," says Piero. "But the Jews have sheltered them in the Ghetto."

"How strange, Jews and Protestants together," I say.

"That's not all," says Piero. "The Ghetto is a hodgepodge of everyone who doesn't have Venetian heritage. Jews from Spain and Portugal, Protestants from Holland, Muslims from Constantinople and Salonika and Cairo. Somehow they all manage."

"It's no mystery how," says Francesco. "They tolerate each other well because they rely on each other for survival. And the Republic of Venice tolerates all of them for the same reason. It's a question of money, little sister. Tolerance is good business."

"But immigrants rarely have money, I thought."

"It's not the immigrants themselves," says Francesco. "It's the countries they come from. We trade with Amsterdam and Barcelona and Alexandria. We trade with almost everyone. If

Venice mistreats the immigrants, the countries they come from will curtail trade."

"We are a tolerant republic," says Piero. "When a complaint is lodged against a Lutheran, the Tribunal and the Committee on Heresy—as well as the locally chosen Inquisitor—listen carefully and decide whether to investigate, or simply to take measures toward absolution, or, even more simply, to drop the whole matter on the grounds of insufficient evidence."

"And the evidence is rarely sufficient," Francesco says. "Yes, tolerance is good business. As I told you girls the other morning, Venice is practical." He winks at me, like Father.

I know Francesco expects me to feel privileged to be part of a discussion that's supposed to be among men only—and I do, and yet . . . The world that's been presented to me by Mother, the world that I hear about at church, that world operates on principles that have to do with goodness and godliness. But despite Piero's talk of not acting like brutes, both brothers spoke mainly of money.

"Any other questions?" asks Piero. "The tutor is waiting for me."

"And for me," says Francesco. "I've returned to my studies. I can't let Piero outshine me too much at the university next fall."

"I have a question," says Laura. "Can we come listen to your tutor with you?"

My lips part involuntarily. Never has Laura asked anything so bold.

Piero looks at Francesco.

"Why not?" Francesco gives a wry smile. "The famous courtesan Veronica Franco got an education, after all. She wrote poems."

Laura's face opens in horror.

"Don't tease," says Piero to Francesco. "All right, little sister, why would you want to do that, anyway? Going to afternoon tutorials would mean missing your music lessons." He looks at Laura. She doesn't flinch.

"In any case," says Francesco, "that's a decision only Father can make. And he's already left for a special meeting of the Senate. You can ask tonight. If you dare."

Piero and Francesco leave.

I turn to Laura. "I didn't know you cared about studies."

"I don't."

"I thought you truly loved the violin," I say.

"I do."

"Why did you ask that, then?"

Laura tilts her head. "Isn't it a request you would have liked to make?"

"Yes."

"That's why, then." Laura smiles sadly. "Paolina was right the other day. We have to make the most of what we love. I love you, Donata."

We hold each other tight.

CHAPTER ELEVEN

THE BROOCH

The first morning light breaks over the roofs across the Canal Grande. I watch it gradually filter through our room, lighting up the painted white and green walls, bringing to life the plaster flowers and ribbons and tassels that decorate our ceilings.

I've been waiting for that light for what seems like hours.

I roll to my side and kiss Laura on the cheek. She murmurs in her sleep. Then I take Bortolo's *bareta* out from under my pillow and stuff my hair up inside it. It all fits, every strand.

The Catholic boys my age wear their hair cut to the chin. With this hat on, my hair looks as if it's very short all over. But that's all right. Some boys do cut their hair that short, especially if it's curly. Some boys and men have beards, others are clean shaven. Some wear wood-bottomed sandals, others wear boots that come up to midcalf. There's a lot of variation. I shouldn't feel sick when I look in the mirror. Everything's going to be all right. I won't stand out as strange.

Besides, in the fisherboy's trousers I look poor, and there's no regulating the dress and appearance of the poor.

But looking poor is precisely the problem. The revolting beggar boy who spat in my face yesterday told me to stay out of his territory. I can't do that, though. I have to pass through his territory to get to the Ghetto. And I have to get to the Ghetto; I owe Noè for the *zoccoli* and the yarmulke.

If only there were a way to get to the Ghetto *campo* without going through the streets and alleys between here and there.

A gondola. Our private *gondoliere* would never take me, naturally. He'd look at me as though I were crazy, just like Father looked at Laura last night at the evening meal when she asked if she and I could listen in on the boys' tutorial. I just sat there like a dummy, so disappointed at his reaction that I was unable to argue in our defense. And the evening meal was *seppie*—those horrible, tough cuttlefish. That made me sadder still.

But in my disguise, a public *gondoliere* would not look at me askance. I can't go on a gondola in the Rio di San Marcuola. That's too close to home. If a neighbor happened to get into the gondola with me, I'd have nowhere to hide and I could be recognized. But I can go over to the next canal—I think it's called the Rio di Noale. I can take a public gondola up to whatever canal runs along the far side of the Ghetto, and never have to risk seeing that beggar boy at all. It's a good plan.

I pull the *bareta* off my head and open the balcony doors. Across the water and down a way, a new *palazzo* is being built. Its arches and columns are different from the other buildings of Venice that I know. I don't like it.

But the Canal Grande itself is a marvelous sight. Fishing boats and fruit and vegetable boats dot the water. A barge goes by, filled with barrel hoops. It's from Padua or Treviso, where the wood is plentiful. It's going to San Polo, just across the Canal Grande, where the barrel-making factories are. I know, because last night I made Mother sit down with me and tell me where all the different factories of Venice are. I thought she wouldn't really know. But after she talked about the wool factories the other day, I wondered. She knew everything.

Another barge passes, piled high with cow hides. The butchers in Dorsoduro and Cannaregio sell the hides to the tanners over in the San Marco section, who sell the finished leather to the shoemakers that line the Merceria. I know all this, some from Mother, some from my brothers, some from listening to Father. I know all this though I've never stepped foot in a butcher's or a tanner's or a shoemaker's.

I look down at my hands. I've twisted Bortolo's *bareta* so hard that it's begun to rip. In a frenzy, I stash the *bareta* back under my pillow and race out of our bedchamber, down the corridor to Mother and Father's chamber. I burst through the door.

Father sits on the end of the bed in his long nightshirt, looking out the window onto the canal, just as I was doing a moment ago. Mother sleeps behind him. He looks at me groggily; clearly he's just woken.

I kneel at his feet. "There are three hundred ninety-three members of butcher guilds. Two hundred forty members of tanner guilds. One hundred four members of shoemaker guilds. There are seven guilds altogether that deal with leather, if you include the guilds of artists who engrave and gild belts and purses."

Father knits his brows. "This is true."

"The fire that burned the Rialto bridge was in 1514."

"Yes," says Father. "How do you know these things?"

"My head is filled with numbers, Father. You put them there. I listen when you talk. But all you talk about is who manufactures what, who sells what, who buys what. The only reason I know the year the bridge burned is that it mattered to the flow of business, so you mention it now and then, Father. You talk about it. Before yesterday I didn't know about the decree of 1516 that said the Jews should live in the Ghetto. I don't know any history at all, I know nothing about the world, unless it has to do with commerce—and then I know whatever you say at meals or in conversations I overhear."

"What are you talking about, daughter?"

"I'm Donata, Father. And I'm talking about an education. Please let Laura and me attend the boys' tutorial."

"The boys have been studying since they were seven. How could you possibly understand anything that goes on, joining them now?"

"We only want to listen. That's all. We don't have to be tutored ourselves. We won't disrupt. We won't slow anyone down."

Father slaps his chest and gives a deep cough, as though to clear his lungs. "You need your lessons on the harpsichord."

"It's Paolina who studies the harpsichord, Father. Laura and I play violin. And we've had lessons for many years—just like the boys, we've been at it since we were seven—why, it's been so many years that all we really need now is practice. And we can do that in the evenings."

Father rests his hands on his knees. He's silent.

"You are a wise father to your sons," I whisper. "Please be wise to your daughters."

Father sucks in air and sits up tall. "Your audacity almost offends me, Donata. I fear for you." He drums the fingers of his right hand on his knee. "But a mind that can hold so many numbers needs more nourishment, or it will languish and die. Yes, Donata. You and your sister may listen in on the tutorial."

I rest my cheek on the back of his right hand. "Thank you, Father. Thank you, thank you."

"But if I hear of any problems, this experiment ends. Immediately."

"I understand." I stand and bend over to kiss him on each cheek.

He pulls me onto his lap and holds me tight. "Be a good girl, Donata."

"I am, Father." I hug him back.

"And I'll look into that map you asked about. The one by Jacopo de' Barbari."

"Thank you, Father."

I return to our bedchamber and shake Laura awake. "Be good when you pretend to be me today, sweet sister."

Laura sits up and rubs her eyes. She looks around the room. "It's barely dawn. What evil possessed you to get up? And what worse evil possessed you to wake me?"

"I'm going out."

"In disguise? But you just went yesterday."

"I have to pay Noè for the *zoccoli* and cap."

"So I have to do all your work plus all mine two days in a row?"

"You get to hear the stories of my adventures."

Laura makes a face. "Some adventures—getting spat upon and having a huge splinter in the middle of your foot."

"And entering the home of a Jew," I say.

"Yes," Laura breathes. "All right, I admit it's exciting. But you're the one who actually gets to live the adventures. All I do is double work."

"How hard was the work yesterday?"

Laura gives a sheepish smile. "Actually, Mother left instructions with Cara and went off early on some errand. So we didn't do much else than a little stitching. Still, work is work, Donata."

"Would you rather be the one who goes out in the streets?"

Laura shivers. "Never."

I smile and poke her in the ribs. "Then stop complaining. Besides, I have a surprise for you."

"Another Jewish cap?"

"No. Noè only gave me one. It's about this afternoon. Or, rather, every afternoon."

Laura curls her legs under her and sits on her feet. She looks like a curious cat. "What?"

"We're going to listen in on the tutorial."

Laura shakes her head. "But Father said . . ."

"He changed his mind. I went to him this morning and he agreed."

"I don't know if that's a good thing or a bad thing," says Laura. "You're the one who loves learning that sort of thing."

"It won't be any particular sort of thing, Laura. The boys learn about everything. History, philosophy. The world. We can learn, too."

Laura gives a weak smile. "I'll give it a try."

"Good." I kiss her on both cheeks. "And now good-bye."

"You're going so early?"

"Yes. And you don't mind if I give Noè my bead bracelet, do you?"

"Why would you do that?" asks Laura.

"I have to pay him somehow. And I don't know how to get my hands on any money."

"I love Murano glass beads. If you give away your bracelet, then I can't wear mine anymore. We wouldn't want people to be able to tell us apart by our jewelry." Laura goes to the dressing table and opens the jewelry box. "Here. Give him this gold brooch, instead. You lost yours, so I can't wear it anyway."

"You're right." I take the brooch. "Wish me luck."

"*In bocca al lupo*—may you wind up in the mouth of the wolf," says Laura.

"*Crepi il lupo*—may the wolf burst," I answer. I spin away, grabbing the *bareta* from under the pillow, and the trousers and shirt I washed last night. I race to the stairwell and down.

No one's about yet except Cook and Giò Giò. They're banging around in the kitchen.

I reach the ground floor and realize with a shock that Uncle Umberto is in the wine storeroom, which is next door to the yarn storeroom, where my shoes are stashed. While he cannot see, he hears everything.

I hold my breath and strain to see into the dark of that windowless room.

Uncle Umberto has clustered maybe twenty bottles on the floor of the storeroom. He fits a short bamboo cane into the spigot of a wine barrel. He takes one of the bottles and fits the other end of the bamboo into its mouth. Then he pulls the stopcock. The wine runs black into the bottle; the strong smell of Vernaccia wets the air. As it nears the top, my breath quickens. But at just the right moment Uncle moves the end of the cane to the next bottle, using his thumb as a stop in that instant between bottles. Though I cannot see the floor clearly from here, I know he doesn't spill a drop—he never does. He fills the next bottle.

Uncle works by sound. He explained that to me when I was little. He made me shut my eyes and listen and try to call out when I heard that the bottle was almost full. It was a good game, but I never mastered it. Uncle can do it with wine and oil and any other liquid I've seen him pour.

It's his job to empty the remains of the barrels so that they can be scrubbed out and brought to our summer home, where they'll be refilled in the fall. He'll probably do the entire job in a single day. Too bad. I like to be his helper at this sort of thing. I wish he weren't doing it precisely today.

As Uncle moves the cane to the next bottle, I tiptoe past and change in the wool storeroom, rolling my nightdress into a tight ball and jamming it in the back corner again. The *bareta* is slightly loose, because of the rip I made on the headband. But it will hold in place, I'm sure.

Then I poke my head out of the storeroom and listen. When the sound of the wine stops for an instant, then restarts, I tiptoe quickly to the door and step out into the alley.

I made it.

I work my way along through the back alleys toward the Rio di Noale, keeping an eye out for beggar boys. But there aren't any here. Naturally. They'll stick to the wide roads where the merchant traffic is heavy.

It's easy not to get lost when my goal is simply to get to the next canal. That's because all I have to do is keep my ear open for the noises of the Canal Grande and stay as close to those noises as I can. I quickly come out on the smaller *rio* and flag down a gondola. "To the Ghetto," I say, climbing aboard.

"The Rio della Misericordia. Right away." The man pushes off from the bank. Then he looks me up and down. "Do you have the fare?"

Oh no. I forgot to bring anything to pay for the gondola ride. How stupid I am.

We're bobbing in the center of the canal and the *gondoliere* is just looking at me. Another *gondoliere* yells at us to get out of the way. My *gondoliere* moves us to the far side of the canal. "Well?"

"All I have is this gold brooch," I say, trying hard to mimic his style of talk. "But it's worth much much more than a simple ride. I can't give it to you. I'm sorry."

"Where did you get that?" The *gondoliere*'s voice is harsh. "Thief."

I get out of the gondola, but I'm on the wrong side of the canal now.

"Thief!" he shouts after me.

I turn into the first alley at a full run, my too-big *zoccoli* slopping wildly. I haven't had the chance to try to adjust them yet. The *gondoliere*'s shout follows me. I turn down the next alley.

Smack. I'm on the ground.

Screaming yowls fill the air.

The big man looks down on me, each of his huge, gloved hands holding a struggling cat by the scruff of the neck. "Ran right into me, buddy."

"I'm sorry, gentle sir." I get to my feet and brush off. I can't hear whether the *gondoliere* is still shouting after me, the cat screams are so loud.

"Now that's a first." The man laughs. "No one calls a cat castrator a 'gentle sir,' and never in such fine diction." He laughs again. "Anyway, there's no need for apology. The cats didn't get away." He purses his lips and throws back his head as though he's sizing me up. "You look like you could use a job. And I could use a helper. Think you could catch cats?"

I back around the man, keeping close to the far wall to avoid the thrashing claws of those feral cats. "I'm on my way somewhere, sir. Thank you anyway."

I go on quickly, but no longer at a run. If the *gondoliere* were going to follow me, he'd have caught me by now. But I should have known he wouldn't follow me—for who, then, would have guarded his gondola?

I follow the noises of daily business out to a wide street. It's the Rio Terrà di Maddalena. Oh, thank everything that's holy, I know where I am again. It's a straight stretch from here to the Ghetto. But I have to avoid the beggar boy, and all beggar boys, no matter what. Somehow I have to find protection to get me down this road, over two bridges this time, to the wide road that marks the border of the Ghetto.

And there's a beggar boy. Not the same one as yesterday, but one who seems just as rough. He's looking at me.

Why can't they leave me alone? I don't have my hand out. I'm not crying for alms. I don't put my *bareta* on the ground and sit beside it forlornly.

He swaggers toward me.

A cart rolls past with a stack of three new mattresses. A

man pushes it, and a boy smaller than me runs along one side with his hand up to steady the load if the wheels should bounce too hard.

I run around to the other side of the cart and hold my hand up to steady the load.

"Get away," calls the man. "I don't need your help. I won't pay."

"I'm not asking for pay, sir." I skip the "gentle" this time and talk in the same colloquial way he does.

"What are you doing, then?"

"I have to go this route anyway. I might as well help till I get where I'm going."

"I don't believe you," says the man. "Scat."

"There are two bridges between here and where I'm going," I say. "If you're going that far, too, I'll be of help getting the cart over them."

"You're up to something. Scat, I said!"

"Please, sir." I look at the man with my most pleading face. "If I'm with you, on this side of the mattresses, a boy I want to avoid won't beat me up."

"Ah." The man looks around and spies the beggar boy. "You should have said that in the first place." He pushes the cart faster, encouraged by the fact that he has a helper on each side now.

We go over the first bridge, clumping up and down the steps. It really is hard work. He wouldn't have managed without extra help. I look over my shoulder. The beggar boy follows. I stare ahead. Shopkeepers call attention to their wares—eyeglasses, pins, needles, papers, Murano glass beads that Laura loves. So much. I want to look at everything, but I can't take the chance of leaving the protection of the cart.

We cross the second bridge, clump clump clump up and clump clump clump down. I look over my shoulder. The beggar boy has disappeared. Maybe I passed out of his territory. Maybe the whole city is marked off in grids by the beggar boys.

We're finally at the edge of the Ghetto. "Thank you, sir," I say. "This is as far as I go."

The man reaches into a cloth bag hanging over his shoulder. He hands me a badly bruised orange. "A mattress-maker isn't rich, but this should be a treat to you. Bet you haven't seen fruit this season yet. That orange came all the way from Sicily."

"You're generous, sir. Thank you, sir." And I am truly grateful, even though in my home such a battered fruit would be considered unfit to eat. I am grateful because the feel of the orange reminds me I didn't stop by the kitchen and grab my usual bread and jam for breakfast. I duck into an alley, peel the orange, and take a bite. The smell of sweet juice mixes with the smell of straw on my hand from the mattresses. It's altogether pleasing. I sigh as I eat.

It's not easy to find Noè's home. Every home seems to have that same metal marker outside it that Noè kissed when he carried me inside yesterday. But I'm almost sure I have the right one. I knock loudly.

After a bit, a girl opens the door. She's a little older than Sara, and I think I see a resemblance. She looks at me blankly.

"Hello," I say. "I've come to see Noè."

"Oh. I know who you are. Sara told me about you."

"I'm sorry about the spoon," I say quickly.

But the girl closes the door in my face before my words are finished.

What do I do now? I lean against the wall and glance up.

A woman across the alley looks out at me from her window.

I turn my face down and study the stone blocks of the ground, which are not in the least remarkable. When I peek up again, the woman is still there.

Noè opens the door. "Hello. Excuse me for taking so long. I was finishing my breakfast."

"Go ahead and eat more," I say. "I can wait."

"I've had enough. Why'd you come back?"

"About the spoon . . ."

"It's already taken care of," says Noè. He seems brusque—much more so than yesterday.

I quickly take the gold brooch out of my pocket. "This is to pay for the *zoccoli* and yarmulke. But it's worth more than them. So you can give me the change in coins."

Noè shakes his head slowly and laughs. "You're a fine bit of amazement, you know that? What makes you think I want a brooch?"

"I told you, it's worth a lot. You can exchange it for coins."

"And where would I exchange it?"

"At a bank. You run a bank, don't you?"

Noè pulls his head back in surprise. "Where'd you get that idea?"

"Jews are bankers. That's what my brother said."

Noè makes a grimace. "Some Jews are bankers. Some Jews are tailors. Some Jews are bakers or musicians or pawnbrokers. We're people, my friend. We do many of the things Catholics do."

I'm breathing so hard from embarrassment, I'm afraid he'll hear the whistle of my nose. I step back. "I'm sorry. It was a stupid thing to think."

"Where'd you get that brooch, anyway?"

I open my hand and look at the brooch dumbly.

Noè takes it and turns it over. "You're right. It's worth a lot."

"I didn't steal it," I say, remembering the *gondoliere*.

"You just took it, is that it? From your sister, maybe?"

"She gave it to me. So I could pay you."

"So she knows about this little game you play. The plot thickens."

I stand stock-still. "What little game?"

Noè flicks his fingertips against the sleeve of my shirt. "People who wear clothes like you have on are many things. Barbers, shop boys, porters, trashmen, hod carriers, street sweepers, itinerant peddlars of ink and rat poison, even. But none of them have feet as tender as yours or . . ." He pauses and takes my hand, turning it palm upward. "Or hands as tender as yours. None of them speak as you do. And none of them have sisters with brooches worth as much as this one."

"It's an innocent game," I say, my voice breaking over the words. "No one gets hurt."

"And you get to see how the rest of us live? Is that it? Is this a thrill for you?"

"You make it sound nasty."

Noè drops the brooch back in my hand. "What's your name?"

I hadn't prepared for this question. Idiot. "Donato," I say. How unoriginal can I get? But the name is already in the air.

"Listen, Donato. I don't want your sister's brooch. If I tried to sell it, I'd probably be accused of stealing it. Besides, I don't have on hand, or even in any bank, as much money as it would take to pay you the change you'd be owed. So I'll make you a proposition."

"I'm listening."

"Come to work with me. Help me every day for two weeks. And I'll declare the debt paid."

Two weeks, just to pay for a cap and a simple pair of shoes? But it's work he's offering me. Real work. Real adventure. "I can only come in the mornings. I have to be home at midday."

Noè laughs. "See? My guess was right. You're out for the thrill."

"How do you know that?"

"You didn't even ask what my work is. You don't care. You're like a scientist and I'm like the strange animal you're studying."

"That's not true." I clamp my jaw shut and will myself not to cry.

"All right, then. If you can come only mornings, it will take a month to work off the *zoccoli* and yarmulke. By the way," Noè says, pointing with his chin toward my head, "what happened to the yarmulke?"

"I traded it to my brother for his *bareta*."

"Your brother's in on it, too, huh? The plot is thicker than pitch." Noè laughs.

CHAPTER TWELVE

LETTERS

Noè has long legs and long strides. I didn't notice that yesterday because I was on his back. But now I practically have to run to keep up with him.

We go quickly down one alley and another and cross a bridge.

"Are we out of the Ghetto?" I ask.

"Yes. The Canale di San Girolamo marks the boundary." Noè's thin arms swing far as he walks the long *fondamenta* beside the canal.

"But don't you work in the Ghetto?"

Noè gives me a sideways glance, not slowing his pace. "Jews are supposed to live in the Ghetto, but we're not confined to it except at nighttime. During the day, we go anywhere we want. And, anyway, I told you, we don't really follow the law. Even at night I'd walk freely here."

I feel scolded unjustly. "Yesterday you were in the Ghetto during work hours."

"You're right. I had a special errand."

A woman comes outside and hangs a string of newly made candles across the top of a door. The smell of hot wax is strong.

"Noè, could you wait? Please, could I watch a little while in the wax-working shop?" I've already stopped, and I'm looking through the window at the huge kettles inside, and the boys lined up on either side, holding strings. This is a factory—my first glimpse of a real factory.

"You can spend your own time how you want, but not my time," Noè calls. He's already halfway down the *fondamenta*.

I run to catch up, past gold-working shops and jewelers, past coopers and ribbon shops. I want to look in all of them. "What's the hurry?"

"In the world of nobles, being late might not be costly. But in the world of the people, being late could cost me my job."

"Oh. I didn't mean to make you late."

"Aha," says Noè. "So you are from a noble family. I knew it."

"Are you going to keep doing that?" I say in annoyance.

"Why not come clean and tell me all about what you're up to?"

"No."

"Well, then, I guess I will keep doing it." Noè crosses another bridge and I recognize that we've passed over the Rio di Noale, where the *gondoliere* called me a thief.

We wind down alley after alley and finally come out on the wide Fondamente Nuove, which looks out over the lagoon. The green water shimmers with the brilliance of morning. I halt and breathe in the beauty.

A barge goes by, piled high with lumber. The way the logs are arranged, it looks vaguely like the sea dragon in the frieze

over the mantelpiece in our dining hall. A giant from some mystical time long ago. I almost expect it to let out a blood-curdling scream.

I run to Noè and grab him by the crook of the arm. "Look at that barge. What does it make you think of?"

"Venice's problems."

"What? It looks like a monster from the deep. Can't you see? Doesn't it seem like it's just about to shoot fire from its mouth?"

"It looks like our future going up in flames, if that's what you mean."

"That isn't what I mean at all. What are you talking about?"

"That barge came down the Brenta River. It's carrying lumber from the mainland, probably from Verona, but maybe even from as far away as Brescia, to the shipyards."

"I knew that," I say with assurance. "Venice makes the most superior sailing vessels in the world."

"Not for long," says Noè. "The oak forests in the Venetian territories are dwindling. Soon we'll have to buy lumber from the territories of Milan. That means it will cost more to build ships, so we won't be able to build them as cheaply as our competitors. Plus the pirates on the Dalmatian and Barbary coasts keep stealing our ships, sometimes with full cargoes. Even European pirates attack us."

Father talked about pirates just last week. But I didn't know how it connected to shipbuilding. And I can't remember him talking about the shortage of timber. I thought Padua and Treviso had plenty of wood. "You can't mean Venice will lose supremacy on the seas."

"And why can't I, my friend?" Noè stops at a door. "Stay here while I talk to the master."

I lean my back against the wall and look out over the waters. The barge is still visible, heading slowly toward Castello and the wide canals that lead to the shipbuilding factories. Noè is like Father, and like Francesco and Piero, too, always thinking about business, about how everything affects business. But I've never heard anyone talk about problems for the future. Father says the Venetian Empire is the greatest economic power in the world. There's never any doubt in his voice.

Noè can't be right.

Noè comes out and puts his arm around my shoulders. He pulls me to the edge of the *fondamenta,* so that I'm looking down directly at the lapping waves. "Listen, Donato," he says quietly, "for the next month your name is Donata."

I gasp and jump back.

He gives a little laugh and pulls me back to him. "Don't worry. Your member won't shrivel at the mere change in name. It has to be this way."

I stand in total confusion. Has he found me out or not?

"Look, to join the guild you have to pay the entrance fee. You don't have any money on you, right?"

"Just the gold brooch," I say.

"Which you'd better not show to anyone," Noè says seriously. "And I don't have enough money to pay the fee. So I said you owed me for a pair of *zoccoli* and you would work every morning for a month to pay me back. I'll get the money you earn. See?"

"No."

"Come on, Donato. If you're a boy, you have to join the guild to work. But if you're a girl, you can't join. Girls work here on and off, unofficially, and their brothers are always the ones to get paid."

"All right," I say, finally getting it. How funny. I'll be a girl pretending to be a boy pretending to be a girl. I smile.

"You do look sort of girly," says Noè.

I stop smiling.

He elbows me in the ribs. "I was joking. We can't do anything about the fact that you're in trousers, but take off that *bareta*."

I hold the *bareta* on my head with both hands. "I can't. My hair's way too short for a girl. This way people can think I've got long hair stuffed up inside the hat."

Noè makes a grimace. "And they can think you're pretty strange, too."

"I'm not taking off the *bareta*. If anyone says I'm strange, tell them I'm trying to look like a boy."

"All right, all right. Come on."

I follow him through a front room full of big machines. I look closely. These must be printing presses. So Noè makes books.

We pass down a corridor with rooms off to each side and out to a back room that has so many windows it's filled with light. The door stands open to a courtyard where two long rows of tables with benches running down one side of the tables stand out in the open.

"There's no one here."

"They'll come," says Noè. "Let me see what the job for today is and I'll get you started. Sit on a bench and wait."

I wander around the courtyard. Except for the occasional lizard, there's nothing of interest. Paolina would have immediate plans for this place. For the past year she's been trying to convince Mother to have the stones of our own courtyard dug up so that she can make a garden. And this courtyard is much bigger than ours. I can imagine Paolina saying, "That corner is perfect for a mulberry tree, and this one for a pomegranate." She'd put a line of plum trees along the far end and a stone reflection pool, far enough from the mulberry to be free of its messy fruits when they fall but close enough to be in its shadows in the afternoon. I smile and twirl around, thinking of my little sister dancing through the garden she'd create here.

"You don't have to act the part yet," says Noè. He watches me with a strange look on his face. His arms hold a stack of papers with a box perched on top.

"I was thinking about my sister." My face grows hot. "She likes gardens."

"This is hardly a garden."

"I know. She'd change it."

Noè puts his tongue in his cheek and pushes it around a bit. He looks as though he's going to say something. Instead, he lays the papers on an end table. From the box he takes out jars and places them at regular intervals along the two rows of tables. Then he takes out quills and scatters them equally on the tables, too. He sits down at the end table and takes one sheet of paper off the top of the stack. He writes.

I stand looking over his shoulder.

He fills the page with big letters. "There. That should do it."

I stare at the letters. "I thought this was a printing house."

"It is, smarty. We do small jobs for the two big printing houses . . ."

"The house of Antonio Galassi in Padua," I say, jumping in to show him that I know some things, that I really am a smarty, even if I didn't know about Venice's timber shortage. I have memorized everything Piero has told me about the book industry. "And the house of Aldus Pius Manutius. Venice is the center of the world book trade. It started out in Germany, but now we do it much bigger."

"That's right." He beckons me toward him with a single finger.

I lean forward.

"You don't have to impress me, my friend," he whispers. "I know you're educated."

Suddenly I feel like a cheat. "I don't know about the book business. Not really. Please tell me about the work here."

"We typeset and print books. In fact, we even do some of the new, small books that you can carry in one hand. The Aldine press—Manutius' press that you mentioned—perfected them. Have you seen them?"

I shake my head.

Noè rushes into the building, then comes out holding a small book bound in red leather. He hands it to me.

I've never held a book before. The ones we have at home are too large. I've seen them lying open on the reading table in the library when I've gone in to fetch Father or one of my brothers. This one feels precious in my hands. A thin gold cord with a tassel on the end marks the reader's place. Gingerly, I use the cord to open the book.

"See? The lettering is squared off. Italic print, it's called. It's not beautiful, I admit. It can't compare to the large books, where the printing mimics script as much as possible. But typecutters can make these simple letters quickly, and the small print allows for small pages. The binding is goat, rather than a more expensive leather, but there's still a vellum flyleaf at the front and back and the pages still have gilt edges." Noè runs his finger lovingly along the edge of a page as he talks. He's like a book himself, so full of information. "Aldus Manutius meant for these books to accompany the rich as they travel. But the result is a book that a man can afford to own—a man like me, not just one like you."

"It's wonderful," I say. "Is this what you work on?"

"No. I'm a journeyman in handmade books. Many people still prefer script, no matter the cost. That's what I do."

I look at the sheet of paper that Noè just covered with script. The letters are equal in size and well placed on the page. But there's nothing beautiful about them. Noè rushed the lettering, and it shows. "This doesn't look like a book page to me," I say hesitantly.

Noè laughs. He puts the small printed book in his pocket and gestures for me to sit on the bench. "It's not. Read it."

I press my lips together. I don't know how to read. But Noè assumes I can because a rich boy should be able to. Then I remember. "Read it to me. If the master looks out, he shouldn't see a girl reading, after all."

Noè gives a half smile. "If the master looks out, he shouldn't see any copyist reading, boy or girl. That's what you are today, my friend, a copyist earning a piece rate. You'll be earning the same *mercede* all copyists earn, which is why it will take you a full month to pay me back. Copyists are poor, my friend. And no copyist gets a private education. Most of them never learn to read."

"But you know how to read. Didn't you start as a copyist?"

"All Jewish boys go to school in the Ghetto. By the time we become apprentices, no matter what the job, we can read anything, in Hebrew, Latin, or Greek. And we can read and write Venetian, too, of course. My uncle often works for the Tribunals during court cases, helping the recorder decide how to write the words of witnesses, many of whom speak in Venetian, even in court, because they're ordinary citizens or just plain people. They don't know Latin."

I'm aghast. "Your uncle's a Jew, isn't he? How can he work for the Tribunals, of all things?"

Noè grins. "He doesn't have a regular job as a civil servant, of course. He's called in for special cases, as the need arises. He translates and acts as an interpreter, too. It's not illegal to be a Jew in Venice, after all. What kind of fool are you? It's illegal to convert from Catholicism to Judaism. Or even from Catholicism to Lutheranism." His voice takes on a sarcastic edge. "To turn from the true way is heretical. You can be denounced as a threat to the State. But if you start out a Jew, well, that's just your bad luck." He laughs. "The Vatican can be clever in its reasoning."

Nothing he has said is in itself blasphemy. Yet I feel sure that Noè is poking fun at my religion. I'm glad no one can hear.

Being denounced is the worst thing that can happen to a Venetian. If a man commits an act that threatens the Republic—if he tells State secrets or tries to buy a seat in the Senate or is somehow else treasonous—and if someone finds out, that person will write up exactly what the man has done in a formal letter, a denunciation, and slip the letter through the opening in the mouth of a carved stone lionhead, a famous *bocca di leone*. The Council of Ten interviews the accused and if there seems to be cause for concern, spies go out and gather information for a full trial. Within fifteen days from the denunciation, the accused is judged and, if guilty, sentenced. If he's lucky, he might spend years in prison. If he's unlucky, he might spend years in exile. And if he's truly wretched, he'll suffer death by hanging, decapitation, or night drowning in the lagoon.

Father's voice lowers to a hush when he speaks of such punishments.

"It's best not to talk about these things," I say.

"Don't be afraid of talk, my friend." Noè sighs. "It's one of the few powers that doesn't cost money. Use it carefully, yes, but use it."

A group of four boys arrive together, noisy and happy. They fall silent when they see me.

"I'll be doing some copy work today." Noè jerks his head toward me and winks. I'm used to Father winking at me—and Francesco did it, too, just yesterday. But for a man outside my family to wink at me is an impertinence. Well, that's a silly way to feel—this man doesn't even know I'm a girl. Still, I feel myself blushing. His eyes are on me and there's something about them that makes him seem handsome. Regal, even, as though he's somehow superior to me. It must be the effect of the wink. He smiles and whispers loudly. "Her name's Donata."

The boys nod and sit on the benches beside me. Noè puts a

piece of paper in front of each of them and places the paper that he wrote on where we can all see it. "Get to work." The boys pick up quills and dip them in the jars, which turn out to be full of black ink. They stare at the paper Noè wrote on, and copy it painstakingly.

Another group of boys arrive. Noè quickly writes on a second sheet of paper. I'm almost sure he's written the same thing that he wrote on the first paper. It looks very similar, at least. The boys fill up the benches along the first row of tables and Noè puts the sheet of paper where they can see it.

More boys and one girl, yes, there's another girl here, line up along the benches at the other row of tables. The girl's not wearing a veil. I wonder if poor girls never wear veils. I smile at her. She sticks her tongue out at me. Then I remember she has no idea I'm a girl—all the people on her bench came in after Noè introduced me. She probably thinks I'm being fresh. I practically gag holding in my laugh.

Noè writes on two more sheets of paper and lays them out as models. He sees me looking at him and comes over. "Get to work," he says quietly. Then he goes inside.

I dip my quill in the ink and try to copy the first letter. The ink puddles, and the puddle spreads to an ugly black splotch.

The boy beside me looks over. "You have to give the tip of the quill a little shake right as you're taking it out of the top of the jar."

I bite my bottom lip. "But I've already ruined it."

"Don't be a blockhead. These are just handbills. So long as everyone can read them, Noè will accept them. Start over, a little to the right."

"Thanks." I dip the quill and shake it. Then I copy the first letter. It doesn't look much like Noè's. I glance at my neighbor's letters. They're good.

"This is your first time, huh?"

"Yes."

"Well, you better speed up or you won't earn anything." He gives a little humming sound. "I'm the fastest one, so don't try to keep up with me. Just speed up."

I copy faster. All morning long. It doesn't get easier, because there are so many different letters. It doesn't get better looking, either, because I still make puddles now and then. And my hand cramps sometimes. And my neck aches. And the bench is hard under my knees, because I have to kneel to reach the top of the page. But after a while, I get to the point where I don't notice my hand or my neck or my knees. I don't notice anything but the quill and the paper and the letters. There's a kind of magic to these letters; the work envelops me.

CHAPTER THIRTEEN

TROUBLE

"It's eleven-thirty," Noè announces, standing in the doorway of the courtyard.

The copyists scribble furiously, me included. Then hands start popping up around the tables.

Noè goes to the boys whose hands are up, collecting the finished papers and marking down the number each boy has done in a ledger.

There are five more letters before the sheet I'm working on will be finished. I concentrate on getting the letters right. Sweat drips from my brow onto the paper.

"Time's up," says Noè.

Finally, I, too, raise my hand. Noè comes over. "Put the stack to one side," he says.

I stack my papers.

Noè counts my sheets and takes them away.

A boy brings a half-finished sheet to my neighbor. They agree to split the payment for this sheet, and my neighbor works like a fiend, finishing a whole line in a few minutes. I can't believe how fast he forms the letters.

A boy goes around collecting the jars of ink and putting them back in the box. Two others collect the quills and rinse them in a bowl of water before replacing them in the box.

My neighbor scribbles furiously.

Noè hands out brooms and buckets with lids on them. He picks up his ledger and checks it. "All right, we have fourteen of you and sixty-six papers, counting the one Emilio is finishing right now. If you work in pairs, that means three pairs can put up ten handbills, and four pairs can only put up nine."

"What about the new guy?" asks the boy sitting beside the girl. "He makes fifteen of us."

"That's Donata. She doesn't count."

"A girl?" the girl says.

"Done!" shouts Emilio. He gets up and hands the finished sheet to Noè. Then he looks at me. "I knew you were odd."

"Girls aren't odd," says the girl. "And Donata should get to put up handbills, too."

I'd love to put up handbills. I want to do everything the copyists do. But my morning is past. "I have to be home by midday."

"See?" says Noè. "That's why I said she doesn't count. So that settles it. Which pairs want ten handbills?"

I expect a fight to break out. After all, these copyists are poor, and work is paid by the piece. So the pairs who put up more handbills will get more pay. I know that because that's how all the guilds work in Venice. It's the only fair way, according to Father. The government declares what the price of each unit of work will be. Then the guilds pay their members for piecework. I stay seated on the bench, to avoid the fray.

But the boys negotiate reasonably. Those who got to put up

more handbills yesterday give way to the others. I shouldn't be surprised. That's the way people ought to work things out. It's the way my brothers and sisters work things out. I'm ashamed of myself for thinking that because these copyists are poor, they'd act badly.

I think back to the beggar boy who spat on me yesterday. And the other beggar boy who followed me this morning. I was outside their group, and they were mean to me. But maybe among the beggar boys, within the group, there's an understanding of how to treat each other. Sort of like an unofficial beggar-boys' guild.

The others run off with buckets and brooms and handbills.

"You can get on home now," says Noè. "It's a quarter to twelve. Hurry."

I stand up slowly. "See you tomorrow."

"Yup." Noè goes inside.

I follow him into the building. He goes into a room off the corridor. I stop in the doorway of that room and watch him.

He looks up at me. "Is something wrong?"

A lot is wrong. But I don't want to tell him. "Aren't you going back to the Ghetto for lunch?"

Noè looks at me silently. "You don't know how to get home from here, do you?"

I smile sheepishly. I hate needing help like this. "Not really."

"I guess I'm hungry, after all." He closes the lid on his ink jar and washes his quill.

"Thanks, Noè."

"Don't mention it."

We go back quickly, through alleys that are more crowded now than this morning. When we get to the Rio Noale, I speak up. "Noè, if it's all the same to you, could we go back by way of the Rio Terrà di Maddalena?"

"It's not all the same." Noè sticks his tongue in his cheek again.

"Do you have a toothache?"

He smiles. "Now who's trying to figure out about people?"

"I asked a direct question. That's different from you trying to trick me."

"All right. Yes, my tooth hurts. Now you answer a direct question. Why do you want to go to the Rio Terrà di Maddalena?"

What's the point of not answering? "It's near my home," I say at last.

"So you want me to go out of my way and spend more time going home so that you can spend less time, is that it?"

"No, that's not it at all. Don't make me sound like a spoiled brat."

"So what is it?" asks Noè.

"There are beggar boys on the paths between the Ghetto and my home. They think I want to beg there, and it's their territory, and they, well, they aren't very nice."

Noè smiles and turns down an alley. "You know, the master's never going to guess you're really a boy."

"And what's that supposed to mean?"

"Sometimes you sound like a girl. And you're really cute, too. Sexy." He holds up a hand with fingers spread and wrist tilted, like a dainty girl, and he wiggles his hips for a few steps. "They aren't very nice," he says in a high falsetto, mimicking me.

"You aren't very nice," I snap.

He laughs and turns down another alley. "And you aren't very fast at your letters. I expected a lot more handbills out of you, given that you have an education."

"I'm supposed to be a girl, right? I have to act the part."

"Some girls have an education."

Really? I thought Laura and I were special—I thought we were the only girls other than courtesans who were about to be allowed into a tutorial. But, oh, could Noè mean courtesans? I take his arm. "Ones you know?"

"I'm in a *havurah*—a study group—that includes girls. The new choral master, Leon Modena—may God his Rock protect him and grant him long life—started it. He says men and women can study together."

I remember the chorus in the Ghetto singing in Hebrew. How lucky the girls in Noè's study group are, to be able to learn that.

Noè looks at my hand on his arm. "But that doesn't mean men and women can touch each other." He carefully lifts my hand off him. "So be sure not to touch me at the printer's, where they think you're a girl."

I step back, alarmed. "Is this a Jewish rule, like with the spoons?"

"Not exactly the same, but yes."

Oh, no. "What would happen to you if a girl touched you?"

"Don't get so upset." Noè smiles at me and walks again. "I wouldn't die. It's just not proper. In any case, go ahead and act like you're struggling with the letters. But don't be too slow."

I rub the back of my neck. "If I don't do enough work by the end of the month to pay for the *zoccoli,* then I'll just work longer. I'll work till you tell me we're even."

Noè looks at me with approval. "*D'accordo*—agreed. Here we are."

The alley opens on the Rio Terrà di Maddalena. And I know exactly where we are. My own alley lies just ahead on the other side of the wide road. "Thank you. I'll stop here."

He lifts his eyebrows. "So you're not going to let me see which *palazzo* you disappear into?"

"No."

He smiles. "All right. And tonight do this." He rolls his head to the side, the back, the other side, and front in a big circle. "Five times in one direction, and five times in the other. That's the only way to avoid a sore neck."

"My neck's all right."

"I saw you rubbing it. And flex your fingers. Like this." He opens and closes both hands. "One hundred times, as fast as you can. That avoids a sore hand."

"All right," I say.

"I'll meet you here tomorrow morning at seven sharp."

"You don't have to do that," I say, though my heart leaps at the offer.

"Beggar boys start work even earlier than copyists." Noè gives a wave and walks off. He's absorbed by the crowd in an instant.

At the first break in traffic, I cross to the other side and wend my way to our alley. I run now.

Francesco and Piero and Antonio and Vincenzo come into the alley right behind me. They're early.

Oh, Lord, help me. I don't dare look over my shoulder. There are other doors on this alley, but I can't just walk into one of them.

I clack one *zoccolo* hard on the stone ground and move to the wall, squatting into a ball, as though there's something wrong with my *zoccolo* and I'm trying to fix it.

My brothers pass by without so much as a pause in their conversation. I wait for them to go into our *palazzo* before I straighten up and run to the door. I hesitate. The door is heavy and thick, and I can't hear what's happening on the other side. But unless they stopped for some strange reason, they should be going up the stairwell by now.

I try the door; it's locked.

Please, Paolina. Remember your promise. I lean my forehead against the door.

In a little while, I think I hear something. I race away, back along the alley. But when no one comes out our door, I return and try the latch again. It opens. There is not much in this world better than a loyal sister.

I race to the storeroom, strip, hide my disguise, put on my nightdress, and run up the stairwell on tiptoe. Paolina waits at the doorway to the *piano nobile*. She looks both ways up and down the corridor, then she nods. I zip past her into the bedchamber.

A moment later, Laura comes in, and I dress exactly like her. Then we go out into the corridor.

Paolina pushes us back into the room. "Pinch your cheeks," she says, pointing to Laura. "Otherwise one of you has redder cheeks than the other."

I put my hands to my cheeks. "Oh, no. I sat in the sun all morning."

Laura puts her hand to her mouth and looks at me. "This is awful. You've got a sunburn."

"It's just a little sunburn," says Paolina. "If you keep pinching yourself, Laura, you'll look the same." She frowns. "Except for Donata's hands."

The fisherboy's shirt has long, loose sleeves, so my arms are white. But the backs of my hands are slightly red.

"I'll keep my hands in my lap as much as I can," I say.

"I'll do the same," says Laura. "I want to, anyway. I'm so tired. Mother insisted we make headway on the giant spools of yarn. She's worried they won't be finished before we leave for the summer. She demanded ten bobbins each from you and me and Paolina. I filled all the bobbins you were supposed to fill, then I had to work on my share. And though I worked as fast as I could, I didn't finish. My fingers hurt from holding the thread so tight."

"I'm sorry." I kiss Laura on both cheeks. "Thank you."

"You'd better have good stories to tell," says Laura.

"I do. And I still have your brooch." I take it out of my pocket.

"It's so pretty." Paolina leans over my hand, her lips forming a perfect circle.

"Here," says Laura. She hands the brooch to Paolina. "This is for you."

"Do you mean it?" Paolina holds the brooch up to the light from the window. "I love it."

"Good. I can't wear it anyway."

"Why not?" asks Paolina.

"Donata lost hers."

"You always wear the same jewelry, the same everything," says Paolina. "Except for fisherboy's clothes." She laughs. "We better get to lunch."

We walk down the corridor in a line and take our places at the table. Everyone talks about their morning. Nicola practically bursts with pride because he mastered a hoop and stick game that boys play in the *campi*. I've never played it, but I've seen it a few times in the *campo* in front of San Marcuola. It's hard, I think. We all congratulate him and tell him how big he's getting. Bortolo pipes up and takes credit for teaching Nicola the game.

Finally, Father comes in, late and clearly upset. "Have you seen this?" He's holding a sheet of paper.

A handbill.

I try to see the lettering, but my older brothers are passing it around and no one passes it to me. At last it rests in Antonio's hands and I crane my neck to get a better look. I was right: It's one of the handbills we made this morning.

"What's it say?" I ask.

"It says we've got trouble," says Francesco.

It can't say merely that. There are so many words on the sheet.

"What are you going to do, Father?" asks Piero.

"We're calling a meeting of the heads of all the guilds related to the wool industry this afternoon to discuss their petition."

"Whose petition?" I ask.

"The wool combers are getting ready to petition the Senate for a raise in their piece rates," says Father. "They put their arguments on handbills all over the Merceria."

"I bet they'll get the raise, too," says Piero. "Their arguments are good. The price of combs has gone from twelve *lire* to thirty *lire*. Their costs have gone up and their pay hasn't."

I remember Mother talking about the wool industry. She talked about the beaters and the carders and the combers and the spinners and the weavers—in that order, the order in which the wool passes hands. "If the cost of combed wool goes up," I say, "what will the spinners do?"

Everyone looks at me. I've never before entered mealtime business talk like this. Mother's and Father's faces are shocked. But I haven't said anything stupid. It's not fair for them to be shocked merely by the fact that I spoke up.

"Donata's right," says Antonio at last, "the spinners will be hurt first."

I look at my brother with love. Good old Antonio.

"They've already been complaining," says Father. "Everyone wants finer wool cloth, and finer wool cloth comes from the very finest spinning. Uncle Alvise won't accept a spool of yarn that isn't completely regular and thin as silk. So a spinning job that used to take a day now takes two. The spinners are working twice as long for the same pay."

"So the spinners will petition for a raise, too," says Piero.

"And that becomes Uncle Alvise's problem," says Francesco. "He either has to oppose the combers' petition, or make a petition of his own."

"Those are the choices," says Father. "And what the Senate decides will affect the tailors, and cloth sellers, like us."

"And our trade abroad," says Piero.

"And our buying at home," I say.

Father acknowledges my words this time with just the quickest of glances. "There's no end to it," he says. "And it doesn't start with the combers. They're the first to petition. The carders complain that the cards for working the weft wool went from thirty-six *soldi* to seventy. And the beaters complain about their costs."

"So, little sister," says Francesco, looking at me, "we've all figured it out together—you included. What the handbills say is that we've got trouble."

"We might as well eat and eat hearty," says Father. "And we better start having lamb even more often, to keep those sheep herders in business."

The food is served and the others are eating, but Mother's eyes are on me, almost as though she's questioning me. I nod at her. Then I look again at the handbill that I quietly took from Antonio. The little splots here and there make me smile.

CHAPTER FOURTEEN

LESSONS

The tutorial takes place in our library. Laura and I sit in chairs at the side of the room. Our older brothers sit in chairs grouped together in the center of the room. The tutor stands in front of them, pacing, now and then circling them. He doesn't look at Laura and me.

Messer Zonico is a private tutor, not a teacher. Most private tutors are members of the clergy, usually priests well known for their skills in preaching. But Messer Zonico is a layman—and a citizen, not a noble. I know a lot about him. Or about his family. Antonio told Laura and me the whole story of intrigue and treachery.

The Zonico family had been a member of Venice's nobility for as far back as anyone knows. They were never wealthy, but they had a good business in luxury items. Today they're known for soap. They import the ingredients—soda ash, quicklime, and olive oil—from other areas on the mainland peninsula, but they actually produce the soaps in Venice. Like everything else wonderful in Venice, these soaps come in startling colors. And they smell of fruits and flowers. Zonico soaps are exported all over Europe. We use them in our family. In fact, Andriana likes to wet her underdresses in little spots here and there and rub on a bit of soap. At parties the other girls ask her how she gets that sweet smell, and Laura and I, on strict instruction from Andriana, insist that it's our sister's natural essence.

The Zonico family was busy developing their connections in the export business and, thus, were not participating in the government of Venice, when the Great Council passed its decree of 1297. This decree officially closed the nobility, limiting it to those who were active in the legislative body during the few years preceding it, and to their descendants. The Great Council drew up its membership roles of all the noblemen over twenty-five years old. The Zonico men were excluded.

It was a terrible blow. And not just for the Zonico family. Dozens of old families were left out. They argued over it for more than ten years, but only the men listed in the membership roles were allowed to vote to select the magistrates for the offices of the Republic. And those men, the electorate, didn't seem to care about the ones left out.

So a group of ex-noblemen formed a plot to overthrow the government. They enlisted the help of some commoners, too—citizens. And even of some outsiders, from Florence and Ferrara. All together there were over thirty men who planned to attack the Palazzo Ducale.

But at the last moment, one of the Venetian ex-noblemen, one who had been a key figure in the conspiracy, went to the Doge himself and reported the whole plot. In return the Doge put the man's name in the register of the Great Council, so his family regained their status.

But the Doge was pitiless toward the others. He had the rebels captured and beheaded. Those few he could not capture were banished from Venice forever.

Two of Messer Zonico's ancestors were beheaded.

The Zonico family, it would seem, has never gotten over this awful event. They have persisted in doing everything that the real noble families do, other than hold office, that is, and in doing it to a greater degree. They send all their sons to the University of Padua, not just those who show an inclination. And they pride themselves on having two or three men in every generation who serve as tutors for the noble families of Venice. They say in that way they are influencing the minds of Venice's rulers more than if they were merely members of the Senate.

This, then, is the history of our tutor. I tried to remind myself of that, when Francesco presented Laura and me to him, because I wanted to excuse him for his rudeness. He kept his lips closed in a thin line and gave us not even a nod. Only the fact that he blinked let us know that he had heard what Francesco said. He immediately pushed the two chairs by the window over to the side of the room and then went about the lesson as though Laura and I didn't exist.

But I cannot really excuse him. Something that happened close to three centuries ago should not intrude itself into this library today. Messer Zonico is a *seppia*—an ugly cuttlefish. A giant cuttlefish, in fact, for he's quite tall. And he's slightly pigeon-toed. It's not nice of me to notice that. I know I'll have to confess this thought before I can receive Communion at Mass next Sunday.

Messer Cuttlefish is talking about architecture. He's describing columns and windows and building materials. His voice drones, but his speech is so packed with information that I listen raptly. Now he opens the giant book lying on the small, wheeled table behind him. He invites our brothers to take a look.

Laura and I are not invited.

I think of the wonderful little book that fit into Noè's hand this morning. The book I held in my own hands. If Messer Cuttlefish had a small book like that, he'd have to pass it around, and then one of our brothers, Piero or Antonio, I'm sure, would pass it to Laura and me. We'd be part of it all—like the Jewish girls in Noè's study group. Instead, Messer Cuttlefish has a massive book, so massive that it has to be wheeled around when it's not sitting on a shelf. He stands over it like a guardsman.

The boys are saying all sorts of things and Messer Cuttlefish keeps asking them "exactly" what they mean and congratulating them. When they ask questions, he answers happily, as though he knows everything in the whole wide world.

While all Laura and I want is to know a little something of this world—this Venice. Just a little something. At least at first. I smile to myself. Then, later, maybe everything.

"What are you doing?" Laura whispers to me. "Sit back down."

But I'm already on my feet. I take her hand and jerk her to her feet as well. I march to the table, pulling her along beside me, and wedge us between Piero and Antonio.

Messer Cuttlefish clears his throat and his eyes dart at me, then away again.

"So this one's Byzantine," says Vincenzo, pointing to a

drawing of columns and arches, "and this one is Romanesque, and this one is Gothic."

"Exactly," says Messer Cuttlefish.

I study the pictures and everything the tutor was saying before makes sense now. "So what is the architecture of the new *palazzo* across the Canal Grande?" I ask.

Messer Cuttlefish stands so still, it's as though he's been turned to stone. Then his tight little mouth wrinkles along the upper lip and his cheeks puff. "Messer Mocenigo," he says, addressing Francesco. "Did you not tell me, did you not explicitly assure me, that the visitors would not disrupt the lessons?"

"I did." Francesco looks at me. His eyes sparkle as though he's enjoying Messer Cuttlefish's discomfort. Somehow I know that if Messer Cuttlefish weren't looking directly at him, Francesco would wink at me. "The question, however, surely seems not a disruption, but, rather, most pertinent," says Francesco.

"Most impertinent, I'd say," says Messer Cuttlefish. "Anyone who had been following the lesson wouldn't ask silly questions."

"I've been following the lesson," Piero says. "The arches on the new *palazzo* aren't pointed like the arches on our *palazzo*—so it's not Gothic. Nor are they high like the horseshoe arches on the Basilica di San Marco—so it's not Byzantine."

"It has simple, rounded arches," says Antonio. "But somehow it doesn't seem like the other examples of Romanesque architecture."

"And the columns go all the way up beside the arches, rather than supporting the bottoms of the arches," says Vincenzo. "That means the arches don't really support any weight. They're purely for decoration."

"Exactly," says Messer Cuttlefish. "You young men have, indeed, understood."

"As did our sister," says Antonio quietly. "She asked the question, after all."

"And none of us can answer it," says Francesco. "Can you?"

Messer Cuttlefish lifts his chin. "Why don't we just take this book into the great hall and look out at that new *palazzo* together?"

Antonio is already wheeling the book table into the corridor. Laura and I follow the troops, her hand squeezing mine hard.

"Please position the book directly in front of the balcony," says Messer Cuttlefish. "Yes, that's perfect. Now come look."

The boys line up along the wide balcony. But they leave spaces between them. I step into one, and give Laura an encouraging look. When she doesn't budge, I give her a commanding look. She pretends not to see me. Finally, I go over and whisper in her ear, "Peace to you, Mark, my evangelist."

Laura looks at me dumbly.

"Pretend you're in a procession," I whisper. "March."

Laura steps forward, between Vincenzo and Piero, and I get back into my spot.

"All right, now, please look through the drawings in this book, starting at the very beginning."

Piero slowly turns the pages as everyone looks on.

"It seems the architect has gone backward," says Vincenzo.

"What exactly do you mean by that?" asks Messer Cuttlefish. His voice rises in excitement.

"The *palazzo* is almost classic in style, like an ancient building."

"Exactly. It harks back to the Greeks. You remember the

lessons on the classical styles. Oh, *bravo bravo!*" Messer Cuttlefish steps from foot to foot and I guess that this is his form of a celebration dance.

"It's ugly," I say. "It doesn't fit our city."

Messer Cuttlefish looks at me and seems unsure. "What exactly do you mean by that?" he says at last.

"Venice is a city of light and water, where colors flourish because of . . . I don't know . . . but maybe a spirit of hope. The architecture in the new *palazzo,* the architecture that harks back to the Greeks, as you said, that architecture is heavy. Too heavy for Venice."

Messer Cuttlefish's face is loose and flaccid for a moment, as though his eyes are open but he's really asleep. Then his eyes come awake and he's looking at me strangely. "I agree," he says. He takes off his eyeglasses and slowly cleans them with a white cloth. Then he puts them back on. "Our buildings reflect how we view the world. Venice thinks anything is possible, so long as we praise the Lord." He closes the big book. "Vincenzo, would you please wheel this back to the library? And I'd like all of you to arrange your chairs around the long library table for individual tutoring now." He looks at Laura and me. But he doesn't have to. I heard what he said—"all of you."

We push our chairs to the table in the library and the boys each take a stack of materials off a side shelf and set it on the table in front of themselves. They work silently at tasks Laura and I have no part of.

Messer Cuttlefish comes to Laura and me and says, "We'll begin with mastering your letters." He lays a sheet of paper in front of each of us, puts a jar of ink between us, and hands us quills. "This is the letter 'A'." He draws it on his own piece of paper. "Form it exactly as I do: stroke one, stroke two, stroke three."

For the second time today, I am faced with paper, ink, and quill. I work hard to do "exactly" as Messer Cuttlefish instructs. I will learn the magic of letters. Praise be to our Lord.

CHAPTER FIFTEEN

GOOD-BYE

A month goes by in a lovely routine. The only really bad parts of it are that Laura must do most of my work and I rarely get to see Mother or the little ones. In the past I spent my mornings with Mother, doing the work that women do in our house. And I spent my evenings with Laura and Paolina, playing with the little ones. I feel almost like they're strangers to me now. I miss them. But, oh, what I'm doing instead is worth that temporary loss.

Every morning I go to work, like most middle-class and poor boys my age. I change in the storeroom and wear my *bareta* out into the world. Noè meets me in the Rio Terrà di Maddalena and we walk together, unmolested by beggar boys, to the book printer's.

I skip Sunday, of course, because I must attend Mass with my family. And I skip Saturday, because that is Noè's holy day, which he passes studying the psalms, even though the printing house still operates. So on Saturday I work like a madwoman, doing both my share of the chores and Laura's. A small payback, to be sure, but anything is better than nothing.

The printing house, it turns out, is owned by Catholics; Jews have been prohibited from owning printing houses since 1548, though they can work in them. Noè told me that. And there's another prohibition against Jews owning the Talmud or even Hebrew versions of the Bible. But this prohibition is not enforced: Catholic printing houses supply sacred Hebrew texts to many Ghetto families. In fact, one of Noè's jobs—for he has many—is to take the daily sermons of the chief rabbi—the man Noè calls his *gaon*—and translate them into Hebrew and deliver them to either the di Gara printing house or the Zanetti printing house. It is Noè, again, who later distributes the printed sermons to those faithful who can pay. So Ghetto homes are full of texts in Hebrew, law or no law.

I don't have a sense yet of what the real rules affecting Jews are. But I know that the interaction between Jews and Catholics is not purely commercial, despite what Francesco and Piero said. One of the magnificent staircases in the Palazzo Ducale leads to a *bocca di leone* where people can insert denunciations against blasphemy in the lion's mouth. *Gli Esecutori contro la Bestemmia*—the Executors against Blasphemy—were founded in 1537 and they punish not only blasphemies of word, but gambling, drunkenness, and sexual relations between Jews and Catholics. Sexual relations? As Noè says, you don't have a law against something that never happens.

And there are religious events that bring Jews and Catholics together. Noè told me that the new Ghetto choral master, that Leon Modena (whose name he never utters without saying swiftly "may God his Rock protect him and grant him long life"), preaches in the *campo*. He's so eloquent that even Catholics come to hear him. And it goes both ways—Jews listen to the famous Catholic Fra Paolo Sarpi, who comes right into the Ghetto to speak with them. Many criticize Fra Sarpi; Pope Clement even denied Fra Sarpi a bishopric because of his friendships with Jews. But Sarpi hasn't been daunted.

I love it when Noè tells me these things. I love every date, every law, every detail of any sort. We walk to work with Noè talking and me learning. It is wonderful, indeed, to be treated like a boy.

When we arrive at the printing house, I take out a plain white cloth and drape it over my head, with enough sticking out in front to act like a visor against the sun. Giuseppe, one of the copyists, questioned this the first time I did it. Noè quickly said it was because I was a girl. Rosaria, the only other girl copyist, piped up with, "A girl who gives herself the airs of nobility." People snickered here and there, but no one has said anything about it since. And when we were alone, Noè commented that it was "a nice touch" to my disguise as a girl. I pull the sleeves of my shirt down over my hands when I'm working in the printer's courtyard so that only the fingers I use for writing are uncovered. It's lucky, after all, that the fisherboy's shirt is so large on me. My writing fingers have turned a little darker with the sun exposure, but no one at home has noticed.

On every afternoon but Sunday I go to tutorial. Laura stopped coming after the first couple of days. She said she was too exhausted from doing double work all morning—or almost double. Sometimes she doesn't finish the work that's supposed to be her share. But she always does my share. She protects me. She winds wool onto the bobbins and she takes care of our younger siblings. She works so hard.

I felt guilty when Laura quit tutorial lessons, and I told her. Then she admitted that she hated the lessons anyway. She much prefers to spend the afternoon with Andriana or playing her violin.

Mother has no suspicions, largely because she's hardly ever home, and, when she is, she's distracted. But also because in the evenings, after I mangle songs on the violin, I run into the workroom and do whatever I can to catch up. A few times Mother has happened by the workroom and given me a surprised smile. I smile back, in genuine happiness, because winding the bobbins for an hour or two isn't dull at all when I have the morning's adventures to think about. But, oh, it is hard to hear the giggles from the little ones as Laura and Paolina play with them while I work.

But I'm happy Laura has this pleasure. And I'm happy when her eyes light up and she laughs as she tells me about her afternoons with Andriana at parties. For Andriana has been invited to small parties ever since Father announced that he would begin thinking about the family marriage plans. Many of these parties are at the homes of noble families, where the mother and the sisters want to look her over. Since Father will undoubtedly give a large dowry, Andriana is the object of immense curiosity. She says she feels as if she's constantly on display. She plays the harp, always the same tune, because Andriana, like me, is not a natural musician. But she's mastered one tune beautifully, and that's all she needs. When they applaud and beg her to play another, she demurely says her own mother plays much better, which is true. Mother taught Andriana the harp, since she wanted her oldest daughter to follow in her footsteps. In any case, Andriana sounds like a paragon of modesty, which is much better than if she had actually played a second tune perfectly.

Laura tells me all this, reporting word for word what the women say. She can't go on the morning outings, of course, but she begged Mother so fervently that Mother relented and allowed her to come along to afternoon parties.

Mother accompanies Andriana every time, as is required to protect her reputation. And when they are not on these outings, they are preparing for them. These facts are exceedingly lucky for me; there is almost no chance that my absence could go on for so long without detection if Mother were not thoroughly preoccupied. Each outing requires a dress for Andriana that no one at the hostess's home is likely to have seen yet. So Mother takes Andriana to the dressmaker to be fitted. Then, when the basic dress is done, Mother and Aunt Angela and Cara and Andriana cluster together—leaving the care of the younger children to Laura—and they embroider the sleeves of the dress or sew on lacy decorations, as they sip the tasty Brognolo wine that Cara's sister brought her from Friuli. When the hostess exclaims over Andriana's dress, it is important that Andriana be able to say, "Thank you, but I really haven't mastered this stitch so well yet," as she points to a section she did—giving the impression she did all the decorations. Home skills are valued, even among the nobility.

Last night Andriana modeled her favorite dress yet for all of us girls. The bodice isn't so low as on some of her dresses, where I fear she'll spill out if she leans forward. But, oh, this bodice is stunning: green silk, lush with pink and green ribbon flowers all over the front. The ribbon flowers were Andriana's idea. So when the next outing comes, she will truly deserve the praise she receives.

Laura will report it all to me.

I can't imagine that it's anything but torture for Laura to bear witness to these events, since she so much wishes she was being looked over, too. And the thought that Andriana is now believed to be a fine musician has to grate on her, as well, since Laura is the true musician of the family. But Laura has said nothing sour to me. Not a word.

Then there are other gatherings where the noble families are trying to show off their daughters to us, so that we'll think about them as potential brides for Antonio. They're smart to do this. Father, naturally, wants a young woman, so that Antonio can have sons and carry on the family line. And Father also wants a noble woman. Given that we are such a wealthy family, Father expects Antonio to marry a woman from a wealthy family as well. Because usually only one son from a noble family marries and because so many noble families have multiple daughters, there are plenty of young and wealthy women to choose from. That means that beauty and personality count. So young women do their best to show off their charms to Mother and Andriana and Laura.

Father is content to leave so much up to the women, for he's overwhelmed with the politics of his business these days. Just as the family predicted, the petition of the wool combers led to more petitions by the other subguilds within the wool industry. The funny thing is, I often know about these other petitions before Father: In the past month I've learned to read Venetian—oh, joy of joys. It's quite simple; each letter corresponds to a single sound, so once I learned all the letters, I could read anything. And I'm quick at it already, because Vincenzo has done me the favor of writing down stories that I practice reading every night. Since the handbills are all in Venetian, even though the actual petitions are in Latin, I can now read what I spend all morning copying. Sometimes I have to bite my tongue at the dinner table to keep from revealing details before Father has brought them up. Other times I simply talk, and no one seems to notice that I know more than I ought.

I haven't gone to any of these women's gatherings, and I never intend to. I am grateful that we are so rich and, therefore, so desirable that it isn't necessary for us to act as host ourselves. I can ignore the matter of matrimony and devote myself to my lessons.

I love studying even the lessons that seem bizarre to me, like those on the book *Vita Nuova*—new life—by the famous Dante Alighieri, in which the author falls in love with a woman solely through reading her eyes. Messer Cuttlefish appears enraptured at this idea, so enraptured that I sometimes wonder if he has been in love. Yes, lessons are far preferable to the women's gatherings.

Nevertheless, Laura tells me all about them in the evenings, when we're alone in our bedchamber. I find myself listening almost against my will. These events have nothing to do with me. I will not marry. And what's the point of taking part in helping to select Antonio's wife? I will probably never live in the same household with Antonio's wife, since Laura is certainly more appropriate for the tasks of maiden aunt than I am. After all, she adores children. And the more I go outside and see other people's children in passing, the more I notice whining and crabbing. I like children when they're funny or sweetly naughty, but not when they're in bad humor—and they seem to be in bad humor often.

When I manage to put all of this confusion about our futures out of my mind, I'm happy indeed. I wish this month would never end.

This is what's on my mind as Noè and I walk home today.

"Your indentured servitude is up, Donato," says Noè.

I laugh more lightheartedly than I feel, and click the heels of my *zoccoli* together. "I've earned my first pair of shoes."

"Actually, you've become a good copyist. Your early work was messy and slow. Now you're fast and accurate."

"Not so fast as Emilio," I say, thinking with admiration of my speedy neighbor at the copyist tables.

"No. But your letters are more pleasing to the eye."

"Who cares whether a handbill pleases the eye?" I say.

"Precisely what I was getting at. You'd make a good scribe, if you'd like to continue your masquerade for a while."

The words stun me. There's nothing I'd rather do. "Are you serious?"

"Of course."

I've learned many things this month. But a scribe? A scribe needs to know so much. "I'm afraid I'm not up to it."

"I'd start you out on simple tasks. We just got an order for a collection of Greek plays. That sounds perfect as your first job."

I make a tsking noise.

"Don't tell me you don't like the Greek plays? I'd have bet you loved them. Especially the tragedies."

"I don't know them," I say, feeling as if I'm speaking the truth to Noè for the first time ever. "I can't read Greek." My cheeks burn, but I have to keep speaking. "I don't know Greek letters."

Noè tilts his head in surprise. "You must be younger than I thought."

I stand tall and square my shoulders. "I'm fourteen."

"Then your tutor's choice of studies is lacking," says Noè.

"I've attended tutorials only for the past month. The same amount of time I've been working for you."

"I don't understand," says Noè.

"Let me keep working as a copyist." I try to keep the tremble from my voice. "Please."

"There are poor boys who need the money, Donato. I can't give you work they can do. I had you work this month more as an indulgence to myself than anything else. I was sure you'd quit on me—and I sort of wanted you to. I wanted to show you that you couldn't do what poor boys have to do all the time. I wanted you to realize how hard the life of the poor is. But you stuck it out." Noè smiles. "I thought you didn't have it in you. You proved me wrong, my friend. I'm glad."

"Noè?" I stop and look away, squeezing my eyes tight to drain the tears back inside me.

"Are you all right?" Noè puts his hand on my shoulder.

The effect is like the shock of cold mountain water when we swim in summer. I shake his hand off quickly. If he knew I was a girl, he'd be aghast at touching me. I'm almost aghast myself. I walk slightly ahead of him. "Am I really your friend? Are you my friend?"

Noè shrugs. "We talk every day. I look forward to being with you. Yes, I'd call us friends. Wouldn't you?"

I've talked to Noè about so many things this month. I feel that he knows me better than almost anyone. But, in fact, he knows so little about me. He doesn't even know my true name. He doesn't know I have no future. "How do Jews marry, Noè?"

"Ah, you're back on the Jewish-Catholic question, are you? Well, we mate the same old way you do, Donato. Human beings have that much in common, no matter what their religion."

"Don't treat me like a half-wit," I say.

"Don't act like one."

"I didn't. You interpreted me in the stupidest way possible. I want to know how marriage works among Jews. Who gets to marry? Who chooses the person you marry?"

"I'm sorry." Noè gives me a little punch in the shoulder. "Anyone who wants to can marry, so long as their proposal is accepted."

"Anyone? Not just one boy in the family? Not just one girl?"

"You're such a rich boy, Donato." Noè laughs. "In my family we have no wealth to protect. And we have more than our share of self-confidence. I have only one brother, and I'm older than him. When he's ready to marry, he will ask me to arrange it. My father would have taken that role, but he died two years ago."

"I'm sorry."

"Thank you. I loved him very much."

"What will you do when you arrange the marriage? What will you look for in a mate for your brother?"

"If you're talking about the size of a dowry, a lot of Jews care about that, just as a lot of Catholics do. It's hard to make ends meet in this world that most of us live in—the world outside the *palazzi*. But, as I said, my family excels in self-confidence. If my brother wants to marry a particular girl, and if she wants to marry him, I'll do whatever I can to get her family to agree to the match. I can take on more jobs if I need to."

"But won't you care anything at all about her? About what kind of person she is?"

"She'll be his wife, not mine."

"What do you want in a wife, Noè?" I ask softly.

"A partner," Noè says without hesitation. "Someone to work through life's problems with, someone to share life's joys." He smiles. "What about you, Donato?"

"I won't get that choice."

Noè pulls on his thin beard. "Has your father decided which brother will get to marry?"

"Yes."

"And it won't be you."

"No," I say.

"But you want to marry."

"Yes," I say.

"I'm sorry, Donato." Noè stops.

I wonder why he's stopped, then I realize we've arrived at the Rio Terrà di Maddalena. I squint against the sun, looking up into Noè's face. He is more handsome than any man I've ever seen.

He shakes my hand. "Visit me the next time you need a pair of shoes, Donato."

"I will," I say.

"Or anytime. I am your friend, Donato. Don't doubt it. Your good friend." He smiles and pulls me into a hug so tight my bound chest hurts. And something else hurts, too. Something deep inside.

I run down the alley, blinded by tears I don't want to understand, and into the ground floor of our *palazzo*. I don't even try to be careful not to be seen. Maybe it would be better if I were seen. Then Father would realize I'm not the sort of girl who could survive in a convent and he'd have to figure out something else to do with me.

But there is nothing else to do with me.

An old proverb comes unbidden, one Aunt Angela taught us girls when we were little—she is a font of proverbs and superstitions. *"Le piegore mate sta fora del sciapo"*—crazy sheep remain outside the flock. What is life like outside the flock?

I change and carry my disguise up the stairs tucked inside my nightdress, as I did the day Paolina and I crept down the stairs to exchange my clothes with the fisherboy's. But that day I was full of the wondrous joy of unknown things to come. Now nothing new lies ahead.

Paolina waits for me, ever faithful. She gives the signal, and I race across the corridor to the bedchamber I share with Laura. I hide the disguise in the back corner of our closet cabinet.

Within minutes, Laura enters and helps me dress, so that we look identical to the world. She murmurs, "It's over. You don't have to go to that printer's anymore. And I don't have to do double duty." She kisses my cheeks. "Welcome home, sister."

I do my best to smile. We go out to the eating table and take our places.

There are *seppie* for the midday meal. I still call our tutor

Messer Cuttlefish in my head, but really I don't dislike him anymore. In fact, I rather like him. He's a good teacher. But I still despise eating *seppie*. Which is fine, since I don't have much appetite today, anyway.

Toward the end of the meal, as the fruit and cheeses are placed on the table, Father says he has an announcement. "The matter of a wife for Antonio will be settled in the future," he says, "but the other matter, well, that's in place." He beams. "We've found not just one husband, but two."

I look at Laura, but she's looking at Father. My heart beats loud in my temples.

"Andriana," says Father, "have you heard good things about the Foscari family?"

Andriana gives an open-mouthed nod of awe.

There's really no need for Father to say more. The Foscari family lives in Cannaregio. They are practically neighbors. The son, Dario, is in his thirties. Mid-thirties, I believe. Older than might be ideal, but not too old. I'm being silly. Why, some men live to their nineties. Dario is definitely not too old.

Dario married years ago, and his wife, the lovely Catarina Trevisan, was rumored to be with child several times, unsuccessfully. A year ago, she died in childbirth. But the baby lived. A boy. Dario Foscari has been one of the most eligible men in Venice ever since, for not only does he have the wealth of his own family behind him, but because his wife left behind a child, her dowry belongs to that child—so it stays with the Foscari family. And her dowry was a summer villa on the mainland near Verona, a very desirable property.

Catarina had a younger sister, Marina. Normally, Dario

would have been expected, at the very least, to seriously consider Marina as a replacement wife. After all, the Trevisan family had invested much in the union. But Dario feared that Marina, like her sister, would not be a good breeder. Everyone knows that. So Dario's choice of Andriana makes sense. Mother is strong and healthy after giving birth to fifteen children, and twelve of them are still alive. There is every reason to hope Andriana will have many healthy babies.

Father is going through the list of Dario Foscari's assets in a singsong tone, almost a litany. I want him to get to the end of it. I want him to get to that second husband.

"And, so," says Father, "he is a wealthy man and will provide well for you."

Andriana's whole face smiles. And I understand. Dario is more handsome at his age than most men are in their twenties. Even I have watched him during Mass. She is lucky. So keep talking, Father, I beg inside my head, get to the second husband.

"And he is so impressed with your charms that he's asked for a smaller dowry than I expected to pay." Father looks at Laura, then at me. "That's why I could afford to arrange a second marriage, with a second dowry, though it is not of a size that would be acceptable to a wealthy family."

I don't care one bit about wealth. And I know Laura doesn't, either. Not when it comes to a husband.

"The groom is of the Priuli family."

I know that name. Oh, yes. Father has talked about the Priuli father. They've been negotiating a joint proposal to the Senate regarding a piece-rate raise that will keep the combers and the weavers equally satisfied. It seems the Priuli family is as much interested in the welfare of the wool industry as our own Mocenigo family. Father has talked about this nonstop for the past month, boring everyone but the older boys to tears. Beyond this, I know nothing of the family. I'm sure Laura does, though, with all these gatherings she's gone to. But I can't remember her talking about them.

"They're nobles, as is only proper," says Father, "but they have nowhere near the worldly wealth that we do. My friend and colleague, Benedetto, the father of the family, wants a partner for his son, Roberto. Someone who will help him hold together a family as well as stand behind him in his business decisions. Someone diligent, with a good head on her shoulders."

There's that word again, that word that Noè used: "partner." Roberto Priuli needs a partner in life, just as Noè does.

Noè's slender face, his ropy arms with those long fingers, stained by ink, his slight sway as he walks, the way the wind ruffles the fine tips of his hair, the way his eyes flicker for a moment before he answers my questions—everything everything about Noè fills my head.

I must be possessed. This is a moment to think about the Priuli son. Roberto. The man who will be husband to either Laura or me. I've wanted so much to be married. I must focus on Father, listen to his words. I must want to drink in those words. I must beg the Lord for Father to say it is me he has chosen for Roberto. Me.

Father lifts his brows. "Which of you is Donata?"

"I am," I say. This is the moment I longed for. Joy should fill me now. Come, joy, fill me. Blot out the image of my Noè.

"You've proven your intelligence in the tutorials. Antonio

tells me all about you—and Messer Zonico assures me it is so. And none of us who shares mealtime conversation with you could fail to see your good mind for business. On top of that, you still practice your music at night, which is commendable, particularly since the Priuli family prizes the musical abilities of their women. You have a fine talent. And the Priuli mother is content with your looks, having seen Laura at these frequent gatherings and being assured that the two of you are as identical as fish eyes. But, more important, more to the point, your mother has told me of your outstanding conscientiousness in the work, as of late. You work much harder than your sisters, even going back to the workroom in the evenings. Diligence is the virtue Messer Priuli wants most in a daughter-in-law. Diligence, modesty, and obedience. You will make Roberto a fine partner, Donata."

I stare at the uneaten meal on my plate. It is not I who has musical abilities. It is not I who has been diligent in work. And, oh, dear Lord, obedient, me? I look up at Laura, whose tear-filled eyes hold mine fast.

"Do I take your silence for gratitude?" says Father.

"I am stunned," I manage to say.

"Life holds its surprises, doesn't it? Laura, you, then, will be the sister to live at home and care for your brother Antonio's children. Mother tells me you've always been patient with your younger siblings, so this is all working out well. And, Paolina, my little flower, Mother tells me you are fast becoming a master gardener."

Paolina smiles. "I could make our courtyard the envy of all Venice."

"There's no need to make a new garden here," says Father.

"There's already a garden that needs you. In a year you will enter the Convent of San Salvador, where the cloisters have a lovely courtyard that can benefit from your skilled hands."

Paolina nods. Her face shows no emotion whatsoever.

And the meal goes on, though I know that three people at this table want to scream and scream and scream.

CHAPTER SIXTEEN

PRAYER

"I'll tell him." I sit on the bed with my knees up to my chest and my arms hugging them as tight as I can. "I'll just tell Father."

"And then what?" Laura makes two fists and holds them under her chin as though she doesn't know what to do with them. "I don't know what the punishment is for a girl doing what you've been doing, but I never want to know. It's got to be horrible."

"That's just like you," I say. "You never want to know the bad things. But sometimes you have to know. Whatever the punishment is, I have to tell him." I get off the bed.

Andriana catches me by the arm. "You're not alone in this. We all knew you were doing it. I'm the oldest; it fell on me to stop you. I did try—remember that, whatever happens. I tried." Her voice shakes. "But not hard enough. So I'm in trouble, too. And Paolina got you the fisherboy's clothes and helped you sneak back to your chamber each day. And Laura played the most important role—she deceived even Mother. If you reveal the deception, we'll all be punished. And who knows what that will mean? Who knows?"

"It couldn't mean anything near as terrible as what will happen if I don't tell."

"Of course it could, Donata. And it's not just family punishment you risk. Girls who conspire—girls who help their sister go out into the city alone. Think about it. Oh, I was so stupid not to stop you. If anyone outside the family learned of this, we'd all become suspect. We'd become pariahs overnight."

I pull myself free and go to Laura. "All right, then, we won't say anything about my going outside the *palazzo*. I'll tell Mother that all month we've been playing a game, that I was you and you were me. Why make it any more complicated than that? As Francesco said to us, the most elegant solution is the most Venetian."

Laura looks at me with a glimmer of hope.

"I'll say you were the one working hard and I was the one who never finished my work. You were the one practicing violin and I was the one never practicing."

"Will you say Laura was the one Antonio and Messer Zonico think is so smart?" asks Paolina.

I flush at being caught in my pride. "Yes, of course."

"That won't work." Laura shakes her head. "Remember what Piero said? Father's always known you're the one with a head on your shoulders. He believed Antonio and Messer Zonico only because that's what he thinks himself. No one, no one at all, would believe it's been me who says all those things about business at meals. And no one would believe I've been saying whatever brilliant things you say in tutorials." Her voice is bitter.

"I don't say brilliant things in tutorial, Laura."

"It doesn't matter, Donata. Father wouldn't believe we've had a game."

"Nor would Mother believe it was Donata who came to the parties with us this month," says Andriana, cupping Laura's chin in her hand. "Donata can't be charming the way you were all month. She could never have won over Roberto Priuli's mother the way you did." She kisses Laura on the cheek.

Laura looks over Andriana's shoulder at me with such savage pain, I can hardly think.

"Then I'll tell Mother and Father that we pretended to be each other only for work," I say. "For work and music."

"But why?" says Paolina. "What kind of game would that be?" She shrugs. "It makes no sense even to me. I wouldn't believe you."

"Nor will Mother," says Andriana, turning to me now. "She'll be alarmed and then she'll force the truth out of you."

"Not out of me," I yelp.

"Then out of one of us. She will, Donata. Oh, I know you want to do the right thing." Andriana holds out her hands to me. "But no one should do anything fast. My wedding will be first, in any case. We've got plenty of time to figure things out before yours."

I'm so confused. "What will waiting solve? An answer isn't going to appear out of nowhere." But, despite my words, I let Andriana fold me into her arms. It's so good to be in the soft warmth of my big sister.

"Donata's right," says Paolina. "And so is Andriana. Answers may not appear out of nowhere, but if you wait and pay attention to what's going on around you, sometimes answers do come."

"You sound like you've already entered the convent," says Laura. "The next thing, you're going to tell us to pray."

"It's not a bad idea," says Andriana.

We get on our knees in a circle, cross ourselves in the name of the Father and the Son and the Holy Spirit, and offer our prayers, eyes closed, heads bowed.

Oh, Lord, merciful Father, have pity on me. I never meant harm to Laura. It cannot be that I am the cause of her being cheated from what she wants so much. No matter who this Roberto is, he wants a partner with the attributes of Laura. And, so, he must be right for her, since she is so right for him. Please, please, Lord, don't put me in Laura's rightful place. Yes, I've begged you for a husband before on so many occasions. But this is not the way I want to get one. I want . . . no no no. I mustn't even think about the kind of man I want. Not in this moment. This is the moment to think about Laura. Roberto Priuli is Laura's man. Help me find a way to right this wrong. Help me, dear Lord. Please. No sin I've ever committed is so terrible as the sin I would commit if I married the man who really wants Laura—the man she really wants, too. Help me. Oh, please, please show me the way.

I open my eyes.

Paolina's eyes are also open. She's looking at the floor and holds herself so still that for a moment I think she's not breathing. Then her eyes rise and meet mine. Her eyes are pools of pain. But her blink is like a door shutting; her eyes go empty. She smiles flatly.

Laura is the next to open her eyes. She avoids mine.

Finally, Andriana opens her eyes. She looks at me pleadingly.

It takes me a few seconds to understand, and then it's all clear. I can't believe how selfish I've been. "Dear Andriana, here we are ignoring your good news. I am so happy for you."

"Dario Foscari is lucky to get such a wife," says Laura, settling back on her heels.

"You'll be happy," says Paolina.

We're all sitting back on our heels now, a circle of sisters on the floor, skirts touching.

"Thank you." Andriana blushes. "He is handsome, isn't he?"

"He's angelic," says Laura.

Andriana laughs.

"No, I mean it," says Laura. "In church with the light behind him, he seems to wear a halo."

So my twin has watched this man in church just as I have. I look at Laura's profile. She steadfastly refuses to turn her face to me, but I know she feels my eyes on her. And she knows I know. How can I have brought such harm to the person I'm closest to in the world?

"Mother and I are going to another gathering today," says Andriana. "The Grimani family wants to show off a daughter for us to consider as a potential wife for Antonio, and from what I've heard, she's better than most. They say she's kind."

"That might mean she's ugly," says Paolina.

I smile—that's exactly the reaction I had.

"We'll see," says Andriana, her voice growing lighter and happier with each word. "Come with us. All of you. Let's have a good afternoon."

"I'll skip my harpsichord lesson gladly," says Paolina.

Laura touches Paolina's cheek. "I thought you enjoyed the harpsichord as much as I enjoy my violin."

"I'll have the rest of my life to play the harpsichord, and only one more year to go to parties." Paolina stands up. "I'm coming." She takes Andriana's hand and pulls her to her feet.

I look at Laura, who is looking down at her hands, folded on her lap. "We'll stay here. Laura and I need to talk."

Andriana leans over Laura. "Is that what you want?"

Laura nods without looking up.

Andriana and Paolina leave.

Bortolo comes in. "What are you doing on the floor?"

"We were praying," I say.

"You're not praying anymore. Why don't you get up?"

"We like it here," I say.

"Laura doesn't. She's crying again. Why is Laura always crying? Is it still that cursed toothache?"

I look at Laura's hands. They're shiny with the tears that fall from her bent head. "It's much worse than a toothache," I say. "Everything hurts today."

Bortolo stares at Laura. Slowly his mouth opens in a circle. "Ah," he practically shouts. "I know what's going on. This is just your trick, not hers."

"What are you talking about, Bortolo?"

"I came to demand you give me a gift to keep silent because you're getting married when really Laura's the one who should be. I thought you were both in on it. But it's just you, Donata. Laura hasn't agreed. It's just your trick. That's why Laura's crying. That's the real reason, isn't it?"

I forgot: Bortolo can tell us apart. He knows Laura's been doing double duty every morning. I should be afraid of his knowledge, but right now I almost wish he'd go blabbing to Father. At least this nightmare would be over. "No, Bartolo. That isn't why Laura's crying. Because I'm not going to get married. Do you understand? I'm not getting married. It's all a terrible mistake. Laura's crying because we haven't yet figured out a way to make everything right again."

Laura looked up when I said I wasn't going to get married, and she's still looking at me.

Bartolo twists his mouth in doubt for a moment, then smiles heartily. "I knew you wouldn't be that bad," he says to me. "I knew you wouldn't steal Laura's husband." He gets on his knees beside Laura. "Don't be sad. You'll find a way. Give me a great treat, and I'll help."

"How, Bortolo?" I ask. "How will you help?"

Laura's looking at Bortolo now, just as tensely as she looked at me a moment ago.

"Tell me what to do," says Bortolo simply. "I'll do anything you say. I'm great at secrets and adventures."

Stupid me, I was hopeful for a moment. Hopeful that my six-year-old brother could actually rescue us. And Laura felt the same way, I'm sure. "I don't know what to tell you to do, Bortolo."

Bortolo reaches inside his vest without a moment's hesitation. He pulls out the yarmulke. "When I don't know what to do, I use my magic hat. It makes me think better." He puts it on his head and closes his eyes. If he were to bow, he'd look as if he were praying, like a perfect little Ghetto boy.

Laura takes the yarmulke off his head. "You mustn't show that to anyone, Bortolo. That's a Jewish hat. Someone might take you for a Jew." Her voice breaks and she's crying again.

This can't happen. Bortolo's right: I can't be this bad—the world can't be this bad. "There's no cause for worry, Laura," I lie. "I have a plan."

CHAPTER SEVENTEEN

STARTING

After the initial horrible celebrations that Mother holds for Andriana and me—a special Mass, a gathering of the closest family friends, little private speeches in which she assures us we'll make good wives and mothers—I can finally get to what I need to do most of all.

Work.

I work like there's no tomorrow—for it is only when I'm working that I can keep myself from thinking of Noè—from missing him. And I don't want to miss him. There's something worrisome about missing him. Besides, it's ridiculous. So much else is important now.

I finish my morning chores in record time, then help Laura finish hers. I play with the younger children enthusiastically, rolling on the floor with them, racing on the staircases, exhausting myself. In the afternoons I study and study and study. At night I play the violin—horribly, it's true, but at least I do it.

There's no way I can make up to Laura for all she did for

me in that one month while I was a copyist, but I try. At mealtimes, I grab the biggest pieces of dessert and place them on Laura's plate before my brothers can get their hands on them. She protests when we're alone, but I know she's glad I'm doing it. I know she feels sorry that I'm suffering so from guilt, and she's happy that I'm finding little ways to assuage that guilt.

And I know, no matter how firmly I speak, that Laura's beginning to lose hope. When Bortolo knelt on our bedchamber floor wearing the yarmulke, I was sure a plan would come to me. I promised Laura to tell all once I had all the details in place. Every day since then Laura has asked me if my plan is ready and every day I've said, "Not yet. But it will be soon." The truth is, no plan has come.

But one thing is clear to me: I must learn more. Answers do not lie in ignorance.

There's no way I can learn all of Latin overnight, though this is my heart's passion. I've memorized the five noun declensions. That was relatively easy. It's all the many verb conjugations that stump me. Sometimes I can guess what tenses the verbs are simply from how similar they are to Venetian verbs. But other times I'm totally wrong. I slave over Latin poetry late at night, by candlelight, when everyone else sleeps, but Ovid gets no easier.

Still, tonight I'm more optimistic than I've been since Father's announcement of my marriage two weeks ago. At tutorial today Messer Cuttlefish handed me a book. A small book, one of those put out by the Aldine press. The very feel of the book pierced me—for the man who first let me hold such a book was my sweet Noè. I had to put the book down on the table, my hand shook so.

This text is bound in dark purple, straight-grain morocco, titled and tooled in gold. Messer Cuttlefish presented it to me like a treasure, almost as though he anticipated my reaction. "It contains several plays by Plautus," he said in a reverential voice. I bent my head to hide my flush when he spoke. The last person to talk to me of plays was Noè, when he asked me to be the scribe for some Greek plays.

Messer Cuttlefish says that Plautus wrote in a unique way: His upper-class characters speak in classical Latin, while their servants speak in common street Latin. He says this will be more satisfying for me, more encouraging, because the street Latin will feel almost familiar. He said it's strange that a woman betrothed, as I am, is so intent on learning Latin fast, but he wants to feed my fervor, whatever its cause. When he said that, I knew he was asking, in an oblique way; I knew he sensed something and wanted to help. And I appreciated his discretion. But I didn't answer.

I'm not the only one our tutor gives personal attention to. Messer Cuttlefish assigns Vincenzo harder problems in mathematics than anyone else, and allows him to explain the problems the rest of us have trouble with. Vincenzo never seems so happy as in these moments. No matter how basic our questions are, he contemplates them and responds respectfully and lucidly. Even I, who am so new to mathematics, can follow most of what Vincenzo says. Messer Cuttlefish says Vincenzo has a gift.

And Messer Cuttlefish gives extra work in philosophy to Antonio, extra work in history to Piero, extra work in geography to Francesco. He has his eye on their futures.

Our tutor is not the prissy pedant I took him for, that first day of lessons. With a heavy heart I realize that. My future, no matter what it may be, will surely take me away from this home, and I'll lose the great privilege of studying with this fine educator. Let me learn while I can.

Thus, I sit tucked in the corner of the bedchamber, the candleholder balanced on my knees, and open the little book by Plautus. Study study study. An answer will come.

Suddenly I fall back, both shoulders meeting the walls. The candle tumbles and hot wax burns the back of my forearm. I right the candleholder and manage to place it by my feet. My stomach heaves.

Everything is clear now. And everything is wrong. Everything. I don't know how I've managed to keep myself from realizing it for so long. The worst will happen unless I do something to prevent it. This is the truth. This, and only this. It is a dishonor to Laura to act like such a fool—to look for the answer in a Latin verb ending.

I lay the book beside the candleholder on the floor and tiptoe past Laura, sleeping in our big bed, and out into the corridor, down to Mother and Father's bedchamber. Their door is closed. I lift my hand to knock, when shakes overcome me again, and I'm on the floor, retching on all fours.

Hands cup my shoulders and pull me back. "What is it, Donata?" I sink into the folds of Mother's dress. Her arms circle me and pull me onto her lap and we're rocking together on the floor in the feeble light of the oil lamp beside her door. "Are you ill?"

"Ill of spirit." It seems like forever since I've been alone with Mother. I twist within her arms till I can face her and hug her tight. "I can't marry Roberto Priuli, Mother."

Her torso stiffens. "And why not?"

"I cannot do this terrible thing to Laura."

"Oh, Donata, my poor, sweet girl." Mother softens around me again. "Of course it's hard for you two to face separate futures—you've always had identical lives. But only one of you can marry. And the very fact that even one of you can marry is an unexpected blessing we should all be grateful for. Be happy for yourself—as I am sure Laura is happy for you."

"You don't understand, Mother. Laura should be Roberto Priuli's wife. She's the diligent one, Mother. She's the musician."

Mother strokes my cheeks. "Laura has always been a hard worker. And she's very fine at the violin. I know that, Donata. But you've matured lately. Your new work habits surprised me."

"You don't know my new habits, Mother. You just think you do."

"Don't be silly, Donata, I know you well. Roberto Priuli needs a partner like you. Father is right to recognize your business acumen."

"The Priuli family cares about the wool industry, Mother. Laura knows as much about that as I do. Laura is the right partner for Roberto Priuli."

"No, Donata, there are things you don't understand."

"Explain them to me, Mother. Please. For God's own sake, please." I clutch her with all my strength.

Mother shakes her head. "Your behavior is exaggerated, Donata. Calm yourself." She runs her hands down my arms and holds me tight.

I flinch in pain.

"What's this? Wax on your arm? You burned yourself?"

"It's nothing, Mother. I was reading by candlelight and I knocked over the holder."

"See? Reading at this hour. Your father and I were standing on the balcony watching Venice sleep—but you were awake, studying. That's why you are the one to marry, Donata. Your mind is restless. You would rage inside if we picked another way of life for you. Even as a wife and mother you will meet challenges disciplining yourself to the confines of proper society. There is much of your father in you, Donata. You're a little too rebellious for your own good."

"But Laura—"

"Laura knows how to accept life."

"That's not fair, Mother."

"Hush, Donata. The decision is made. And it's the right one. Go back to bed now."

"It's—"

"Discipline yourself," Mother says firmly. "Good night, Donata." She goes into her bedchamber and shuts the door behind her.

I walk back to my room. The candle flickers in the corner. Laura rolls over in her sleep and sighs. My eyes blur with sadness.

What if there is no answer at all?

I envy Bortolo, who puts the yarmulke on his head and yields to belief in magic.

I cannot even yield to sleep; my entire body quivers.

I lie on my stomach on the floor and open the little book hesitantly. I force myself to read.

Soon I'm lost in the play. It is about a legal trial. At once my body grows rigid. I rise to a sitting position and read faster.

The protagonist of this play is wrongly accused of a heinous murder. The servants give testimony that is true, entirely true, but misleading for reasons that have nothing to do with treachery, but purely with innocent misunderstandings. The circumstances sweep me away. I read deep into the night.

When I finish the play, I hold the book to my chest until my racing blood slows to normal. Then I put the book under my pillow and blow out the candle.

Trials can end in death. But those that don't can change life radically. Sometimes even for the better, if Plautus is to be believed.

But is he?

I close my eyes and still I see the image of Bortolo in the yarmulke, eyes shut, hands folded together. I toss and turn in frustration.

The next day at tutorial when it's my turn for individual instruction, Messer Cuttlefish asks me how far along I am in the Plautus play.

"Dearest Tutor," I ask, "has anyone ever found himself in better circumstances after a trial?"

Without hesitation, Messer Cuttlefish answers, "Andrea Donà."

"Andrea Donà stood trial?" I am astonished. "We know the family. Mother is friends with the Donà mother. We girls have gone with Mother to their *palazzo* on many occasions, just as the Donà girls have come with their mother to our *palazzo*. Signora Donà even came to the private gathering that celebrated Andriana's and my betrothals but ten days ago."

Messer Cuttlefish shakes his head. "The Andrea I'm talking about is not the father of the Donà family today. The trial took place over a hundred and fifty years ago."

I sigh in relief. I would not want my friends to have suffered the humiliation of a trial. "What happened?"

"He was ambassador to the court of Francesco Sforza in Milan. He was accused of taking a bribe from Sforza to reveal secrets of the Venetian Empire. He was tortured until he confessed. Then he was fined, imprisoned for two years, and banished. He lived in exile until the state pardoned him and—"

"Why?" I interrupt. "Why did they pardon him?"

"The Senate never made public their deliberations." He stops short from saying more.

But I can guess the nature of what he was about to say. Since that day when Francesco and Piero came into Laura's and my bedchamber and talked about how tolerance is good business, I've come to learn that Venice's history has always been guided by good business. "What trade was the family responsible for then?"

"They didn't dominate any single trade. Instead, they exported many things—paper, pins, needles, ship riggings. And they imported just as many—spices, cotton, wheat, almonds. Why do you ask?"

"They must have been involved in something in a crucial way," I say, "because the pardon must have been to Venice's economic benefit somehow."

A corner of Messer Cuttlefish's mouth twitches; he fights a smile for sure. "The Donà men were mercenary generals. Venice wanted to use them in wars against the dukes of Milan."

"Oh, no. So a man who had been ambassador to Milan was asked to come back from exile in order to lead wars against the very place that had hosted him?"

Messer Cuttlefish nods.

"But he must have been close friends with his old hosts, or he wouldn't have been accused of accepting bribes from them in the first place. So how could Venice expect him to cooperate—and how could he consider it?"

Messer Cuttlefish just looks at me.

"All this treachery is hard to understand," I say. "Did Andrea do it? Did he really come back to Venice?"

"Indeed."

"And did the Donà men lead troops in battle against Milan?" I ask.

"Yes. But Andrea was not a general—he was always a statesman. And he went on to hold higher offices than he'd held before the conviction and exile. He was ambassador to Cosimo de' Medici in Florence and to the sultan of Egypt and, finally, to Pope Nicholas V."

"I don't understand," I say. "I don't see how anyone could have trusted him, and I don't see how he could have trusted them. I don't understand politics."

"But you do, Signorina Mocenigo. You knew his pardon had to be to Venice's benefit. You used the word 'treachery.' You understand perfectly."

I shake my head. "This conversation has gone astray from what really interests me."

"Exactly what interests you, Signorina Mocenigo?"

Oh, how I want to ask him direct questions. I long for Messer Cuttlefish's counsel in the things I must do now. But I cannot confide in my tutor. Whatever plan I devise, no one must know of it. No one must be put at risk for my sake ever again. Finally, I say, "What happened to Andrea Donà's family while they were in disgrace?"

"The man was disgraced," says Messer Cuttlefish, "not the family. In these situations, a brother will step in and make sure the family affairs don't go awry. Nobility prevails."

His voice gives no hint of sarcasm, though in his own family's history nobility did not prevail. Perhaps in this moment he's uncomfortable. Perhaps he even suffers. I wish I knew the right thing to say. "Thank you," I murmur at last. "Thank you for answering my questions."

Messer Cuttlefish licks his lips. "This is my duty, Signorina Mocenigo. Is there anything else you wish to ask?"

"Yes. Today when a person is convicted, does the family suffer?"

"Not if they have resources."

Money, he means. And now everything makes sense. Of course a family is not disgraced when a man is disgraced. The family owns the wealth—not the individual man—and wealth cannot be disgraced. "And if the accused isn't found guilty, what happens?"

"A frivolous denunciation is punishable." Messer Cuttlefish rubs his lip. "Anyone who tries to tarnish a man's good name for capricious reasons deserves punishment fitting to the degree of slander." He looks at me in silence for a while. "Is that all?"

"Yes. Thank you."

"You have interesting questions, Signorina Mocenigo. You are a person of discretion beyond your years." He walks around the table and begins Piero's instruction.

Discretion. I don't believe anyone has ever considered me a person of discretion before.

I go to bed that night without a word to Laura, though a

plan has finally formed. I cannot tell Laura this plan because she'd stop me.

I rise early the next day and take my fisherboy's disguise out of the closet cabinet.

"I thought that was all behind you," says Laura, pushing herself up on one elbow.

"I thought so, too." Too bad, I think now. These clothes let off a sour odor. The last time I put them away, they were due for a rinsing. If I had realized I'd need them again, I would have washed them well. "I'm going out today."

"You're crazy. After everything Andriana said, how could you?"

I clutch the clothes in silence.

"Don't expect me to hide your absence," says Laura. "I won't be any part of this." Her voice, though, is not unkind, but sad.

"I don't want you to do anything for me." I kiss Laura on both cheeks. "It's important, in fact, that you don't." I stuff the disguise under my nightdress. "Do you know where I'm going?"

"No," says Laura.

"Good. That's important, too." I go to the door and peek out into the corridor.

Laura gets out of bed and runs to me. She pushes the door closed. "You're worrying me, Donata. What are you up to?"

"Only good, Laura. I promise."

"So you have a plan at last?" Her voice rises to a thin screech.

"Perhaps."

Laura bites her bottom lip. "Can you do it alone? Without help?"

I blink as her question makes sense. There is something I need help with: the lock on the side door of the *palazzo*. "If I'm not home before the boys, tell Paolina to do the usual."

"What do you mean? What's the usual?"

"Just tell her."

"Will she get in trouble?"

"I pray not. I don't want to hurt anyone ever again. But I need this one thing." I peek into the corridor, then dash for the stairwell. Within minutes, I'm in disguise and out in the alley.

Suddenly, I'm fearful. Noè will not be on the Rio Terrà di Maddalena to meet me, and I will have no defenses against the beggar boys. My best chance is to move as quickly as I can.

It's wrong of Noè to leave me so unprotected.

Even as I think that, I realize it's irrational. Noè has no idea I'm coming to the printer's today. Nevertheless, I'm angry at him. And afraid of the beggars. And afraid of what I'm about to do.

I run out into the wide street, keeping my head down, refusing to make eye contact with anyone.

"Stop, boy!"

At the shout I run faster.

Slam, smack. A crushing weight crosses my middle, then it's over.

I'm lying on the stone ground, looking up at the bottom of a cart.

A man drags me out and pulls me to my feet. "You ran in front of me," he says loudly. "I can't be held responsible." He scurries about, gathering the wood and bone carvings that litter the ground. He tosses them back in the cart. "You ran in front of me."

I bend to clutch my middle. The front wheel of this three-wheeled cart went entirely over me. I heave, but it's dry, for I've had no breakfast.

Still, there's a stickiness on my chin. I wipe it; the back of my hand comes away smeared with blood.

The man stares at me as though he's seeing some horrible specter. He picks up my *bareta* from under the cart.

I snatch it and twist my hair into a clump that I stuff back inside the hat. My chin drips blood.

"Come on," says the man. "I've got a friend up the road here. She can take care of you. It was your fault," he says again loudly, looking around at anyone who might be watching. "So it's just the kindness of a spectator that moves me now. The kindness of a poor carver."

I stagger beside the cart. The man soon stops and leans into an open shop door. "Chiara, someone ran in my path without looking, right under my front wheel. Could you help?"

A heavyset woman comes to the door.

"Thanks," says the man, and he's back to his cart before she can respond.

Chiara mutters a few complaints in the man's direction. She puts a hand on my shoulder and guides me inside to a stool. I've got my own hands cupping my chin, so I won't bleed all over everything, but she pries them away. Now her mutters change to words of comfort. She tells a small boy who emerges from the corner to grab a basin and go for water. Then she washes my chin.

I'm thanking her and trying not to cry out as she picks bits of rubble from the gash. To divert myself, I let my eyes wander the room. Boxes of all sizes are stacked around the walls. Some are plain, but most are made of beautifully painted or printed paper. Laura loves paper boxes. She has a collection of particularly small and delicate ones. "Your boxes are exquisite," I say. "My sister would love this store."

Chiara hands me a small square of clean cloth. "Hold this to your chin and press. And you can get up now." No sooner do I get up than she sinks onto the stool with a little wuff sound. "So you know fine craftsmanship, do you? You've got good taste. I love this shop. I'm a slave to it, working every day, dawn to dusk, but I love it. This one's my own design." She reaches for a box, but her arm isn't long enough. The little boy who brought the basin obliges again, knowing exactly which box she means and putting it in her hand, then going back to settle in the corner once more.

Chiara holds the box before my eyes and rotates it. It has eight sides of equal dimension and it's about the size of a man's hand, with fingers spread. The corners are perfectly tucked. The lid is made of narrow folds of paper that radiate out from the center in a swirl, so that you expect it to be round. But somehow she managed to make perfect tucks at the eight corners.

"It's marvelous," I say.

"My best seller. I'd let you hold it, but for the blood and all."

I realize Chiara is the keeper of this shop. I didn't even know women could be shopkeepers. Barmaids and laundresses and servants, yes. Prostitutes, yes. And I know that women do all sorts of work at home that serves the factories. But here's a woman who runs a business from beginning to end. She's in charge of her own destiny.

Chiara puts the box on the closest stack and peeks at my chin. "It's stopped bleeding. You'll be good as new before long. Wash your hands now."

I rinse my hands in the basin and wipe them on the back of my trousers. "Thank you," I say quietly. Then I kiss Chiara's hand, as a gentle boy would.

She laughs. "Now, aren't you the ladies' man? Go on, get out of here."

I look at her steady eyes. "I need help getting over to the Fondamente Nuove," I say.

"What do you mean, help?"

"If I walk alone, I'll get beat up by beggar boys."

Chiara looks out the door past me. "Is that why you were running without looking where you were going?"

"Yes, kind woman."

"What's your name?"

"Donato."

Chiara puts one hand on her hip and regards me with piercing eyes. "The Donà family has a *palazzo* on that *fondamenta*."

I stand stupefied. Yesterday Messer Cuttlefish talked to me about the conviction of Andrea Donà. Now Chiara is talking about that same family. I feel as though Chiara has seen into my thoughts. I stare at her in dread.

"They've placed a large order with me. I was waiting for my sister's boy to deliver it. But if you'll deliver it, I'll pay the passage on the gondola. It'll get you to the *fondamenta* in one piece, at least."

"You've put your trust in the right boy, kind woman," I say with genuine gratitude.

"I'm a good judge of character," says Chiara.

I begin to smile, but it hurts my chin, so I simply give a single bow of the head. "I won't let you down."

"You'd better not."

Moments later I'm in a gondola with a large package wrapped in brown paper and tied with string. The *gondoliere* knows the *palazzo* of the Donà family, which is good, since I don't know how to get there by canal starting from here. All I have to do is carry the package into the *palazzo*.

I sit back in the gondola and am enjoying the rhythmic motion when I notice that the *gondoliere* is looking at me oddly. I jump to my feet and almost knock Chiara's package in the water. I have to leap to catch it in time, and the whole gondola rocks dangerously.

"*Cretino!*—hare-brain," shouts the *gondoliere*.

Stupid me. Girls sit in gondolas. Boys stand. It's not a rule, it's just the way it happens. I stand as tall as I can.

When we arrive at the *fondamenta*, I get out quickly, mutter a thank-you, and carry the package to the entrance of the *palazzo*.

A servant girl answers my call. She comes down the stairs in quiet slippers and opens the gate. She eyes the package while I eye her, my head turned to one side so she won't see my full face. She doesn't look in the least familiar, thank heavens. "Follow me," she says.

"It's not heavy." I hold the package in one hand to show her. "You can carry it easily."

"It's a boy's job to carry packages that big, lazybones. Can't you give a good girl a hand?" She leads the way up the stairs to the kitchen.

Baskets and pots clutter this kitchen. Several rounds of hot bread steam on the counter. The heavenly smell brings water to my mouth. I've gone out without eating again.

The girl looks at me a moment in silence. I don't know what to do, but I'm almost sure she doesn't have any inkling who I am, so I just look back. "Set it on the table," she says at last, "and I'll call the mistress."

"Good-bye, then." I put down the package and quickly head for the stairwell.

"Stay put. Don't you have any manners?"

"I'm in a hurry," I say.

"Too much of a hurry for a tip? How about a thank-you kiss, then?" The girl smiles, and I realize with shock that she's flirting with me.

"Who's there?" Signora Donà comes into the kitchen.

I look down at the floor instantly. For a moment I think that I'm going to pass out.

"This boy brought a package," says the servant girl.

"Who's it from?" asks Signora Donà. "What is it?"

"The boxes," I mumble.

"Oh, yes, the boxes. Thank you, young man." She gives a little flustery noise. "I didn't realize you were coming so early. I don't have even a *soldo* on me. I'll send Diana to get a coin."

"Or we could give him bread," says Diana. "Would you prefer that?" she asks coyly. She's an observant one, that's for sure.

"Thank you," I mumble.

Diana hands me a round of bread and I turn to go.

"Just one minute," says Signora Donà. "Let me have a look at your face."

She recognized me. How could she not—she was in my

home so recently? So it's over. I'm caught. I look into the signora's face with resignation.

"What's this?" She frowns. "Have you been fighting?"

I shake my head, confused.

"Yes you have. Look at that chin. And the dirt across your shirt. I won't have ruffians in my house. Tell the shopkeeper to send someone else next time. Now get on your way." She flicks the back of her hand at me, as though I'm a piece of trash.

I race down the stairs and out to the *fondamenta*. Signora Donà peered right in my face, a face she's seen so many times before, and didn't recognize me. She didn't even really look at me. Not really. She looked only at the wound on my chin. Why should she really look at a poor boy who's come on an errand? Such a boy could never be anything to her.

The bread is chewy and salty and wonderful. I rip it ferociously with my teeth. And I practically run to the printer's.

A group of five boys comes right toward me. Five. How can I possibly get away from five?

But one of them smiles and I realize I know these boys.

"Are you coming back to work, Donata?" asks Giuseppe.

"I have to talk with Noè and see," I say.

"He'll take you back in a minute," says Rosaria. "You do good work."

I'm touched by her words of confidence. For the month that I worked here, I kept a good distance between us. I was afraid that if I tried to make friends, Rosaria would discover some inconsistency in my story—or maybe somehow sense that I was different. As a result, she considered me haughty—she said as much more than once.

Well, I'll make friends with her now. She can't possibly get in trouble if things go wrong for me.

As though Rosaria can read my mind, she reaches into a fold of her shirt and hands me something. A lily petal. It's been crushed, and black lines run crisscross at the folds. I wonder if she picked it off the ground at a flower market. I think of the flowers we have on our dining table every day. Fresh flowers. Not a single black line on them. Rosaria watches me and her face tells me this is a treasure. I kiss the lily petal and tuck it inside my own shirt. Rosaria smiles.

We go through the entrance door and down the central hall together, but at the last moment I hold back and let the rest of the boys and Rosaria go out to the courtyard. I stand in the rear room and watch through the window, feeling nervous and silly.

Noè does everything I've seen him do so many times before. He moves with a long, confident stride, making sure everyone has the proper tools and space to work well, making sure everyone can see his models to copy from.

He stands back a moment and looks over them almost like a proud father. I smile. This is something I hadn't seen before, because when I used to sit at those tables, I'd be bent over my work, giving all my concentration to the letters.

Noè turns to come in and I'm struck with an inexplicable panic of shyness. I flatten myself against the wall and hardly breathe as he passes through the doorway and goes down the corridor to the room that I know is his workplace.

I stay pressed against the cool, inner wall, trembling, well after he's out of sight.

Have I come here just to back out of my plan like a coward?

Yet the plan hasn't even been on my mind. It's Noè who makes me tremble.

Slowly I walk to his workroom. My *zoccoli* click on the floor. I wish I could be like a Venetian cat, silent and quick, ready to disappear at the least threat. In contrast, I feel huge and clumsy and loud.

Noè is already seated, quill in hand, writing some ancient Greek work. He hasn't heard me yet. He's oblivious to everything but the words in front of his eyes. I imagine them dancing inside his head. His yarmulke is on crooked; I can't help smiling.

I stand in the doorway while he finishes a line of script. Then I whisper, "Hello, my friend."

Noè looks up with a start. His smile is immediate and genuine. How could I have been afraid? He rests the quill on its little tray and almost lunges toward me, with a hug and kisses on each cheek.

I was too late to stop the kisses, but this dear friend will never know I'm a girl, and what he does not know cannot hurt him. Still, I step away and smile from a proper distance.

"What happened to your chin?"

I think of Signora Donà. "You know what a ruffian I am."

Noè smiles but he pulls me to the window for a closer look. "Did you wash this?"

"A woman did."

"You'll live, I guess," he says. "How's the other guy?"

"You don't want to know."

Noè plays with the tips of his beard. "Still not talking, huh? I thought when we parted last time that you'd given up hiding from me."

I reach up and straighten his yarmulke, careful not to touch his head. What's the point of hiding? "Noè, do you recognize errand boys?"

"What do you mean?"

"When a boy delivers something here, do you look at his face?" I ask. "Do you remember him the next time?"

"It's good business to recognize errand boys. If you treat them kindly, they do their best for you the next time. I should know," says Noè. "I was an errand boy before I was a copyist."

I wonder now if the servant girl at the Donà *palazzo* is someone I've seen many times before, but never taken the care to notice. I fight off the sadness. "I met a woman who runs her own box shop."

"Is that remarkable?" asks Noè.

"I don't even know. Is it?"

"She's done well for herself, I guess," says Noè. "Probably she's a widow who took over the family business when there was no one else to do it."

"But maybe not," I say. "Maybe she just loved paper and she found herself folding it into shapes as a little girl and before long she was making boxes and then someone bought one and then everyone wanted her boxes." I'm practically out of breath. "Is that possible, Noè? Is it?" I pant.

Noè hesitates. "I suppose so, Donato."

"Don't look at me so worried, Noè." I give him a smile. "Sometimes my head just fills with silly questions."

"They're not silly." Noè's eyes change. "You know, I was thinking about you yesterday." He races to a shelf and grabs a manuscript. "Look at this."

I read aloud, "*Water Monsters*. An unusual title."

Noè laughs, that deep-throated laugh I've missed so much. "A child wrote it. A boy called Giulio, but a mere seven years old. If you want to talk about remarkable things, this is one, for sure. His adult brother, Maurizio Strozzi, acted as scribe, for the boy's own handwriting still leaves something to be desired, apparently."

"A boy with bad handwriting made you think of me?" I say, pretending to take offense.

"Yes." Noè grins. "It's a play, for five characters. And it's written in Venetian. The Strozzi family plans to have it performed at a special party for Giulio. They want five quick copies, one for each of the actors. And one professional copy to save in their library. I'll do that one. But the others . . . well . . . I have to find someone."

"The quick copies don't have to look perfect," I say, as though on cue.

"That's right."

"And someone who knows only one language could do the job," I say.

"That's right."

"Hmmm. Who might that be?" I make my lips protrude, as though in deep thought.

Noè laughs again. "Take the job, Donato. It's a good start."

"I know a bit of Latin. I never told you that. So I know more than one language—maybe I'm overqualified," I tease.

"A bit of Latin," he mimics in a snooty tone. Then he breaks into a grin. "Actually, that's good, because at three points in the play a character crosses the stage holding the Venetian banner, shouting the Latin words on it. No big deal—but it helps in copying without mistakes if you know the Latin."

I hand him back the manuscript. "I don't have the time," I say seriously.

Noè's cheek twitches. He flips through the pages. "It's short. You can do a whole copy in a day, I'm sure."

"I have lessons in the afternoon."

"Right. Well, then, two mornings per copy. You could finish in ten sessions."

"Will you pay me what I want?" I ask.

Noè looks surprised. "I'll pay you the piece rate. The amount the master will pay me."

"I don't want money, Noè. I want help."

He looks a bit wary. "What kind of help?"

"Help with my Latin," I say.

Noè smiles in relief. "That's the kind of help I'm best at. Count on me."

I will, I'm thinking. I've put the first step of my plan in your hands. It's real now. My Great Plan.

CHAPTER EIGHTEEN

ARGUMENTS

"Donata," comes Mother's voice, firmer than usual.

I'm in the corridor with Laura and Paolina, heading for the eating table. It's a surprise to see Mother standing before the entrance to the hall. "What is it?" I ask.

Mother gasps. "What happened to your chin?"

"I fell. It barely hurts now."

"How did you fall?" Mother holds me by the shoulder with one hand, while she carefully tilts my chin upward with the other. She examines me, just as Noè did. "Run along, girls." She gestures for the others to go ahead. "What happened, Donata?"

I remember the comfort of her arms last night and suddenly I'm hungry for that closeness again. I move toward her so that our skirts press together. "I was rushing and not watching where I was going."

"Well, it's not surprising, given how much is on your mind." She tucks my hair back behind my ears.

My hair hangs loose and curly, hardly brushed. Laura's hair, on the other hand, is in a bun of several complicated twists, undoubtedly the work of Andriana. But Andriana was so mad at me for going out again, she wouldn't speak to me, much less offer to do my hair. I was upset at first. Still, there's no point in Laura's and my doing ourselves up identically now, though I did put on the same dress as her. It would have felt just too strange not to.

"I'm sure it will heal evenly," says Mother, giving me an approving look. "You'll be just as lovely as you've always been."

It's funny; until Mother said this, I hadn't thought at all about what my accident would do to my looks. Even my sisters didn't say anything about that. Instead, when I came home, they immediately clucked around me, fussing to check that the wound was clean, asking over and over if it hurt. "It doesn't matter, Mother. I don't care what my chin looks like."

Mother frowns. "Don't think because you're engaged you can forget your looks. Every woman benefits from appearing her best." She walks back down the corridor, out of earshot of my hovering sisters, and I go after her obediently. "And don't think that if you forget your looks, we will cancel the wedding plans."

"I wasn't thinking that, Mother."

"Good. Where were you this morning?" she says quietly.

"Working."

Mother folds one hand inside the other. "Not the work I set out for you, that much I know."

"Different work."

"You're expected to fulfill your family duties, Donata. You haven't left us yet. I looked for you everywhere."

"I'm sorry, Mother. I have something I must do."

"Tell me about it."

"I can't, Mother. It's a secret."

"A secret?" Mother looks bewildered. "What kind of secret could a proper girl keep?"

I take her hand and hold it to my cheek, but I'm almost sure it doesn't reassure Mother, for it doesn't reassure me.

"Did your secret cause your fall?" she asks in a nervous hush.

"I told you about the fall. I didn't watch where I was going."

"Does your secret have anything to do with your marriage?"

"If I answer your questions, it won't be much of a secret, now, will it?"

Mother pulls her hand away and hugs herself. "You exasperate me, Donata."

There's nothing to answer to that.

"If Laura and you—"

"Laura is not involved," I say quickly.

"All right, then. So this is a new worry of yours." Mother sighs. "You are so high-strung. Marriage makes young women think of things—intimate things—in a new way. They can get frightened. It can help to talk."

I almost laugh. "It's not anything like that, Mother. You've always answered that sort of question. I don't need to talk."

"If you're sure . . . but don't keep secrets from me," she says with a shake of her head.

"I have no choice, Mother."

"Of course you have choices, Donata. These are important times for you. Your engagement carries with it responsibilities—toward the family, not just yourself."

"I'm being responsible, Mother. That's precisely what I'm being."

Mother looks at me and I can see her face change to one of resolve. She smiles. She has decided to believe the best. "All right, then. Give me your word that you will perform your duties from now on."

"I'll do the best I can," I say.

Mother takes my hand now. "The meal is waiting."

I allow myself to be led to the table like a dumb animal. I practically dream through the conversation, dream through chewing and swallowing. I know I'm worried, but I'm not wiggling around, popping with ideas to try, the way I normally am when a problem presents itself. And this is a dreadful problem: Without someone to hide my absence over the next two weeks, I may well not be able to finish what I've started.

And I won't be able to see Noè.

I chew and swallow.

Afternoon tutorial is on biology. Messer Cuttlefish has brought a book of drawings of the animals of Africa by the Dutch artist Albrecht Dürer. My older brothers and I crowd around the little wheeled table that holds the enormous book. They ask questions and Messer Cuttlefish answers.

After a while, Messer Cuttlefish gives me a curious look. "Signorina Mocenigo, what would you like to ask?"

"I hardly believe Africa exists," I say, though that isn't what I meant to say at all. I meant not to speak.

"And why is that, Signorina?"

"I've never seen it." What a foolish thing to say, I think, even as the words still hang in the air.

"You've never seen God," says Messer Cuttlefish, "yet you know He exists."

I should drown in a wave of embarrassment for making this prattling exchange take place. But I feel nothing. I wonder briefly if I'm getting sick. This sense of detachment isn't like me.

Finally, it's time for working on our own. We sit at the study table and I take out the book of Plautus plays. I read silently until it's my turn with Messer Cuttlefish.

"Shall I try again today?" asks Messer Cuttlefish.

I look at him, confused.

"Yesterday you managed not to talk about Plautus at all. Tell me the truth, Signorina Mocenigo, have you read any of his work?"

"I've finished the first play and am halfway through the second."

He gives an appreciative nod. "I take it you enjoyed the first play, then."

"The language was easier to understand, as you said. But the workings of the trial confused me," I say.

"What didn't you understand?"

It isn't that I didn't understand—it's that I couldn't glean the information that I wanted. I have to find the right phrasing to get what I want from Messer Cuttlefish now. But nothing clever comes into my thick skull. "I wonder how modern trials work. Here in Venice. Could I read something about that?"

"Modern trials? Criminal trials? You mean like the one we talked about yesterday—the one involving Andrea Donà?"

"Yes."

Messer Cuttlefish observes me for a moment. "Is it the law that interests you, Signorina Mocenigo? Or is it questions of right and wrong?"

"Aren't they the same thing?" I ask.

Messer Cuttlefish smiles—he actually smiles at me. "In theory, yes." He goes to the shelves of books and walks along, scanning the titles. He opens the glass door, selects a volume, and brings it to the table, setting it before me. "Have you heard of Saint Thomas Aquinas?"

"No."

"He was a pious scholar from the south who lived three centuries ago. Pope Giovanni XXII canonized him on July 18, 1323." Messer Cuttlefish says the date as easily as he'd report his own birthdate. I feel sure he knows the canonization dates of all the saints, just as he must know the smallest details of their lives. Envy stings me—there's so much to learn and my tutorial days are almost over. "This is what you should read next," he says. "It's not the easiest Latin prose, but the ideas within merit the time spent. It's incomplete; yet even in its incompleteness, it's better than anything else you can read on the subject."

"Thank you," I say, swallowing. "I hope I'm up to it."

"I wouldn't give it to you if you weren't. Start now." Messer Cuttlefish moves on around the table to Piero.

I open the book and struggle along. This volume is not one of the small editions; I cannot carry it away with me to read tonight. Just as well. The intricate arguments in it tire me.

They seem never ending. I should have asked Messer Cuttlefish for a book simply on trials—that's what I really care about, after all. I want to know what happens to the accused, from beginning to end.

I want to know what to expect.

The rest of the day moves slowly. After the evening meal, I go into the music room for violin practice, but I can't manage to lift the bow. I stand there and wait. Finally, I put the violin in its case, go down the corridor, and slip into Paolina's bedchamber.

Paolina squeals with delight. "Oh, I'm so glad you came. Tell me about your plan."

I frown. "Did Laura tell you I had one?"

"Laura and Andriana won't talk about you at all. But they didn't need to. When you went out this morning, I knew it. Even Bortolo guessed."

"But he didn't see me leave. I'm sure of it."

"Nevertheless, he knew you were gone. Mother went all over the *palazzo* calling for you."

"She's a problem," I say.

"Who? Mother?"

"Yes. She insists I be responsible for my morning work, but I can't do the work, because I have to go out."

"So?"

"So will you do my work for me?" I ask.

Paolina looks incredulous. "Have you lost your senses? Laura can be taken for you, but I can't. If I did your work, Mother would see."

"If you do my work, at least the work will be done. And I'd have been responsible enough to make sure it got done.

When Mother asks, tell her outright that I begged you to do it."

"She'll get angry."

"But at me, not you. And it's the best I can think of right now, Paolina. Will you do it?"

"Yes. Tell me your plan."

"I can't. I don't want to involve you. It's bad enough that I need you to unlock the side door for me."

Paolina gasps.

"What's the matter?"

"The lock. You asked me to unlock the door for you and I forgot all about it. I'm so sorry."

"Well, that's all right," I say. "By chance the door was open today anyway."

"I don't mean today." Paolina looks confused. "How could I know you wanted me to unlock the door today? You didn't even tell me you were going out."

"But didn't Laura deliver my message?"

"Of course she did—that's the only thing she was willing to say about you. She told me to 'do the usual'—so I waited for you at the top of the stairs—but Mother shooed me away."

"What are you telling me?" I feel sick. "Aren't you the one who unlocked the door for me the whole month I was working at the printer's?"

"No."

"Then who?" I put my fingers to my temples and walk in a circle around Paolina, my stomach growing more jumbled with every step. "Could our brothers have been so careless as to leave the door unlocked behind them every day?"

"Not Piero," says Paolina. "He's never careless."

I circle her again, my fingers in my hair now, pressing hard. "Who, then?"

"Don't brood on it, Donata. You were lucky. But you don't have to be lucky again. I'll unlock the door for you tomorrow. Tell me where you're going."

"I can't. If Mother asks, tell her I didn't speak about it. And then hush. Please, Paolina. There are dangers you don't understand. Do what Andriana and Laura do—know as little as you can and say nothing." I kiss my sister and go back to the bedchamber I share with Laura.

She's already in bed, lying there with the oil lamp lit beside the bed and her eyes wide open. Now she rolls on her side so her back is to me.

I get into my nightdress, kneel at the little prayer stand beside the bed, and say my prayers—extra prayers tonight. Then I blow out the light and climb into bed.

"Is it dangerous, this plan of yours?" Laura whispers.

I don't answer.

"Will you get beaten up?" she asks.

"My chin isn't from anything like that," I say. "I fell. That's all."

"Do you think your plan will work?"

"I don't know."

Laura's silent for a long time, but I know she's not asleep. "I'm mad at you," she says at last.

"I know."

"You can't know. You can't know how hard it is to try to be good all the time, because you've never tried. But I have, Donata. I've tried to be as good as I can be my whole life."

"You are good, Laura."

"I wish I wasn't. I wish I was mean enough to go to Father and tell him. I wish I didn't care what happened to any of us, so long as you didn't get to marry Roberto Priuli."

"Don't wish that, Laura. I've been the mean one. Don't you wish to be mean."

Laura says nothing.

I hear the quiet splash of a gondola oar from outside the window.

"I'm sorry I'm so mad at you, Donata," Laura whispers. "I know you didn't do this on purpose. You're not really mean. I tell myself that. But I can't help the anger." She gropes for my hand behind her back.

I lace my fingers through hers. "No matter what, Laura, I won't marry Roberto Priuli." I won't marry anyone but the man I love, I think.

"Don't promise that, Donata. You don't know if your plan will work. And if I can't marry him, then you might as well. At least one of us should have a good life."

I can't answer, my mouth is so full of sadness.

"Mother and Andriana talked about her wedding this morning."

"I'm sorry you had to listen to that," I manage to say. "I'm sorry for everything. Sleep now, Laura. I love you."

Eventually her breathing tells me she sleeps. Eventually, I, too, yield to the night.

But I'm up at the first hint of dawn, waking from a nightmare. My heart thumps as if it will burst, so loud I fear it will wake Laura.

Slowly I realize the noise is not my heart at all. It's coming from the corridor. I open the door.

Little Maria bumps along the floor on her bottom.

"Good morning," I say, closing the door behind me, so that Laura won't wake.

"Who are you?" asks Maria.

"Donata."

"That's what I thought from your chin." Maria wrinkles her nose. "You never play with me anymore. You never give me rides."

I get on all fours. "Climb on me now. But we mustn't wake the others, so speak softly."

Maria jumps on my back and rides me up and down the corridor. I have to stop frequently to untangle my nightdress, but that doesn't disturb her joy. She whispers happy little words in my ears. And once, when she leans down to whisper, she lets herself collapse on my back and hugs me around the chest with all her might. Oh, how I've missed this.

I turn at the end of the corridor to make one last, long run, such as it is, when Maria says, "Look, Mother, Donata's my horsie."

Mother stands there with a sleepy smile on her face. "When we go to the country next month, you can ride a real horse. You're old enough now."

"Hooray!" Maria jumps off me and runs to Mother, hugging her around the legs. Then she runs back to me with a wrinkle of worry in her small brow. "But I love riding you, too, Donata. You're a good horsie."

I gather her into my arms and kiss and kiss and kiss her. Thank you, Lord, for a four-year-old sister.

"And you'll be a good mother, Donata," says Mother.

I wince. "What's the point of having children and watching the girls go off to convents?"

"Donata!" Mother looks stricken. My words hurt her as much as hers hurt me.

But I won't take them back. Even if she doesn't feel sorry for her daughters, I feel sorry for us. I feel sorry for every daughter of Venice.

"Father said Paolina is going to the Convent of San Salvador next year," says Maria. "What's a convent, Mother?"

"It's a wonderful place, Maria. We'll talk about it later. And, Donata, you are not to say anything like this ever again." Mother beckons with her hand. "Maria, come here."

I grab Maria and give her one last kiss on the forehead. "I'll play with you tonight," I whisper in her ear. "Before I practice violin."

She puts her lips to my ear. "All right," she whispers loudly. Then she runs back to Mother and they go into the bedchamber she shares with Giovanni and the wet nurse Cara.

I rush to my room and grab the silk cloth. There's no time to bind my chest now. I have to get downstairs before Mother comes out of Maria's bedchamber. I race to the stairwell and run down as fast as I can. I go into the storeroom, bind my chest, and change. Then I realize it's way too early to go outside. Noè has agreed to meet me in our usual spot, but that won't be for a while yet. So I perch on a giant spool of yarn like a watchful bird.

This storeroom has a little window high up, because it's against the alley side of our *palazzo*, the side away from the church of San Marcuola. Will I be able to hear the church bells? But I can judge by the light, what there is of it. I lean my back against the wall and wait.

THE HEAVY CLUNK OF wet wood against stone wakes me. How long have I slept?

The fisherman talks with Cook, chattering of the goings-on about town.

What seemed interminable finally ends. I hear someone close the canal gates and secure them. Footsteps ring on the stairs.

I run out into the alley and pass to the next alley and the next, out to the Rio Terrà di Maddalena. Noè isn't waiting for me. It's not terribly late, but it's late enough. I've missed him.

I set out walking with the big strides of Noè, the strides that should tell anyone who sees me that I've got a destination, I'm not a beggar.

I haven't gone fifteen meters before the beggar boy's face is in mine.

"I told you not to hang around here."

"I'm not," I said. "I'm passing through." I move on around him.

He pushes me against the wall. "You can't pass through here."

"I have to," I argue as firmly as I dare. "This is the path I must take."

"I don't like you," says the beggar boy. "I don't like your white skin or your fancy talk. The only good thing about you is that wound on your face." He smiles suddenly. "Let's make it last, eh?" With a swipe of his nails, he rakes the scab from my chin.

"Ahiii!" The blood streams. I press the heel of my hand hard against my chin to stop the flow. "What'll it take to get you to allow me free passage from here to the Fondamente Nuove?"

"You're going all the way over there?"

"I am." I blink. Then I add, "If you'll protect me."

"You don't need his protection," comes an angry voice. Chiara, the shopkeeper, holds a broom over her head. "This'll come down on your back if you bother my errand boy again," she shouts.

The beggar boy turns and runs.

"Come on, Donato." Chiara pulls me by the elbow across the wide street and into her box shop. "I hope you're not planning on bleeding all over the place every day."

"Don't make me laugh," I say. "It hurts this chin of mine."

She takes my hand away and looks close. "At least it's not full of dirt this time." She hands me a clean square of cloth. "Seriously," she says. "If I hadn't been standing outside my door, I'd have never seen what was going on. What'd you do to that boy, anyway?"

"Nothing," I say, pressing the cloth hard. "He just hates me."

"Signora Donà doesn't like you, either. She said you're a ruffian."

"Because of my chin," I say.

"I thought as much."

"Need anything delivered to the Fondamente Nuove today?" I ask.

"No."

"I thought as much," I say.

We both laugh, though it makes the blood flood more.

I kiss her hand, as I did yesterday. "Thank you again, kind woman."

"God be with you. But just in case, learn to run, young man. With your eyes open this time."

I leave at a run, staying close to the wall, dodging in and out of the peddlers and shoppers. Whether it's the determination in my gait or the gory sight of my chin, I don't know, but no one else bothers me the whole way.

I walk into the printer's, past the two journeymen busy at setting type, down the corridor, and into Noè's workroom.

He gets up, shaking his head as Chiara did. "Again?"

"Don't say anything funny," I warn quickly. "When I laugh, it bleeds more."

"Have you washed it?"

"It wasn't dirty this time."

Noè grimaces. "Fool. Stay here while I get water."

I go toward his stool.

"No." He quickly drags the stool away from his desk. "I've been slaving over this page. I can't take the chance of your blood getting on it." He puts the stool in the center of the floor and beckons me to sit.

He's back fast, with a basin of water, a bar of soap, and a clean cloth. Printers always have soap on hand, though it hardly helps against the stain of ink. "What happened this time?" he asks roughly, but he's washing my chin as gently as if I were a baby. And his other hand is on my neck, steadying himself so that the hand that tends my wound will press no harder than absolutely necessary.

My insides stir at his touch. I can hardly stay still. And I'm ashamed that I allow him a touch that is forbidden by his religion. The moment he stops tending my wound, I get up and step away. "There's no time to talk about it," I say. I go to the table Noè set up for me yesterday and I take up my work where I left off.

Noè gives me no arguments.

CHAPTER NINETEEN

LAND ANIMALS

I'm in my nightdress, having left the disguise down in the storeroom. I come racing up the stairs and burst through my door, only to find Mother waiting in my bedchamber.

Mother presses her lips together so hard they turn white. "Your chin is raw again," she says in a thin, high voice.

"It looks worse than it is," I say, which is senseless, since I haven't seen how it looks.

"You haven't dressed yet. And you didn't do your work."

"Paolina did it for me, didn't she?" I say.

"She began to. But I stopped her. You didn't keep your promise, Donata."

"That's not fair," I say.

"That's what you said when we talked about Laura the other night. Stop it, Donata. Stop saying everything is unfair!"

"But if you'd have let Paolina, my work would be done. Then I'd have taken the responsibility for getting it done. That's the best I can do—and that's all I promised."

"Leading your sister into the path of perdition is not the best you can do, Donata."

The way she says that gives me the shivers. "Have you punished her?"

"She's confined to her room."

"I asked Paolina to help me. She agreed to do my chores. Please, Mother, that's not something that merits punishment."

"She wouldn't tell me where you were. That merits punishment."

"She didn't know. It's a secret."

"A secret. The way you talk—and what you said this morning about not wanting children because the girls will go to convents—such crazy talk—and in front of little Maria."

"I spoke only the truth."

"What truth? All of my children are fortunate to be part of a noble tradition. Your children will be fortunate, too."

"You said yourself, Mother, that if you had been born a man, you'd have broken with tradition and used bright colors in wool weaving. Your face glowed when you said it."

"We were both born women, Donata."

"That doesn't stop us from knowing there are lives better than what tradition affords us."

"And there are lives much worse. Look at your life and be grateful." Mother's eyes glitter with tears. "I'm at my wits' end. You've been stubborn before, but never like this. And this secret. A secret that involves bloodshed is indecent."

How have I reduced my strong mother so severely? I put my hand on her arm to console her. "My chin is an accident. It's not part of the secret. It won't happen again."

"But it did happen again. And the other night you burned yourself with wax."

"The candle fell, Mother. I told you that."

Mother hugs herself, as she did yesterday morning. "Cara and Aunt Angela and I searched the *palazzo*. Where were you?"

"I didn't want to be found, Mother."

"We looked in closets, under beds, on balconies."

"I didn't stay in a single place."

"Were you . . ." Mother grimaces in fear and sucks air in through her clenched teeth. "Were you outside the *palazzo*?"

"Do I look as though I went outside? I'd never go outside in my nightdress, Mother."

Mother blinks and a tear escapes. It runs down the side of her long nose. "Do you swear before the Lord?"

My tongue feels too thick to move. But I'm swearing that I didn't go outside in my nightdress. That's what I'm swearing, no matter what Mother thinks I'm swearing. "I do."

"Thank the Lord for that at least." Mother brushes away the tear. "Would you rather I ask your father to talk with you?"

"No. Please, Mother. I have nothing to say."

"Of course you do." She drops her arms. "Hiding in your nightdress, tearing your chin open, burning your arm. Oh, Donata, you're beside yourself. You're one of those girls who . . ."

"Who what? What girls, Mother?"

She heaves a sigh. "Speak your mind, Donata. Ask about what troubles you."

"The questions that trouble me are not ones you can answer."

Tears well in her eyes again. "Do you want to talk with a priest, then? Don Zuanne could be fetched immediately."

I can see that she won't give up. "Not a priest, no, Mother. But if you insist, I'll talk with the tutor."

"Messer Zonico? I never heard of such a thing—a girl turning to a tutor for counsel."

"Boys turn to tutors for counsel."

Mother makes a tsking noise and I can see she wants to snap at me for saying that. But then she seems to think better of it. "Messer Zonico is sensible." She rubs my hands now, though the day is hot already. "I'll tell him to take you aside this afternoon for a private talk. For now, stay in your room."

The air in the corridor was full of the odor of roasted lamb when I came up the stairs. Now it curls in under my door. "I haven't eaten anything yet today, Mother."

Mother's eyes widen. "You're not eating?" She puts her hand over her mouth; then she shakes her head slowly. "Perhaps an empty stomach can help clear the brain."

"I'll accept that," I say. "But please let Paolina eat with the family. I swear she doesn't know my secret. No one does."

"Don't use your sister ever again, Donata. It can lead to nothing but problems for both of you." She leaves.

I watch the closed door, half-expectant. But none of my sisters comes in to talk with me.

I look briefly in the mirror. My chin is a mess. My hair falls in tangles. I have the air of a madwoman. No wonder Mother is so frightened for me. I dress slowly.

And now it hits me: Paolina was confined to her room. And both Father and the boys came in before me. Surely one of them must have thought to lock the door behind them. So who unlocked it for me?

Who in this *palazzo* knows my comings and goings? Bortolo, perhaps. But is he reliable enough to come down and unlock the door at just the right time every day?

I can't figure this one out. And, surely, whoever it is means me no harm, or harm would have come already.

I work on my hair, combing loose every last knot. I wrap my hair with one of my white veils, so that my face and shoulders are free of locks. The young woman in the mirror now seems subdued, though the telltale wound on the chin can't be ignored. I go out on the balcony.

The Canal Grande is almost empty. No one works during the midday mealtime. The water is green as precious stone. It laps sweetly at the *fondamenta* on the far side.

Venice is deceptive when the canals are empty. It seems the perfect city, the Serene Republic, completely and lastingly peaceful and innocuous. But Noè and I talked today about how far from innocuous it is. Violations of voting procedures have been increasing, as has the harshness of punishments for offenders. The copyists' handbills today detailed those punishments.

Now if a noble is found guilty of seeking to influence votes to advance the interests of a foreign lord, he will be excluded from offices and commands for ten years, and he will pay a fine of 500 ducats. A citizen will likewise be excluded from office, though he cannot hold commands in any case, and he'll pay 200 ducats. And a member of the people, who has no voting rights anyway, will be exiled for ten years and pay 100 ducats.

All of this does not seem so terrible. How can a republic survive if the voting process is not protected against such assaults, after all?

But there is something awful. The handbills list one more proclamation: If someone knows of a voting wrongdoing and does not report it, his right hand will be cut off.

Noè says this barbaric punishment proves Venice has not risen far from its Byzantine past. He predicts that corruption will persist, and, with no benefit whatsoever, we will become a sorry republic in which each member acts like a watchdog against his neighbor.

I said nothing. The difficulty of creating a society in which all can flourish seems greater now than I would have believed possible a couple of months ago. So many people, with so many needs. Poor people. Women. In some ways Venice is already a sorry republic.

I have the urge to jump into the Canal Grande and swim away. Forever.

My stomach growls in hunger. Mother told me to stay here, but what she really meant is that I should be excluded from the midday meal. She won't care if I go to the library. I open my door.

Giò Giò stands in the corridor. He looks at me.

"Why aren't you serving the meal?" I ask.

"Your mother told me to keep an eye on you."

A chaperone within the house. But I can't blame Mother—she's right. "I'm going to the library."

Giò Giò follows me down the stairs, but he stays in the hall, while I go inside and sit at the long study table.

I open the volume by Saint Thomas Aquinas and read. The arguments seem less tedious today. There's a strange attraction about the clean way they proceed, their tightness. I read with growing interest.

At some point Messer Zonico comes in. He doesn't utter a

greeting. Instead, he lays a large book on the little wheeled table and flips through the pages. I know his silence is not out of any disrespect, but, to the contrary, out of deep respect for the fact that I am reading this work of theology. And I realize that in my head I have called him by his rightful name for the first time since that very first lesson. I smile to myself and keep reading.

When my brothers come in, we move to the cluster of chairs by the window and the lesson begins. It is a continuation of yesterday's lesson, the nature of life on land. Messer Zonico goes on and on about the habits and life cycles of wild creatures that do not live in Venice proper. Our mainland summer home allows us just "a bit of countryside," as Father says. Mother has already starting packing our things to go there, muttering little complaints about how the heat here is becoming unbearable. Most of my knowledge of land animals comes from our visits to that country house. I've seen goats there, and rabbits, squirrels, foxes, badgers, ferrets. I've chased snakes and frogs through the grasses by the little lake. I've climbed trees and looked out on hillsides covered with flocks of sheep. And, of course, we ride horseback—a great pleasure. Other than that, land animals are known to me in the form of food or leather or wool.

And of course, Venice bursts with cats. And there are rats, big and fat.

I wonder if the beggar boy who torments me has ever had the privilege of seeing a fox.

And now that I think about our summer home, I realize I've never seen beggar boys from our coach as we ride along. But surely there are poor people in the country, too.

Messer Zonico solicits questions now.

"What do poor people on the mainland do?" I ask.

Messer Zonico looks at me blank-faced.

"What's the matter with you, Donata?" asks Vincenzo. "Haven't you been listening?"

"People are land animals," I say in defense, though I know my question is misplaced. "Poor people in Venice are greengrocers and ribbon makers and box makers and cat castrators and servants and thieves and beggars and so many things. What are poor people on the mainland?"

"They are dirt farmers," says Francesco. "And sharecroppers and day laborers."

"They dig irrigation ditches and serve as stable boys and lackeys," says Piero.

"Why should you care?" asks Vincenzo.

"We should all care," says Antonio.

"Exactly," says Messer Zonico. "Life is life, whatever its quality. And human life is sacred." He pulls up a chair and sits in front of us. "Everywhere you go, some poor people work, scrabbling to make a livable life, and some poor people struggle in misery or prey upon the more fortunate."

"Tell us about the habits of poor people," I say, thinking about my friend Chiara and the copyists Giuseppe and Rosaria and Emilio. "Where they live, what they eat. Tell us about their life cycle."

"I don't want to hear this," says Francesco. "We have little to do with poor people."

"On the contrary, we deal with poor people every day," I say. "Consider how much our family talks about the combers' petition for a raise. Why should any one of us care about whether it costs one *soldo* or two and a half to adjust the teeth of a comb? A *soldo* is worth so little to us. Nothing. But the people who made those leggings you wear count their *soldi*. As do the people who made the glass in this window and those who fitted it in place, and the people who cut down the wood for that shelf and those who carved it, and the people who printed the books that surround us and those who bound them. Oh, yes, we build our life on the backs of poor people." I have risen at some point during this stream of words and my hands have been jabbing at the air, pointing here and there about the room.

My brothers stare.

I sink into my seat.

"Be grateful we do," says Francesco at last. He gets up and goes to the long study table. "I'm doing my own work now."

"Me too," says Piero. He goes to the study table.

Vincenzo follows.

Antonio and I remain with our tutor.

"Some live in tenements right beside the rest of us," says Messer Zonico in a low voice. "But some live in wooden sheds on the edges of the city. If they're lucky, a family occupies a single floor. If they're not, they might crowd into a single room."

"A dark room," I say.

"I've never been inside a home of the poorest people," says Messer Zonico. "But I imagine that's right. And most of the poor die young."

"Almost half the people of Venice die before reaching the age of twenty-one," I say. "Father talked about that."

"Yes," says Messer Zonico. "But if you take out the nobles and citizens, if you look only at the poor people, you find that sixty percent of them never reach adulthood. They have many babies, but few live."

"Why?" I ask. "Why do the babies die?"

"Sickness, lack of food." Messer Zonico lifts his hands toward us, as though apologizing. "The sorghum we use for making brooms—do you know it? The state doesn't even tax it because it's considered inedible. But some poor make their bread from it. And bread is the mainstay of their diet."

"Mother sometimes takes hot bread and puts it on our chests inside our clothes in winter," I say. "To give us a special warm feeling—so we're cozy. Bread made from wheat flour. When the bread grows cold, we throw it out." I clench my teeth as I remember.

"We should be ashamed," says Antonio so softly I can barely hear him.

"The very worst part of poverty, however, is probably not any of these physical discomforts." Messer Zonico looks right at me now. "It's the monotony. They have no education. We can take respite in our books, in our philosophy and theology. Our spirits can take flight no matter what happens to our bodies. The poor have none of this."

Nor would I, I think, if I hadn't fallen into this tutorial almost by accident, as it were.

"Antonio," says Messer Zonico. "You can go to your individual study now."

Antonio goes to the study table.

"Your mother has asked me to talk with you," says Messer Zonico to me. "She says something troubles you."

"Many things trouble me."

"I can see that. And rightfully, Signorina Mocenigo.

Rightfully. But your mother says there is something else—a secret."

"Many things are secret," I say. "Before I studied with you, all the things you've taught me were secret so far as I was concerned. They were kept from me."

Messer Zonico takes off his eyeglasses. He rubs his eyelids with the thumb and forefinger of his right hand. Without opening his eyes, he says, "Your mother fears you have taken up a practice that has, unfortunately, become popular among certain young women these days."

"I have no idea what you're talking about. I don't know what's popular among young women. I haven't spent time with any of my old friends for months."

"She thinks you've entered a period of self-flagellation," he says.

"What does that mean?"

"She thinks you close yourself away from light and food and all comfort—that you harm yourself, to atone for some real or imagined transgression. Young women do that sometimes—particularly when they believe they have received a gift they don't merit . . ." He pauses. "Such as an unexpected betrothal."

"Mother is wrong," I say. "I don't consider the betrothal a gift I don't merit. Anyone merits getting married. Marriage should not be reserved for the privileged few." I didn't know how strongly I believed this until now, as the words come out of my mouth.

Messer Zonico looks at me and his eyes seem huge and vague. "Then perhaps something else weighs on you, something else makes you punish yourself. You are about to enter into a noble marriage, but with a family of more modest means. Your outburst earlier—which I do not disparage in the least—indeed, we all benefited from hearing it—your outburst indicates a serious concern about economic matters. Signora Mocenigo, do you feel guilty for your wealth?"

"I don't know," I say honestly. "I've never asked myself that question. But the answer is not relevant to my secret, Messer Zonico, for I do not practice self-flagellation."

"I see." Messer Zonico puts together lightly the tips of the fingers of both his hands. He looks at me imploringly. "Whatever it is you do—whatever secret—can you at least tell me why you've been doing it?"

"I'm trying to do the right thing."

Messer Zonico's chest rises and falls in deep breaths. He seems to struggle with my answer. He looks pitiful.

Why do I make so many problems for so many people? Why can't I simply be like Laura, naturally good?

"The right thing in general, or in particular?" he asks.

"If one does the former, how can one not do the latter?" I say.

"Quite right. But I cannot return to your mother with no answers," says Messer Zonico. "I must tell her something. If I tell her that you are concerned with questions of right and wrong—with questions of theology—would that be a deception?"

Questions of theology. Questions of and for God. "No," I answer.

He puts his eyeglasses back on. "Then that is what I shall say. Do you want to return to your reading now?"

I get up and go to the long table and take up reading where

I left off. It's hard to concentrate after the discussion of tutorial today. But gradually the words on the page command my attention. I dig deeper and deeper into the beauty of Saint Thomas Aquinas' arguments for the existence of our dear Lord.

CHAPTER TWENTY

FINISHING WORK

I wake to a noise in the corridor, like yesterday. Little Maria? I open the door stealthily.

Cara sits in a chair directly across from my bedchamber. She's looking around and tapping her feet, probably to try to keep herself awake. Has she been out there all night? Or did Giò Giò take the first shift? When Cara finally turns her head to me, her mouth opens uncertainly.

"Are you my prison guard?" I ask, which isn't totally kind, since I know that Cara isn't to blame. She's a slow woman, but an earnest one. I'm immediately ashamed of myself.

But the offense flies past Cara's unsuspecting nature. She smiles her usual smile, just a bit more weary than normal. "The mistress told me to alert her when you came out of your bedchamber."

I return her smile and step into the corridor. "You had better do so, then."

Cara gets up heavily and walks up the corridor.

I am already on the stairs, taking them at breakneck speed, by the time I hear her knuckles rap on Mother and Father's bedchamber door. I get over to the outer edge of the stairwell and run as close to the wall as I can, so no one looking down from above will see me.

"Donata!" Mother shouts. "Where are you? Did she go up or down, Cara? Which way?"

Bortolo and Nicola are playing already in their corridor. They both see me coming down.

I put my finger to my mouth in the hush sign and keep running.

Nicola opens his mouth to greet me, but Bortolo slaps his hand over Nicola's mouth and wrestles him to the floor. They roll like kittens as I race past and down the last flight. I duck into the storeroom.

I'm afraid to stay here, though, even for the few minutes it takes to dress. Bortolo won't say he saw me. But Nicola probably will. He's never yet kept a secret. And I can hear Mother's shouts. Everyone will be awake soon.

I climb over the large wool spool, grab my fisherboy's clothes, and go out the *palazzo* door.

I'm in the alley in my nightdress—something unthinkable only yesterday. My arms feel chilled, though the morning is already warm. I jam the fisherboy's clothes underneath the nightdress. I have to go left, because on my right the alley ends at the Canal Grande. And I have to go fast. One alley, the next, the next.

The traffic on the Rio Terrà di Maddalena is just picking up. Noè won't be here for a while.

I wish I were invisible. I shake my head wildly, till my hair bushes out around me, half covering my face. A kind of natural veil.

A chimney sweep goes by with brooms and buckets. He looks at me, his eyes amazed, then quickly lowers his head, as though he's afraid he'll get in trouble for what he's seen.

I press my back against a wall.

A man opens the shop next to me. He glances over his shoulder at me as he fiddles with the door lock, trying not to drop the sack under his arm. He goes inside, his head turned away. I'm almost sure he purposely avoided looking at me.

I need help.

Chiara. She'll be opening her shop soon, if she hasn't already.

I put on the *zoccoli* and cross the road, looking both ways. The beggar boy comes out of nowhere, sees me, then spins on his heel and goes the other way.

They're afraid of me, these men and the boy. Afraid of a girl who's somewhere she shouldn't be, acting erratic. Maybe this is better than being invisible.

I knock on the door of Chiara's shop. No one answers. I press my back against the door and slide my bottom down till I'm sitting, as small and inconspicuous as I can be.

"What manner of person are you, child?" comes the muttering voice.

I jump up in relief. "Oh, Chiara, kind woman, can I come inside just to change my clothes? Please, kind woman."

Chiara draws back with a frown. "How is it you know my name?"

I smooth my hair back, hold it down with one hand while the other hand keeps my fisherboy's clothes safe in place under my nightdress, and thrust my face into hers.

"Donato?" she asks, as though she can't believe her eyes.

"I have to get out of sight fast. Please, Chiara."

Her eyes burn into me. "Turn left at the next alley," she whispers. "Then again left at the one after that. Count the windows. Stop at the seventh one. Don't knock." She steps back and raises her hands as though in alarm. "Get away," she says loudly. "Scat."

I race for the alley, stumbling at her rough words.

"And good riddance to you," she shouts after me.

What's going on? But I can't think what else to do. I turn fast into the alley, run to the next one and turn again. Most of the windows are shuttered. I go to the seventh one and wait.

One side opens a crack. "Is anyone about?" she whispers.

I look up and down the alley. "I don't see anyone."

Chiara opens the shutter a bit more. She grabs me by the elbow and half pulls me in, as my legs and arms scrabble to help me climb.

Once my feet are on the floor, she closes the shutter again immediately. Dank darkness swallows us.

"Have you got a change of clothes with you?" asks Chiara.

"Yes."

"Be quick," she says. "Then come through to the front shop." She walks away, knocking into things in the dark as she goes.

I'm accustomed to changing in the dimness of the storeroom, so I have no problem here. Then I roll my nightdress tight and feel my way across the room and into a little corridor. Now the light from the front windows guides me. I go into the box shop.

Chiara sits on her stool and stares at me. "It is you." She puts her hands to her cheeks. "Are you bringing me trouble?"

"I don't intend to. Someone's coming to meet me out on the street soon. Can I stay just until he gets here?"

"Tell me, are you boy or girl?"

"Girl."

"So is this a forbidden romance, you and the someone who's coming to meet you? Are you running off together?"

"No," I say.

"But it is trouble, it is something you're not supposed to be doing."

"Yes," I say, though her comment wasn't a question.

"You look like a normal Catholic child now." Chiara regards me carefully. "Do you know what you looked like in the street?"

"I have some idea," I said.

"But not a good enough one, I bet. You looked like a girl the devil had snatched and planted a child in. A lost soul. A witch."

I shake my head in horror. "I'm no witch."

"I know that. But others might not. You cannot go about looking like that."

"I never will again," I say.

"Keep that promise, for your own sake." Chiara walks to the door of the shop. Then she rushes back in, grabs her broom, and returns to the doorway, shaking the broom over her head threateningly. She turns to me. "I just reminded your enemy not to bother my errand boy. You'd better go now, while his memory is still good."

"Thank you, Chiara. I won't forget your kindness."

"Don't think of repaying me, child. I may not be able to afford the consequences of another visit from you."

"Take this, at least," I say, handing her my rolled-up nightdress. "I can't carry it around with me all day, and maybe you can sell it."

Chiara feels the nightdress, her fingers measuring its fine quality. She looks at me in surprise.

"*Addio*—be with God." I kiss her on each cheek. I'm sad to think I cannot come to her shop again. But after today, I will be saying good-bye to so many things—so what does it matter, one more good-bye? Why should it hurt this much? I go into the street without a backward glance.

Noè comes walking toward me.

Francesco walks not far behind him.

Oh, Lord, what mischief have you designed?

I turn my back to them. Have they seen me? I want to run, but that might draw attention. I get to the side wall and kneel over my shoe, as though adjusting it. That trick worked once before, it must work again.

Francesco passes by.

"Hello," calls Noè.

I hold perfectly still. Don't let him call my name. Don't, don't, please.

"Donato," calls Noè.

Francesco stops and looks back.

At least Noè said the male version of my name. I should have known he wouldn't use the female—he uses that only at the printer's when someone else might hear. Francesco shouldn't think long about it; Donato is a common enough name.

Noè has reached me now.

"I'm having trouble with my shoe," I say out of the side of my mouth to Noè, my head lowered so close to my foot it almost touches it. "Just a minute, please. And, please, don't say my name again."

Noè bends over to take a look. "Can I help?"

"There's someone up ahead. Someone I don't want to see me. Please don't look around. But tell me if the noble in the blue hose is still looking at us."

Noè squats beside me and fumbles with my *zoccolo*. His face is all concentration. He lowers his chest and twists a little, as though to get a better look at my shoe. The position allows him to see up the road. He's more adept at deception than I would have expected. "The young man has moved on."

"As soon as he's out of sight, we must go fast," I say.

Noè takes a *zoccolo* off my foot and fools around with the straps. He puts it back on me. "Give me the other one." I do, and he adjusts that one, too.

"They fit much better now," I say.

"It was easy. You should have told me when I gave them to you," he says.

"Sold them to me," I correct him.

"He's out of sight."

I stand and walk so quickly even Noè's long strides have trouble keeping up.

"Who was he?" asks Noè.

"My brother."

"But I thought your brother knew about your escapades among the poor."

"Only Bortolo. I have seven brothers."

Noè lets out a whistle. "And a sister, who has a gold brooch."

"Four sisters."

"Your mother's been lucky."

"Three other sisters died."

"I didn't even keep track of how many of my brothers and sisters died."

"Is that true?" I ask, horribly saddened at the idea.

"No. Four brothers died. Three sisters died. The only ones who lived are Sara and Isaia and me. I'm the oldest. Then there's Isaia."

This is what Messer Zonico talked about, but it's worse than I imagined. "Did they starve?"

"No one in the Ghetto starves, Donato, unless everyone starves together. If a family needs, everyone gives. Sometimes we don't give as much as we should, but we give. No, they died in epidemics."

"Epidemics?"

"Sicknesses that sweep large parts of the city."

"My sisters died in epidemics, too. And my mother's sisters and some of my Father's brothers and sisters. And my uncle Umberto went blind from the smallpox." Then I remember. "Another girl answered your door once. She looked a lot like Sara."

"My cousin Neomi. Our families live together."

"I have cousins, too. But they live in Padua."

"You can stop running now, you know. Your brother is far away."

I slow down. "I can work all day today. I'll finish the job." I look up at him and give in to pride. "You're amazed, admit it."

"Not at all."

"Really?"

Noè laughs. "My amazement passed late yesterday afternoon." He gives an appreciative bob of the head. "I looked over your work before going home. In two mornings you finished two copies and did most of the third. The work is easy for you. In fact, I'm surprised you think it'll take all day to finish it." His voice rises as he teases me. "You must be feeling lazy."

"Very funny." But I'm pleased. "I'll need that help you promised me with Latin, as soon as I finish the fifth copy."

"But I thought you knew Latin."

"Not enough," I say.

"All right. I suppose I can give you ten minutes of my time."

"Ten minutes?" I squeal.

Noè laughs. "I was just joking. How long a lesson do you want?"

"I don't want a lesson. I want help writing a letter."

"That's easy enough."

We arrive and I go straight to Noè's workroom. With no delay, I'm bent over the third copy of the noble boy's play. But now I hear Noè talking with another man. His voice is loud. I can't afford to take the time to go into the corridor to listen better. I have to finish this job today. With all probability, I'd never make it out of the *palazzo* if I waited till tomorrow. Mother will realize now that I do, indeed, go outside. She'll think I lied to her yesterday. And I guess I did. I violated her trust.

What has become of me?

What will become of me next?

I set to work.

After a long while, Noè comes in. He paces in agitation.

I give up. "I can't work with you acting like that, so you might as well tell me what's bothering you."

Noè rushes to me. "It's today's handbill. The Inquisition is heating up again."

I press my fists together in alarm. "But I thought Venice wouldn't risk offending its Jews or Protestants because of business."

"Right," says Noè. "And the Vatican has noticed. They question Venice's devotion to Catholicism. So the Senate has decided to prove its piety by clamping down."

"Oh, no. What will happen to the Jews?"

"Nothing. They won't bother the Jews, because we bring prosperity to Venice. Today's handbills proclaim that there will be no more tolerance of blasphemy, sodomy, prostitution, or procurement. A new tribunal has been formed to enforce these bans."

"That's good, though, Noè," I say in relief. "These other things are sins."

"Have you ever been with a prostitute?" His voice is angry.

My face goes hot. "Of course not."

"Then what do you know about them, Donato?"

"In selling their bodies they sell their souls."

"You told me your father has not chosen you as the son to get married. Sooner or later, you'll find yourself frequenting prostitutes, like most Venetian men."

"I will not," I say. "But even if I did, that wouldn't make what the women do right."

"Nor what the men do," says Noè.

"I agree. There are two sins for each act. They willingly choose to sin."

Noè puts his hands on his head in exasperation. When he takes them down, his yarmulke is off center. I realize that's why his yarmulke is so often off center—this is his habit. Now he holds his hands out to me. "Some sins are worse than others, Donato. Some of these women choose the life of a prostitute, yes. Some are courtesans who live in luxury. But there are twelve thousand prostitutes in Venice, at the last census. Twelve thousand, in a city of one hundred thousand. That's too many for you to believe the nonsense you just spoke. Not all of them freely choose to sell their bodies, and the vast majority live in quarters that are far from luxurious. They are simply poor and trying to make enough money so they won't starve, so they have a bed to sleep in when the customers go home. Maybe you have never imagined that kind of misery, Donato. But I ask you to now. What would you be willing to do if you had no money?"

I have imagined misery—just such misery. And I know I would never turn to prostitution.

Still, Noè's question disturbs me. Why does my heart harden in the face of a prostitute's misery, when in tutorial only yesterday I was able to feel sympathy for the misery of the beggar boy who has plagued me? Jesus himself said, "Let him who is without sin cast the first stone." And certainly I am not without sin, yet my hand holds a stone.

I'm crying now. I am sad for myself. I am sad for every prostitute, every lost soul. I am so very sad.

Noè puts his hand on my back. It is warm and much too welcome for me to find the moral strength to shake it off.

"That's right, Donato. What should be done about these problems, I don't know. But one thing is certain: Prison does not cure poverty." He goes to his desk and works.

I look through my tears at this wonderful man who has helped me in so many ways. I love him.

I wipe my eyes and work again.

CHAPTER TWENTY-ONE

GOD AND OTHER THINGS

Yesterday I ate only one meal: the evening meal. And while I filled my plate, it wasn't enough. Today I've had no food yet. At the mid-day mealtime, everyone else left the printer's to post the morning handbills in the Merceria, then go home to eat, while I stayed and worked. It's late afternoon now and the copyists have gone off again, this time to post the afternoon handbills. I've finished the fifth copy of the boy's play and I'm waiting for Noè, who left a while ago on an errand. There's nothing to keep my mind off the aching emptiness of my stomach. I feel faint.

I lean forward from my stool and let my head drop. When the wooziness passes, I walk out to the courtyard. An unfinished handbill lies on a table. That's unlike Noè. But he disliked these afternoon handbills, too, almost as much as he disliked the morning handbills. That must be why he didn't ask Emilio, the fastest copyist, to finish it.

At first I didn't understand Noè's commotion at the afternoon handbills; they were simply about a proposal to build a new Rialto bridge, out of stone this time, so it cannot burn down. But then Noè explained. The architects had gotten word early about the harsh new proclamation—and the part about clamping down on prostitution interested them especially. They gathered last night, and by today they had this proposal. The Rialto area has the most squalid brothels of all Venice. If the prostitutes are rounded up and thrown in prison, the area can be developed as a place for expensive stores.

Everyone wants to profit from any change. That's what Noè said. They forget at whose expense their profit comes.

I fold the unfinished handbill and bring it inside to the stack of papers that cannot be used because of scribe mistakes. When the pile is high enough, it will be sent to the papermaker, who will soak it and make new paper. I know so many things about this bookmaking industry now. This is a good industry, for nothing nourishes the whole self better than books.

I can imagine Noè's response to that. He would say a hungry body must be fed before a hungry mind. He's seen so many more troubles than I have. Yet even if I lived a thousand lives and each one was as a poor person, I feel sure that I'd take a book before a loaf of bread.

After all, I'm hungry now, but that hunger doesn't shake my belief.

I laugh out loud. What a rich girl I am, through and through, that I can hold on to such lofty beliefs.

And how can I think this is hunger? All I've missed is a couple of meals. I'm a complete dolt.

"What's funny, Donato?" Noè walks past me and into his workroom, giving a smile as he goes.

"Nothing worth talking about." I follow. "Will you help me with the letter now?"

"That's why I came back. Where is it?"

"I haven't written it yet. I want you to write it."

"If I write it, how can you learn?" Noè sits at his desk and takes out some work. "Write a draft and I'll correct it, then you can write the finished letter."

This is a better plan, I see immediately. If Noè were to write the letter, there's the chance, no matter how slim, that someone might recognize the handwriting from some book Noè has scribed for him.

I sit down and write the letter. Short and blunt. "I'm through," I say.

"So fast?" Noè gets up to come over. In a flash of clarity, I realize my error. I turn the paper over.

"What? Now you won't let me see it?"

"It turned out to be easier than I'd thought." Which is true. I don't need Noè's help. I must have been crazy to think I did. The letter has only two sentences in it; even if there are errors in the Latin, I'm sure it is comprehensible. And if Noè reads it, he will try to stop me.

Maybe Noè should stop me. Maybe if Noè knew everything, he would come up with a better solution.

Maybe that's why I wanted him to write the letter.

Wretched me, that I almost involved him—and after I'd sworn to myself never to put anyone else at risk again.

Noè gives a confused laugh. "All right, then, I'll pay you the piecework rate for the copies of the plays you just finished."

"Thank you."

Noè gets his ledger off the shelf. He writes in it.

"But can't you pay me now?" I ask.

"I don't have that much money on me. And the master pays

me only once the customer pays him. I'm sorry, Donato. But I'll ask the master if we can have the copies delivered tomorrow, for I've already finished the clean library copy, too. So the job is done." Noè smiles. "With luck, I can pay you midday tomorrow."

I can't wait till then. If I don't carry out my Great Plan tonight, I won't get another chance. Mother will never let me out of her sight again. "Could you give me enough money to pay for two gondola rides?"

"Here, there are three *soldi* in my pocket. You can have them and I'll deduct them from your pay." Noè lays the *soldi* in my outstretched hand. Then he goes about putting away the things on his desk. "Think you'd like another job?"

"No."

"Why not, Donato? We have fun together. I missed you when you stopped coming, you know." He fumbles through a pile. "I think I have something here you'd be perfect for."

"Noè?"

"What is it, Donato?"

"Who will you marry?"

"We already talked about this. Why torture yourself?"

Has he guessed how I feel about him? Did he understand even before I did? "What do you mean?"

He sits on his stool, so that now we are each sitting on stools, with half the room between us. "You told me you can't marry and you want to marry, right?"

Ah, yes. This is what I told Noè, before Father announced my engagement. It's almost funny how I thought I was sad then.

"But if you can't do something," continues Noè, "what's the

point in dwelling on it, my friend? The world is full of satisfactions for a noble like you."

Satisfactions for a noble man. "Humor me, Noè. Tell me about the woman you'll marry."

"I'm not betrothed."

"Have you ever loved a girl?"

Noè smiles.

"Answer me. Please."

"When my father died, I put girls out of my mind for the short term. My family needs me too much now."

"Then tell me about the sort of woman you'd like to marry," I say.

"That has no meaning," says Noè.

"But surely there are some things about her that must be so in order for you to choose her."

Noè lifts his shoulders.

I won't let this go. This may be my only chance to know. "Must she be Jewish?"

"That goes without saying," says Noè.

I swallow. "And could she be a convert?"

Noè looks long at me. "No. I'm not against conversion, Donato. And you know I have no trouble caring about a Christian. I've grown closer to you than I ever expected. But a mother holds a special place in a Jewish family. She is the bearer of tradition. A Jewish child needs a mother steeped in Jewish tradition. My children need such a mother."

"But you are steeped in Jewish tradition. Why couldn't you teach your wife?"

"It wouldn't be the same," says Noè.

The four meters between our stools might as well be the

whole lagoon of Venice. "I thought your mind was wider, Noè." I take off my *bareta* and shake my hair out.

Noè stares. "Are you a girl?"

Now it's my turn to lift my shoulders.

He stands, his face stricken, his eyes bright. Then he sinks back onto his stool and stares down at his own hands.

"You didn't sin when you touched me," I say quickly. "Sin takes conscious choice—whether you be Jew or Catholic, right?"

"Yes."

"Well, you didn't choose to touch a girl."

Noè gives the smallest laugh. "And here we were pretending you were a girl."

"It got complicated," I say, with my own sad laugh.

"Donata, after all," says Noè softly. He leans forward with his elbows on his knees and his hands folded in front of him. "You're a girl and your father has not chosen you to be the one to get married. I'm beginning to understand." He speaks very slowly. He's wrong, of course. "But you dressed like a boy. Why?"

"It was the only way to go outside my *palazzo* without being in danger." I wrinkle my nose at my own words. "Or at least that's what I thought when I first went out. Then I learned going out as a poor boy carries dangers I didn't guess at."

"Why did you want to go outside your *palazzo*?"

"Wouldn't you want to?" I ask.

Noè sits up straight. "What's the letter about?"

I put my hand on the turned-over letter, as though to weigh it down. "I don't want you to know. It's false, anyway."

"False?"

"Do you believe my God is false, Noè?"

"There is only one God."

"I believe that, too," I say. "People are different. People make up different ways of believing. But God is one and the same."

Noè stands up and comes to me. He kneels before me. "That's not all there is to it, Donata. God is not the whole thing."

"Yes, I know," I say through my tears. "There are spoons that have to stay with their mates on special shelves."

"You are my good friend, Donata. I cherish you."

We bow our heads toward one another. But they do not touch.

CHAPTER TWENTY-TWO

IT'S DONE

I go by gondola to the Piazza San Marco—for the second time in my life. It's getting late and people rush past every which way, going home for the evening meal. Boys pick up litter from the wide *piazza*. Pigeons flutter from spot to spot. Nothing has any direction.

I'm lost.

Then I see the tall bell tower. I rush to it. I know facts about this tower from Messer Zonico. He spread an illuminated codex out before us and explained that the bell tower was originally a lighthouse and lookout, and it rose not nearly so high. Now it stands alone, the buildings nearby having recently been leveled. Everything Messer Zonico said stays clear in my head.

Last time I was here, I didn't understand what I was seeing. I didn't know what anything stood for, where anything came from. But now I do.

The bell gongs loudly. I look up and see the two statues of Moors striking the hour with their hammers. I see the sign of the zodiac. I am filled with the pride of my heritage. This is my birthright. I kiss the air.

Beyond the bell tower is the Basilica di San Marco. I walk to it, as though drawn forward with an invisible string. When I came here with my family that one time so long ago, we didn't enter the church. Mother felt too poorly to battle the crowds in the *piazza*. But the *piazza* is not crowded now. And who knows when and if I'll ever get another chance.

There are so many columns, on so many levels, and arches within arches. The Quadriga—the four gilded bronze horse statues above the great central arch, which were brought to Venice from Constantinople during the Fourth Crusade—are even more massive and majestic than I remembered them. Messer Zonico says no one knows where they were made. I'm glad of that. Their mystery wraps me as I enter the church. First five steps, a landing, then another two. Seven. A mystical number.

The light is immediately reduced, yet the height of the ceilings lifts. I walk as in clouds. Little windows run along the bases of the cupolas allowing me to see better as I reach the transept. I look at the mosaics above archways, on the cupolas themselves, even under my feet. I know about these mosaics. Messer Zonico has shown us drawings, and discussed their history and artistry. But seeing them, seeing the glittering gold and grays and reds, seeing Adam asleep and God causing Eve to be born from his side, seeing Adam and Eve summoned to God's judgment after their sin, seeing all of it dazzles me. Light comes through a rose window at the right end of the transept, a window resembling delicate lacework. It's Gothic, I think to myself with a smile. Messer Zonico has taught me well.

"What are you doing here, child?"

I jump at the voice, which seems to come from some heavenly source.

A priest walks along a side aisle. Just an ordinary priest.

"Looking, my Don," I say, with a bow.

The priest walks past and disappears beyond curtains near the altar. On the other side of the altar is the Doge's chair for popular assemblies and aulic ceremonials. Oh, yes, Messer Zonico has done his job.

But no amount of talk could have prepared me for the ecstasy of being before the Divine.

I don't know how long I spend going from mosaic to mosaic, but I realize finally that my eyes cannot strain hard enough through the dark to make out the details any longer. I go out the great archway that I entered by.

The evening sky is pink and deep blue. A few stars show, more with every second. From the tops of the two colossal columns by the Palazzo Ducale the statues of the winged lion and of Saint Theodore reign over the city.

Here and there people walk in groups or alone. But very few now—and none that I dare ask for directions.

I need to find a *bocca di leone*—a lion's mouth—but I don't know which walls to search. I need to find one because I am about to deliver the letter I wrote at the printer's. It reads:

This is a denunciation of Donata Aurelia Mocenigo,
daughter of Augustino Marcantonio Mocenigo of the Sestiere di Cannaregio.
She has converted to Judaism.

Reciting the words in my head sends chills deep inside, so that my bones would splinter. This denunciation is false. And yet . . .

I never converted. I never even explicitly thought about conversion.

Nevertheless, the idea was intimate with me. Like fingers brushing lightly on my back—hardly felt, but nonetheless demanding.

Talking to Noè ended that elusive intimacy.

Even if he would have me—and he will not have me, I know that now, I have to know that—I could not be a good wife to him, not so long as he wants children. I am a Catholic, in every part of my soul and body. I revere Saint Thomas Aquinas, though I love Noè.

Noè is Jewish; I am Catholic.

What does that mean?

Noè is Jewish; I am Catholic.

Maybe Messer Zonico was more right than I guessed—maybe I am obsessed with questions of theology. Yet I am a dunce; I get no closer to sense.

Noè is Jewish; I am Catholic.

There are differences here—there must be differences. And these differences must matter. Though I keep forgetting just how.

I keep wanting to straighten his yarmulke and run my fingers lightly over his ears and hold that thin chin with the straggly beard. I keep crying.

I collapse against the nearest wall, my head hanging back, face to the sky. The water of my eyes blurs the stars into one glowing heaven. I sit and watch, a long time, until finally each point of light grows distinct again.

It's time to remember Laura. It's time to carry out my Great Plan.

My Great Plan is this. I will search this *piazza* until I find a *bocca di leone*. Then I will deliver my letter through its mouth. Tomorrow I will be arrested and stand trial.

I will be found innocent. After all, there is no evidence that I have converted to Judaism. No worldly evidence, at least.

Nevertheless, I will become suspect, for a woman who draws the public eye is always suspect. But the Mocenigo family name—with all its wealth—will still shine. My betrothal will be unthinkable. And, as is custom, when a girl withdraws from a betrothal, a sister takes her place. Laura will marry Roberto Priuli. She will have children.

I will have done the right thing.

There are consequences.

The most devastating is that I will never have children.

The thought does not torment me, for the idea of children is joined to the idea of a husband; and I would not want Roberto Priuli's children. I would not want any noble's children. I could not bear to send my daughters to a convent.

This denunciation means I will never even marry.

This thought does not torment me, either. Marriage is not a goal in and of itself. The lure of marriage for me was the lure of love. I don't love Roberto Priuli. I love Noè. It would be a travesty of all I hold dear to marry anyone else.

Noè is the husband of my soul.

Dear Lord, how could you teach me such profound love of the soul and deny me love of the body? Never to feel the weight of his hand, the heat of his breath on my skin. Never to touch him, to embrace him. Never. What wretched loss.

But at least Laura will know a more complete love than I

do. At least the denunciation will have benefits, rather than costs.

So long as I am found innocent.

And now Noè's news about the new tribunal worries me. I don't know anything about trials. Not really. What if the new tribunal decides to make an example of me and, despite all reason, finds me guilty? What if I'm locked up or worse, much worse, what if I'm exiled from Venice just when I've learned so much of her glory? Lost and alone. Without my family. Who am I then?

I put the side of my index finger in my mouth and bite down hard. I will not allow terror to wipe out reason.

And I will not look for excuses to back out.

I will be true to Laura and, most of all, to myself.

I wander along the edge of the Palazzo Ducale looking for a *bocca di leone*. I wander back again along the outer walls of the Basilica and around to the small *piazzetta* at the side. Again and again. It is only by chance that my hand finds letters carved into smooth stone. With a fingertip, I read, *"Denoncie secrete contro ministri et autri che cometessero Fraudi a . . ."* —secret denunciations against magistrates and others who would commit fraud. There's no need to read further. This is not the correct *bocca*—the one for heresy is inside the Palazzo Ducale—but this one will do. My hands run down the cool of the stone to the lion's head. To the open mouth.

I look around. No one appears to be looking this way. But I cannot see who might watch from inside a window. Still, who would watch at this hour? And what would they see? A shadow of a poor boy standing by the wall. They cannot see this *bocca di leone,* even if they know it's right here. They cannot see my hand reach inside my shirt and pull out the letter.

The white paper catches a bit of starlight at the last moment, before the lion devours it.

It's done.

And the details of the moment press upon me suddenly, with all their necessities. I walk past the Palazzo Ducale again, quickly now. The *fondamenta* along the wide Canale di San Marco is mostly empty. I have to find a gondola soon. Night carries too many dangers. But my nose detects the scent of food. I walk along the *fondamenta* and over a bridge.

"Have pity," comes a scream.

A hand stretches out through bars from a window only a meter above the water level. I can barely make out a face pressed against those bars, lit from behind by a weak oil lamp. The prison beneath the Palazzo Ducale. Messer Zonico talked about this, too.

What happens to the prisoners when the high water comes in autumn and winter? I didn't ask this when Messer Zonico talked of the prison. None of it seemed particularly real to me then.

A morbid sense of curiosity consumes me. "Tell me, kind sir," I call from the bridge, "what's it like inside there?"

"Pity," he screams. "Have pity, you scoundrel. A crumb of bread. Pity."

"The walls are damp," says a stronger voice.

I peer into the dark, but I see no one.

"The stench makes it hard to breathe. Summer bakes and winter ices." He laughs. "Disease comes in every season. Food is always scarce."

I see him now—he's not behind bars. Instead, he squats outside in the shadows by the wall beyond the bridge.

"Pity!" screams the prisoner.

I turn my back on both of them and walk quickly along the *fondamenta,* staying close to the water's edge. I go toward the smell of food.

A man cooks in a pot over an open fire. Others crowd around him. He fills a bowl from the pot and hands it to one man. The man eats it with his fingers. Rapidly. He hands the bowl back to the cook. The cook fills it again. Another man gives him a coin and takes the bowl, slurping it down. He hands back the empty bowl. I push forward with the crowd. I've never eaten from a shared bowl. I've never eaten without utensils.

I've never been this hungry.

Finally, it's my turn. I give the man a *soldo.* He hands me a bowl full of rice with a fish head in the middle. I eat it as fast as I can. It's hot and the rice fills the maw of my stomach. I give back the bowl, holding onto the fish head. I suck out its tasty juices.

I want another bowlful. But the single coin left in my pocket is my passage home.

I turn and walk back over the bridge, keeping to the open water side again, as far as possible from the sighs of prisoners. I stop at the place where the gondola left me off. Surely another gondola will come along.

The air off the water is warm. This was a very hot day.

A man limps past. He looks at me, but doesn't talk. I don't know if he was the man who squatted in the shadows before.

I can't stay here. So long as I stand alone like this, I'm a target for who knows what. Panic creeps up on me.

But there are things I know. I'm not helpless. The Merceria runs from the Piazza San Marco all the way across to where the Rialto bridge used to be. If I can find the Merceria, I can at least get that far toward home without having to ask my way. And I realize with an involuntary laugh that I can recognize the Merceria easily, though I've never been there, for that's where the copyists put up the handbills.

I walk around the *piazza* now, checking every alley that runs off it. At last there they are, the handbills I know so well, on the large passage that opens close to the Basilica. I walk as fast as I can, staying close to one wall, even though that makes my steps fall practically in blackness. A cat hisses. I kick something that clatters away. A man's voice calls out. I have to work at not running; it would be stupid to run when I can't even see the ground.

Finally the Merceria opens onto the Canal Grande. I wave my hands over my head, calling to a gondola. It passes.

I walk along the water in the direction of my home, but the *fondamenta* stops at the site of the old Rialto bridge.

Another gondola comes along. I shout and jump in place, waving like a maniac.

The gondola comes to me.

I climb in fast. "The Palazzo Mocenigo," I say.

"Do you have the fare?"

I hand him my last *soldo*.

And I sit. What's the point of pretending to be a boy anymore? I'm afraid to stand, anyway. The water looks black at night. And the Canal Grande is deep.

It doesn't take long to round the curve and make our way to my *palazzo*. "The alley beside it will do," I say.

The *gondoliere* lets me off.

I go to the side door. It's locked, of course.

I could wake them—after all, there's nothing they can do to me now that will be worse than what will happen tomorrow.

But I'm dressed in fisherboy's clothes.

With Bortolo's *bareta* in my hands.

Paolina and Bortolo would get in trouble.

How could I have failed to think of this?

I sit with my back pressed against the door and I laugh at what a sad and stupid person I am. I have failed to think about anything after my Great Plan. Now so many thoughts come. I have no idea what Father will do to me. But it hardly matters, for there is no future I could have had that wouldn't have meant great loss.

I have known freedom. True freedom. Dressed in these fisherboy's clothes, I have enjoyed the license of observing the world firsthand. And sitting in Messer Zonico's tutorial, I have read and argued. I cannot bear the thought of losing all that. But it's already lost. My laughter turns to sobs. Stupid, wretched me. There is no place in Venice for a girl like me. I might as well run away—banish myself.

The door opens and I barely manage to keep myself from falling onto my back.

"Come in, Donata."

"Uncle Umberto? What are you doing here?"

"I've been waiting for you. Making sure the lock is open has become a tiring job."

I jump up and into his arms.

He holds me tight.

"So you're the one." The risk Uncle Umberto has been running hits me hard. He's Mother's brother, not Father's. He lives with us on Father's charity. "Father would be outraged if he found out," I whisper.

"No one suspects me. Most of the time they don't notice I'm around. It's as though they can't see me—as though they're the blind ones." He reaches past me and secures the latch.

"Well, you won't have to open the latch for me anymore. I'm through going out."

"Ah." Uncle Umberto touches the *bareta* on my head. "I'm glad it ended well, with you safe and sound."

His voice tells me he was worried. And still he didn't give me away. "Why did you help me?"

"You needed adventures. Later on you can remember them. As I remember mine."

My mouth opens, but I don't let the sound of the gasp out. Uncle Umberto wouldn't want me to feel sorry for him. "Thank you for keeping my secret."

"I've had a lot of practice. Everyone thinks because I can't see them, I don't know what they're doing, so they do it right in front of me." He laughs. "There are more secrets in this family than you can guess."

"And you know them all?" I say with wonder.

"No, I'm sure I don't. But I know plenty."

"And you help everyone without their knowing?"

"Only some people," says Uncle Umberto.

"Thank you for helping me." I kiss his cheeks. "Thank you."

"Hush now. Get upstairs to bed."

I take off my *zoccoli* and run up the stairs, straight to Laura's and my bedchamber and out to the balcony. I strip and throw my clothes into the water. They drift on the surface, slowly sinking. I throw my *zoccoli* on top of them.

And the boy Donato is gone.

"What are you doing?"

I turn around.

Mother rushes past me to the balcony. "What did you throw in the canal?"

"My clothes."

"Your clothes? Why?"

Everything is happening too fast. I thought I wouldn't have to face questions till morning. I look toward the bed with longing.

"Where have you been?"

"Out doing the right thing."

"Outside the *palazzo*?"

"Yes," I say.

"Ahi!" she cries, as though she's been wounded.

Laura sits up in bed with a start, her nightdress a gray bird in the dark of the room. I want to be a bird with her. I want to fly somewhere quiet and safe, and cuddle against her in a nest.

"Get something on," says Mother. "Now."

I grab my old nightdress from the bottom of the closet. It's barely over my head when Mother pulls me by the arm, out into the corridor and down to the dining hall, where Father sits at the table with his head in his hands.

He looks up at me.

I straighten my nightdress and gather my courage.

"Where were you, Daughter?"

I don't answer.

"She was outside," says Mother. "Outside, in the night. Our daughter. Alone in the night." She sounds as frightened as I feel. "And she threw her clothes off the balcony into the water."

Father stands. "Were you outside the *palazzo* for the past three days?"

My knees threaten to give way. I grip the table edge. "Yes, Father."

"You lied to me," says Mother in a voice weak with pain.

"I swore only that I hadn't gone out in my nightdress, and I hadn't, Mother."

"You knew what I was asking, Donata."

"What have you been doing?" says Father, with naked fury.

"I went out to see the city." They're looking at me with pained surprise. "It's my city, too." I look from one to the other of them. "My Venice. You both knew it so well by the time you were my age. Mother should understand. Someone should understand."

Father's face is aghast. "You must tell me. Have you done anything to put your betrothal in jeopardy?"

I look at him in silence.

Mother bursts into sobs.

"Speak!" he shouts.

CHAPTER TWENTY-THREE

EVIDENCE

Laura comes into the bedchamber. "Come, Donata."

"So you're talking to me again?"

She nods. "You look so pathetic, how could I not? And, anyway, I missed you."

I get off the bed and hug Laura.

"Father says you're to come to the midday meal."

"Did he tell you himself?" I ask.

"No. Mother told me."

"Then you don't know what he looked like," I say.

Laura furrows her brow. "What are you talking about?"

"You don't know whether he was wild with anger or not. You don't know why he wants me at the table. That's what I mean."

"Their anger can't have grown, Donata. Last night was the worst of it, I'm sure."

I'm equally sure last night was just the beginning. Last night they were angry because they'd been half-crazed with fear at my absence, and they were angry because I wouldn't tell them anything about where I'd been, and they were angry because they feared my behavior would ruin the marriage plans. But I persisted in saying I'd done the right thing, and finally their questions stopped and even Father's anger seemed to wane. Perhaps because they wanted so much to believe me; perhaps because they were worn down. But today is a new day, with new energies, and new problems. Now follows the denunciation and, undoubtedly, a tempest.

Beyond that, I have no idea what's to become of me.

Laura takes my hand. "Come to the table."

"If you'll keep holding my hand. No matter what Father says, keep holding my hand."

Laura's fingers tighten around mine. "I will." She reaches for the doorknob.

I pull back. "I'm afraid, Laura."

"Pretend you're brave. March," says Laura. "Peace to you, Mark, my evangelist."

I stare at her, astonished.

"Don't look at me like you don't know what I'm talking about. You're the one who's always saying that."

"Laura, oh, Laura, those words are exactly the words on the banner of Venice. But on the banner, it's in Latin." I can't believe I didn't realize that before. I wrote those words three times in each of the five copies of the boy's play over the last three days—but I simply copied the Latin, I didn't translate it in my head.

Laura puts her hands on her hips and looks at me doubtfully. "Come on, Donata, how can words you made up be the words of Venice's banner?"

"I didn't make them up. The woman said them—the

woman who sat beside me on the balcony at the festival in Piazza San Marco." I let out a little laugh. "She was translating. '*Pax tibi, Marce, evangelista meus.*' Don't you see? She knew Latin. She was a noble—she wasn't a courtesan, and, still, she was educated."

"What on earth are you talking about?" asks Laura.

"Maybe my future." I may actually have a future, if I can get past this denunciation in one piece. I kiss Laura. "Let's go."

Laura opens the door.

Andriana and Paolina stand in the corridor. They arrange themselves in front and to the other side of me, instinctively protecting me. I've been so lucky to grow up in this family. So very lucky. We move down the corridor like a formal procession in Piazza San Marco, and I chant under my breath, "*Pax tibi, Marce, evangelista meus.*"

We take our seats. Laura stays beside me, holding my hand. True to her word.

No sooner have I sat than Father speaks. "This morning the Council found a denunciation in a *bocca di leone*." He looks right at me.

I feel Laura's hand tense up. I look around the table. My older brothers know; their faces are loquacious. Uncle Umberto knows; his face is guarded. Mother knows, too. The rest keep their eyes on Father. Even the little ones look grave, alerted by the tone of Father's voice.

Now it all begins. Father will take me before the tribunal.

And Laura will marry Roberto Priuli.

It is a good plan. I made this happen. I wanted this. Still, my teeth clench so hard the bones in my head hurt.

Father reads the denunciation aloud in Latin, then translates into Venetian.

When he finishes, Laura gives a little shriek.

I'm shaking now. I know everyone's eyes are on me, but I can't stop shaking.

Laura closes my hand in both hers.

"Who signed it?" asks Andriana. Her boldness in speaking first after such an announcement clearly surprises everyone. Her face is fierce with loyalty. I have never loved her more.

"It's anonymous."

"The coward," says Laura.

"Precisely," says Father. "The Council of Ten pays no attention to anonymous denunciations."

I gasp. How could they pay no attention? No one told me a denunciation had to be signed. No no no! All this for naught!

Father looks at me hard. "But the fact that the denunciation is anonymous doesn't mean it is false."

I blink in confusion.

"Have you anything to say to this charge, Donata?"

"I am a good Catholic, Father."

Father puts his hand to his head in a gesture of such wrenching relief, I want to cry for the anguish I've caused him. "Donata, what have you done outside this *palazzo*?"

"I did the right thing, Father. That's what matters."

"I am the one to judge what matters."

Laura's hands squeeze mine so tight, I fight not to cry out.

Father puts his hands together as in a prayer and shakes them at me. "Have you been in the Ghetto these past three days?"

"No," I answer truthfully.

"You sat at this table not long ago and asked about the Jews being confined to live in the Ghetto," says Father. "What—"

"I have never been in a synagogue, Father," I say quickly. "I have made no inquiries about conversion."

"And, Father," says Antonio, "it means nothing that Donata asked about the Ghetto. Donata asks questions in tutorial all the time, about all sorts of things. She asks about the poor. About disease. About anything at all. She simply wants to know things. She wants to know everything."

Father seems to think about Antonio's words. He looks at Mother, then he turns back to me. "Your mother and I have faith that you are telling the truth."

"But, Donata," says Mother, "denunciations, even false, anonymous ones, are costly. Everyone will know."

My ears ring. Scandal. Thank you, Lord.

"I can't understand this, Daughter," Mother says. "How could you be the center of something that even remotely hints of heresy, no matter how frivolous the charge?"

"I have never believed in our faith more fervently than I do now, Mother."

Mother comes around the table and stands beside me. "Be very careful as you answer my next questions, Donata. Much rides on them. Don't play games—don't try to get around the truth. Did you do anything in the past three days that would ruin your reputation as a lady were it to be known?"

"I did nothing indecent, Mother."

"Which people know what you did these past three days?"

"No one you will ever meet knows what I did. But it was nothing wrong in the eyes of God. I promise you that, Mother."

Mother strokes the hair back from my forehead. "You sound rational today, Donata. Like your old self. You seem well."

"I am well, Mother."

"You seem peaceful," she says wistfully.

"Trust your senses, Mother."

"They're all I have to go on right now." Mother looks at Father with resolve. "I will pay a visit to Margherita Priuli. I will ask her to prevail on her husband, Benedetto, to hold true to his marriage promise."

"Don't do that, Mother," I blurt out.

"Please, Donata, you said the foolishness is past."

"Marriage is not for me, Mother. This much I know."

"Donata's right," says Father. "Whatever has happened, it wouldn't have if Donata had behaved properly. She would not thrive within the bounds that a husband would set for her. And a failed marriage will do neither family any good."

"But Margherita and I—" begins Mother.

"No," says Father. "It would be a mistake for Donata."

"It would not be a mistake for Laura, though," I say.

Laura's grip is fierce once more.

Mother's eyes go from me to Laura and back. For an instant I see suspicion in them, as though she almost guesses that I have somehow devised this result.

"This is something we women can work out, Father," says Andriana in a burst. "I'll go with Mother to talk to Margherita."

"Yes," says Father, with renewed strength. "If Margherita can be convinced, Benedetto will see the wisdom of it."

He's nodding to himself and the anger and fear and disappointment that disfigured his face since last night are gone.

Just like that—the world is going right again, everything is going right, my Great Plan is working. Father is almost happy—he can think clearly. I am no longer the huge problem. Now is the time to ask the new question that has come to me—the question of a future for me. *Pax tibi, Marce, evangelista meus.*

But before I can speak, Father says, "The men must also follow a path: I want to know who wrote this denunciation. Malevolence of this level must be punished."

Francesco looks at his brothers. "Does anyone have an enemy so low as to try to harm him by slandering our sister?"

"If I have an enemy, I don't know who it is," says Piero.

"Nor I," says Vincenzo. "And Antonio couldn't possibly have an enemy."

"Unless it's someone who wants to undermine the Priuli betrothal," says Francesco slowly. "After all, with both families being in the wool business, this marriage has financial consequences for the industry."

"I thought of that," says Father. "But who? There's no one obvious."

"May I take the letter, Father?" Piero pulls the paper toward him. "Let me show it to Messer Zonico. He might at least look at the handwriting and tell us what he can guess about the man."

My lungs deflate. Messer Zonico cannot fail to recognize my script, for he has taught me to write, he has harped on certain weaknesses, he will know from the very first word of the letter.

"I will show it to him myself." Father looks around the table. "Does anyone have anything else to add?"

No one speaks, but Maria looks at my face. She comes around the table and climbs onto my lap.

"Then let us try to eat."

The meal is silent.

I have little appetite. Maria insists on feeding me. I swallow, more for her sake than my own. Exposure is imminent. My thoughts are scrambled. I can offer no explanation for my erratic behavior. They will never forgive me.

Finally, we walk downstairs to the library, Father leading, with Mother close behind.

Maria holds me by one hand, Laura by the other. Andriana precedes me. Paolina follows.

"We are now a circle of sisters again," I say in despair, for in all probability this is the last time.

"With you in the center," says Laura.

"A flower," says Paolina.

"I like flowers," says Maria.

Messer Zonico comes in. He looks alarmed, faced with this mob in the room he's so used to commanding. "Senator Mocenigo, I am pleased to see you." He folds his hands in front and doesn't look pleased at all. "But I do not understand. What has happened?"

"A most grievous offense," says Father. "A false denunciation of my daughter Donata."

"A denunciation of a girl?" Messer Zonico presses on the bridge of his eyeglasses in bewilderment. "What offense could a girl be accused of that would threaten the state and warrant a denunciation?"

"Probably the only one a girl could ever commit." Father spreads the letter flat on the wheeled book table. "Would you look at this handwriting and give us your ideas about what the accuser might be like?"

"Ah, it is anonymous. Thank the Lord for that, at least.

Certainly, Senator Mocenigo. I'll do whatever I can to help." Messer Zonico looks down at the letter. Immediately he glances up at me.

I move closer to Laura and press my arm against hers for support.

Messer Zonico looks back at the letter and seems to study it. Now he steps away and wipes his hands off against each other, though they cannot be dirty. "These letters, while well formed in many respects, still need improvement. My guess is that the writer is a new scholar. Someone who's been studying only for a short while."

"A child?" says Mother.

"Exactly."

"Why would a child accuse our daughter?"

"Such speculation is beyond my capacity as a tutor," says Messer Zonico.

I don't know why he doesn't expose me. He knows I wrote it.

Father folds the letter. "A child or, perhaps, a childish mind."

"The Latin, however, is impeccable," says Messer Zonico, quietly, and irrelevantly to everyone but me.

Messer Zonico is my ally. Yes. And now it's so clear: Messer Zonico is the one who should propose my future to Father.

"Fire!" comes the shout.

We run out of the library.

"Fire, fire!"

Francesco points to the stairs. "It's Cook."

We race down to the kitchen.

Bortolo stands in the center of the room, drenched, beside

an ashy puddle on the marble floor. He's moaning and clutching his hand.

Mother runs to him and examines his palm. The burn already blisters. "Get lard. Quick."

Cook drops the empty water bucket he's holding and gets a handful of lard. He smears it on Bortolo's burn. "I don't know what got into the boy," he says. "He was feeding a fire, right here on my floor."

"How could you do such a dangerous thing?" cries Mother, hugging Bortolo and rocking side to side.

"I had to destroy my magic hat," says Bortolo.

"You're too old to do such crazy things." Mother moans as she kisses the top of his head over and over. "My crazy boy."

His magic hat! That crazy boy has destroyed the only piece of evidence that ties me to Judaism. And he hasn't even asked for a treat.

What a wonderful family I have. What a wonderful tutor I have. Now all I need is a wonderful future.

"Please, Messer Zonico, please, could I talk with you in the library?"

CHAPTER TWENTY-FOUR

A FUTURE

I am folding Antonio's clothes into the leather-bound trunk for our move to our summer home in the hills. Antonio will accompany Mother and the girls and the youngest boys and Uncle Umberto. Father will stay here with Francesco and Piero, and attend to various business odds and ends before joining us. It is my job to pack the boys.

An unexpected breeze comes through Antonio's window. I pause and drink its sweetness. But I know it is deceptive. A summer storm to the north has brought a brief reprieve in the heat. Once it passes, the air will grow oppressive, unbreathable.

I move mechanically, performing my assigned duties without thought. I feel I hardly know who I am anymore. All I do is wait for a determination that is entirely beyond my control.

But others' futures have been determined, which makes me truly glad and grateful.

Andriana will marry early in the new year, as she wanted.

Laura will marry in the spring.

Margherita Priuli talked with Laura and decided she was an even lovelier choice than I had been. Laura and I chuckled over that, of course. And Benedetto Priuli was delighted at his wife's decision, since an alignment with a family so powerful as ours would have been hard to give up.

My twin is happy. And she has since met her betrothed and speaks of him with joy, her eyes alight.

And even Antonio's wife is chosen, though they won't marry until his education is completed. His fiancée is the eldest daughter in the Donà family. I blanched at the announcement. But I know that Signora Donà will never recognize me as the ruffian errand boy who delivered her boxes so recently. And I must admit that Franceschina is both beautiful and kind, a better person than her mother by far. It is a good match.

Paolina is not going to a convent, after all. She will be the aunt to stay at home and look after Antonio and Franceschina's children. I wasn't even considered for that position, after all that has happened. Headstrong women don't make good maiden aunts. But I'm willing to bet that Paolina, with all her funny ways, will prove an unusual maiden aunt herself. Franceschina will face lessons in patience, that is assured.

In any case, Paolina is delighted. She has already convinced Father to have the stones in our courtyard dug up over the winter. She's going to make a garden there, starting in the spring. And she's enlisted Vincenzo, of all people, to accompany her on visits to the best gardens of Venice. So far they've explored a convent garden on Giudecca known for its trees, and the Cornaro family's garden on that same island, where lemon and orange trees grow in huge pots.

Mother begs them not to make decisions without her. She's as excited about the garden as Paolina, and promises to give it her attention as soon as the weddings are over. At first I was surprised at her enthusiasm. In the past when Paolina asked to make a garden in our courtyard, she never agreed. But then, her change of heart made sense to me, as so many things do now. Mother never allowed Paolina a garden before because she knew a garden would make Paolina want even more to stay at home. In her own way, Mother was protecting Paolina.

Mother would like to protect me now, too. I can tell from the way she flutters about me. She's on edge, always wondering if the evil that made me leave the *palazzo* for those three days will return. She tries to hide her fear by talking calmly and asking me to do the same sort of tasks she asks of everyone else. I know that she wants so very much to help me, to give sense to my life.

My future has become the silent topic, the thing everyone purposely does not talk about. Father said the matter was in his hands, and that he would announce his decision when he was ready. His words gave the whole family the jitters. My brothers and sisters have persisted in little acts of kindness toward me ever since. I put my hand in the cloth purse that hangs from my wrist now and finger the lacquered scarab that Francesco bought for me at the Greek market. They feel sorry for me, all of them.

No one knows of my hope—no one except Messer Zonico.

I fervently hope to become a tutor, like him. Then I can be of use here in the *palazzo*. I can be the tutor to Antonio's children.

And maybe, when Antonio is in charge of the family, maybe he will allow me to tutor other noble children, too. Maybe I can even tutor girls. And women. After all, that woman beside me on the balcony was a noble and she somehow got an education. There are women and girls who would want me to tutor them. If only Father will allow me to study with Messer Zonico for a few more years, then I'll know enough to be a good tutor.

Messer Zonico promised to talk with Father. But he was called unexpectedly out of town. I can only pray that Father does not decide my future before Messer Zonico returns. The wait is agony.

I close the trunk and leave it for Antonio to carry to Vincenzo's room later, so that I can continue the packing. For now, I'm free.

I head for the library. I miss my studies. In the past ten days, there have been no tutorials in this house because of Messer Zonico's absence.

I hurry into the library. "Oh, excuse me."

Father and Messer Zonico sit across from each other at the study table.

"Welcome back," I say to my tutor uncertainly. I clasp my hands together and wait. Why did he not tell me he had returned?

"Take a seat, Donata." Father now recognizes me easily. It is not simply the fact that Laura would never come into the library like this. It is also that Laura and I have decided to no longer look exactly alike. My hair is in a single braid down my back every day. Laura's is however she wants, but never a single braid.

I take the chair beside Messer Zonico.

"Messer Zonico has reminded me of important facts."

This is a good beginning. I want to look at my tutor's face to learn what I can from his eyes, but I don't dare.

"The daughter of our fine poet Pietro Bembo lived her life in a convent," says Father. "She studied Greek and Latin there."

My insides fold and wither. "If my wishes matter at all, Father, I do not want to enter a convent, though I would gladly study Greek and Latin for the rest of my life."

"Your mother and I have already concluded that a convent is out of the question." Father clears his throat. "My words lead toward a different end." Father looks at Messer Zonico. "Would you like to tell her of some of the other women you mentioned to me?"

Messer Zonico touches his beard, which I now notice is thin—sweetly thin, like Noè's.

I swallow the lump of longing that rises so faithfully every time I think of Noè. I blink at the burn in my eyes.

"Bembo's daughter was named Elena, by the way," Messer Zonico says quickly. His eyes radiate intensity.

A rush of gratitude fills me. Somehow this small act, this naming of the woman, is an immense kindness. I lean toward Messer Zonico.

"Marcella Marcello was a wife and a scholar," he says evenly. "And her daughter Giulia, who married Girolamo della Torre, was a superb scholar of Plutarch's works. Cassandra Fedele was known for her beauty and her accomplishments in Latin. Modesta da Pozzo, the wife of the citizen, Filippo de Zorzi, even today writes poetry."

"I'm glad to know these things," I say. I look at Father, hoping he has absorbed their import. "Thank you for telling me.

Those are reputable women, wonderful women. I want to be like them, Father."

Father nods.

That's all the encouragement I need. "I want to study with Messer Zonico," I say, speaking so fast he cannot interrupt, "and then be a tutor to Antonio's children. And, if I'm good at it, if Antonio approves, then I'd like to tutor other nobles' children, too."

"We can't talk about that now, Donata."

"What do you mean?"

"Tutors must be people of impeccable reputation—for study of the sciences is study of the Lord's work. A good tutor is trusted to instill that respect in his students."

I rush around the table and fall to my knees before Father. "I will instill the utmost respect for the Lord and His work in my students. You know I will. Please, Father." I put my cheek on his knee. "Please. We are a wealthy family—and Venice is practical. That frivolous denunciation can be overcome."

"Precisely, Donata. Yet again you've proven how well you understand our homeland. I didn't say we could never talk about it—I said we couldn't talk about it now. Your reputation must be rehabilitated," says Father, "and your credentials must be beyond reproach. To that end Messer Zonico has spent the past week at the University of Padua, pleading your case."

"My case?" I sit back on my heels, dumbfounded.

"The university has admitted women into its classes before," says Messer Zonico, "but no woman has ever formally entered a program leading to a degree. I requested that you be allowed to enter the doctoral program in theology when you are finished with your tutorials."

I cannot speak.

"My request was denied," he says. "They believe it is inappropriate for a woman to obtain a degree in theology. But they were sufficiently impressed with my description of how much you have learned in so little time that they have agreed to allow you into the doctoral program in philosophy."

Never did I dare to dream of this. I look from Messer Zonico to Father, who is smiling at me. I throw myself into Father's arms.

Father pats my hair. "You'll need at least another two years of tutorials before you are ready for the university, Donata. And in that time, you will have to earn the right to your studies."

I stand and put my hand on Father's shoulder. "I will earn that right gladly. What must I do?"

"Your brother Bortolo turns seven in August. There's no doubt he's bright and ready for tutorials. On the advice of Messer Zonico, Vincenzo will aid Bortolo in mathematics. Messer Zonico will tutor Bortolo in all other subjects except writing, where you will serve as Bortolo's aide, always under the supervision of Messer Zonico, of course."

I look at Messer Zonico. The twitch of his lips threatens laughter. Me, an aide in writing. I grin. The man has a sense of humor I am only too happy to discover. "Father," I say, "you haven't made a mistake. I will do my very best with Bortolo." I hesitate. Should I ask now? "Paolina is older than Bortolo," I say. "And she's bright, too, Father. As bright as Bortolo."

Father looks at me sharply. "Does she want tutoring?"

"I'll ask her. And if she does, I'll do everything I can to aid her, too, Father."

Father drums his fingers on his right knee, in that way of his. Then he slaps his knee in a gesture of decisiveness. "I'm sure you will. Maybe you will tutor little Maria and my grandchildren someday as well." He takes my hand. "But, no matter what, you have important skills that the family needs. You have a sharp sense of business. And your brother Antonio, with his gentle ways, will benefit from having you by his side."

Me, helping Antonio? But why not? I do care about the way business is run. I care about the way all Venice is run. Why shouldn't it be possible for me to help my brother? I remember Messer Zonico's words at my very first tutorial: "Venice believes anything is possible, so long as we praise the Lord." And I do praise the Lord, as a true daughter of Venice. "I will study my hardest, Father. I will prove myself useful in business."

"I have no doubt you will prove yourself useful in many things, Donata. And I also have no doubt that I cannot guess yet what they will be." Father laughs.

Messer Zonico laughs.

But my mind is already racing ahead, guessing.

Author's Note

This story is dedicated to the spirit of Elena Lucrezia Cornaro Piscopia, scholar, musician, artist. Many people of her time considered her no more than a trained monkey. In spite of this, she persisted and became the first woman ever to be awarded a doctoral degree: Doctor of Philosophy, University of Padua, 1678. This story is also dedicated to the spirits of the women in the centuries before (like the Donata of this story) and since who have longed for such an opportunity but were not so fortunate.

Much has been written on the history of Venice, and not all works agree, sometimes reporting dates for events that can differ by decades or even centuries (such as the dates when certain canals were filled in). Whenever possible, I checked primary sources, including autobiographies, legal documents, portraits and other art of the period, and maps of the period. And I consulted with several historians (again, not all of whom agreed on the pertinent data). What errors remain are entirely my fault.

While most details of daily life and history are as close to accurate as I know how to make them, the individuals in this story are fictional, as is the Palazzo Mocenigo (which isn't even on the same side of the Canal Grande as the museum of that name today). Any similarities to people or personal events of the late 1500s in Venice are fortuitous.

About the Author

Donna Jo Napoli is the author of many distinguished books for young readers, among them *Crazy Jack, The Magic Circle, Zel, Sirena, Beast,* and *Stones in Water*. She has a B.A. in mathematics and a Ph.D. in Romance linguistics from Harvard University and has taught widely at major universities in America and abroad. She lives in Swarthmore, Pennsylvania, with her family, where she is professor of linguistics and chair of the linguistics program at Swarthmore College.